THE LONG ATTENTION

A NOVEL

G. J. STEIN

G. J. Stein

The Long Attention

First published by GJ Stein Books 2026

First edition

This book was professionally typeset on Reedsy
Find out more at reedsy.com

Contents

The Legacy Index

Mara Keene arrived early, which was unnecessary and therefore noticeable.

The Aurelian Lineage Bureau did not open before eight, but the atrium beneath it filled well in advance, as if people feared the building might forget them if they were not present. From the mezzanine where the Index offices were kept, the city revealed itself only indirectly — refracted through layered glass and polished surfaces, reduced to movement and light. It was possible to sit above the Reach in comfort and forget that anything beyond data existed.

Mara did neither.

She paused at the threshold until the access panel acknowledged her presence. The corridor beyond adjusted its temperature by half a degree, reading her biometric profile as something familiar but no longer primary. She noted the change and said nothing. Not everything needed contesting.

The waiting area was narrow, tasteful, and intentionally neutral. Two chairs faced a single desk, and behind it the far wall held the Index display — currently dormant, its surface a matt grey interrupted only by faint calibration lines. The quiet was not absolute. Systems breathed softly. Somewhere far below, transit rails hummed as carriages shifted loads with mechanical restraint.

Mara sat.

She folded her hands in her lap and waited.

Keene Holdings had undergone twelve legacy reviews in her lifetime. She remembered the earlier ones dimly — adults speaking in lowered voices, her mother's hand resting lightly on her shoulder, the sense that something important was occurring just outside her comprehension. Those reviews had been brief, almost ceremonial. The Index had confirmed what was already assumed.

This time, she suspected, the confirmation would be of a different kind.

The auditor entered without announcement. He moved with practiced efficiency, neither hurried nor indulgent of delay, his presence calibrated to suggest importance without dominance. His hair was precisely trimmed, his jacket unremarkable. Nothing about him drew attention except the fact that he was here to pass judgment while appearing not to do so.

"Ms. Keene," he said, as if greeting her were optional.

She stood, nodded once, and sat again when he gestured. The chair reconfigured beneath her, responding to posture, spine alignment, stress indicators. She let it.

"Thank you for coming in person," he added. "Not everyone does."

"I find it simplifies matters," Mara replied.

"Indeed." He settled behind the desk and activated the display.

The Index bloomed into life.

Lines traced backward and outward, branching into intersections that reorganized themselves as parameters shifted. Family names appeared briefly, then receded, giving prominence to others. Some glowed with confident steadiness. Others were dimmer, thinner, their trajectories bending subtly away from the center.

The Keene line appeared after a moment, neither prominent nor obscure, occupying a careful middle space. Stable, but no longer exemplary.

"This is a routine continuity evaluation," the auditor said. "No extraordinary triggers."

"Of course."

"Keene Holdings," he continued, voice even, "has historically maintained dispersion across three major infrastructure classes. Residential, transport-adjacent commercial, and offshore energy shares."

"Yes."

"However, recent reallocation activity suggests strain on the first category."

Residential.

She did not ask him to elaborate.

He glanced at her then, briefly, as if to confirm she understood the language being used. Mara returned his look calmly. She had learned early that confusion was treated as weakness in rooms like this.

"The primary residence," he said, "remains Keene Tower."

"It does," Mara said.

The display shifted, isolating a tall structure rendered in translucent blue. Upper floors curved outward — beautiful, inefficient. A relic of architectural optimism.

"Usage rates have declined," he continued. "Maintenance overhead has increased. Environmental exposure has become a factor."

"The building is sound."

"No one disputes that," he said gently. "But soundness and suitability are not equivalent."

Mara inhaled slowly.

Keene Tower had never been practical. Even at its height, it had been a statement rather than an asset. Her grandfather had believed permanence could be willed into existence if it were made elegant enough. For a time, he had been right.

"The Index flags underutilization," the auditor added. "It invites discussion."

"That discussion tends to arrive prepared," she said.

He smiled faintly. "Prepared discussions save time."

The display rearranged, overlaying forecast curves across the Keene line. None were dramatic. That, she knew, was the most dangerous configuration of all. Dramatic declines inspired intervention. Gradual erosion was allowed to proceed.

"There are interested parties," he said, as if discovering the thought rather than introducing it. "Operators with relevant capacity. Strong reliability assessments."

Leasing, then.

Mara nodded once.

"And where," she asked, "does the Index place our internal distribution of responsibility?"

He tapped the desk lightly, calling up a second layer of data. This one did not display publicly; it reflected back at her in faint shapes, just enough to register its presence.

"Your personal profile remains a stabilizing factor," he said. "Professional engagement, cross-sector competency, and allocation efficiency have all scored positively."

She heard the unspoken clause: *for someone in your position.*

"I aim to be of use," she said.

"Yes. You are."

The words carried relief more than praise.

The moment passed. He deactivated the Index and the room seemed to exhale with it.

"There is no immediate mandate," he concluded. "Only advisory pressure. But timing matters. Families who engage early tend to preserve optionality."

Mara rose smoothly.

"Thank you for your clarity," she said.

He stood in response. That, at least, was still observed.

As she turned to leave, he spoke again.

"Ms. Keene."

She paused.

"The Index is reflective, not directive," he said. "It assesses consensus."

"I understand."

She did. Consensus existed to ensure that no individual could be blamed for the outcome.

The lift carried her down through calibrated strata, descending from curated quiet into managed movement. The atrium below pulsed with afternoon traffic — executives, couriers, families moving with different permissions and priorities. Advertisements adjusted mid-display as her presence passed beneath them, then returned to brighter palette and higher contrast once she was gone.

She exited without breaking stride.

Her own building was not far, though it sat just outside Crestline itself, close enough to be mistaken as belonging until one noticed the marginal differences. Public transit did not stop directly outside. Invitations were delivered with careful phrasing.

From her apartment windows, the Reach unfurled in widening arcs — seawall lines glowing against rising water, transport corridors threading between towers like illuminated veins. The sight still steadied her, though the steadiness changed year by year.

She ignored her message queue at first, setting her bag down and crossing to the glass instead. The window vibrated faintly with distant motion, a reminder that the city never paused for appraisal.

Her father's voice reached her memory unbidden.

Optics, Mara. Always consider optics.

The message queue pulsed once more, insistently.

She accepted the call.

Her father appeared precisely framed, Crestline light lending his features the careful sharpness he preferred. He did not waste time.

"You've seen the Index."

"Yes."

"They're positioning faultlessly. No ultimatums."

"That's correct."

He nodded, satisfied with her assessment.

"It may be prudent," he continued, "to explore transitional arrangements."

"Leasing," she said, not unkindly.

He exhaled. "Shared stewardship," he corrected.

"Of course."

"They'll expect speed."

"They always do."

He watched her for a moment, expression unreadable, then softened slightly.

"You've been handling these things exceptionally well," he said. "Better than I could, if I'm honest."

The admission surprised her with its weight.

"I'll review the proposals," she said. "And coordinate accordingly."

"Yes. Good."

The transmission ended neatly, as if punctured cleanly from existence.

Mara remained standing.

Only then did she open the system alert waiting beneath the call.

Infrastructure Allocation Notice

Keene Tower scheduled for preliminary stewardship review.

She closed it without response and turned back to the window.

The tide was higher than it had been an hour ago.

She rested her palm against the glass, feeling the faint vibration beneath her skin. Somewhere below, water pressed patiently against the barrier built to contain it.

Containment, she thought, was never the same as certainty.

Her wrist interface buzzed once more — a legacy feed she had never disabled, though she rarely remembered it was there.

The identifier surfaced before she could stop it.

E. Calder

The update was brief.

Contract completed. Return vector logged.

No elaboration. No location.

Mara set her wrist down on the sill and looked back out at the Reach, forcing herself to remain still until the initial stir of pressure settled.

The system accepted the update.

She did not yet decide what it meant.

Mara did not return directly to her apartment after receiving the update.

Instead, she took the service lift down past Midway, ignoring the advisory prompts that suggested a faster route. Efficiency had its place, but so did familiarity, and she preferred corridors that had not yet been entirely revised. The Reach changed in increments; one learned its moods only by walking through them.

The lift opened onto a lower concourse where the ceilings dipped and the lighting lost its polish. Here, the city's older layers pressed closer together, joints reinforced rather than concealed. The air carried a faint mineral tang from the seawall pumps cycling beneath the floor. Conversations struck softer tones, as if people understood instinctively that voices did not need to carry far to be heard.

She walked along the railing that separated the concourse from the submerged tier below. Through the glass, she could see the outlines of structures long converted to aquaculture platforms, their original functions barely discernible beneath growth and modification. Light pulled across the water's surface in warped bands.

When she had been younger, she had imagined that downward movement meant loss. Later, she learned that adaptation often occurred where conditions were least accommodating.

A small café occupied the corner nearest the railing. Its sign flickered between white and amber, undecided. Mara took a table by the window and ordered tea, specifying manual preparation instead of rapid infusion. The delay was marginal, but it allowed her to remain undisturbed for several minutes longer.

While she waited, she watched the water.

The Reach did not pretend stability. Tides rose and fell according to forces no one in the Crestline liked to acknowledge, and the city answered with adjustments rather than resistance. Most people trusted the systems to manage those negotiations on their behalf. Those who lived closer to the seams were less inclined to optimism.

Her wrist interface buzzed again. She ignored it this time, folding her hands around the warm ceramic cup when it was set before her. Steam curled upward, indistinct, dissolving quickly in the air.

She took a sip and let the heat settle.

Eight years ago, she had come to this same place on a night that felt very much unlike this one.

She had been younger, though she did not think of herself in those terms now. At the time, the difference between twenty-seven and thirty-five seemed abstract, theoretical. Now it felt measurable, as if time had added weight she could feel in her movements.

Elias Calder had been late that night. She remembered the irritation clearly, how it had flared and then faded into something gentler when she saw him approaching along the concourse, jacket unfastened, hair still damp from rain. He had always moved as if space were provisional, something to be negotiated moment by moment rather than accepted as given.

"Sorry," he had said then, smiling in slight apology rather than carelessness. "Transit stalled."

She had believed him without hesitation. She believed many things then.

They had sat where she sat now, close enough that their shoulders nearly touched, watching the light shift across the water. He had spoken about contracts — not specifics, never specifics — only trajectories and timelines, the kind of language used by people who suspected they might soon be in motion again.

"It's temporary," he had said. "Just until the next offer."

She had nodded. Temporary things had always sounded manageable.

What she remembered most was not the conversation itself, but the sense of anticipation beneath it, the belief that decisions unfolded in a generous universe, one that would meet careful planning more than halfway.

She did not think that way anymore.

The interface buzzed again, impatient.

She turned it face-up and scanned the message before she could stop herself. This one was not from Infrastructure Allocation. It was from the

Transit Authority — an automated notice routed through her personal credentials.

Incoming operator clearance granted.

Duration: provisional.

No name attached.

She closed the notification slowly.

Across the café, a couple argued in low voices over the partitioned table, their disagreement more procedural than emotional. The Reach trained people to navigate conflict with restraint. Those who did not learn quickly were sorted into environments better suited to them.

Mara finished her tea, placed the cup back on the tray, and stood. She did not look again at the water.

By the time she returned to her apartment, dusk had deepened into evening. The city's illumination rose to meet it, brightening corridors and facades in calculated increments. From above, the Reach might have resembled a diagram in motion, each light marking a function rather than an intention.

She moved through her rooms without turning on additional lighting. The ambient glow from outside was sufficient, softening edges and leaving some corners deliberately indistinct.

Her apartment bore few marks of occupation that might have been mistaken for legacy. There were no family portraits, no crests or insignia. She had learned early that preservation required selectivity. Some things endured more securely when not displayed.

She removed her coat, folded it carefully, and placed it back in the storage niche. Only then did she notice the weight at the foot of the door.

A sealed delivery packet lay on the floor, its surface matte, unmarked but for the faint impression of a sigil she had not seen in years. Her muscles tightened before her mind fully recognized the design.

Independent operator authorization.

She stood very still.

There were proper channels for such notices, formal notifications routed through civilian systems, framed by reassuring language. This packet was not one of those. It bypassed filters deliberately. That alone made it a statement.

She did not open it immediately.

Instead, she moved to the window once more and looked out at the Reach, as if confirming its persistence before engaging with something that threatened to disrupt it. The seawall lights burned steadily. Transport lanes traced predictable arcs. The city appeared untroubled by the arrival or return of any single individual.

Finally, she crossed back and knelt to retrieve the packet.

The seal disengaged at her touch.

Inside was a single data wafer, its edge worn, not freshly minted. He had always preferred devices that looked as though they had been used. The habit had once annoyed her. She understood it better now.

She did not activate it.

Instead, she placed the wafer on the table and sat opposite it, hands resting flat on the surface, as if proximity alone might satisfy the moment. Her pulse had accelerated despite her efforts to remain composed, a reminder that discipline did not eliminate response so much as postpone its expression.

After a full minute, she spoke aloud, though there was no one present to hear her.

"Of course," she said quietly.

There was no reply.

When she finally accessed the wafer, the display resolved into a simple transmission header. No embellishment. No recorded message. Just a location marker and a timestamp.

Azure Quarter — Dock Six.

Tomorrow. 19:00.

No signature, though none was required.

Mara leaned back in her chair and closed her eyes.

Azure Quarter was not a place of chance encounters. It favored intention, performance, and carefully managed visibility. To arrange a meeting there was not a neutral choice. It suggested equality, or at least the appearance of it.

She exhaled slowly.

Eight years, she thought again. Enough time to have justified her decision, to have made peace with it. Enough time for him to have become someone else entirely.

She reopened her eyes and regarded the wafer without touching it again.

Her refusal, all those years ago, had not been impulsive. That much she could still say with confidence. At the time, Elias had no fixed contracts, no standing within the Reach. His work took him beyond consistent communication windows, beyond insurance thresholds her family considered acceptable. What he offered, earnestly and without guile, was possibility.

What she had chosen instead was stability.

It had not felt like cowardice then. It had felt like responsibility. Her mother had been gone less than a year. Her father's composure had concealed more anxiety than he meant her to see, and the Index had already begun its quiet recalibrations.

"You're young," her aunt had said, not unkindly. "You'll understand later."

Mara understood many things later. She was not certain that was one of them.

The system chimed gently, pulling her back into the present. A reminder from her professional queue, flagged as time-sensitive.

She acknowledged it automatically, scanning assignment updates, expected deliverables, forecast meetings. The familiar structure steadied her. She read through the list until her breath returned to its usual cadence.

Only then did she allow herself to consider the meeting again.

Dock Six sat at the edge of Azure Quarter, near the refurbished public platforms where older transport infrastructure intersected with the newer promenade. It was visible without being central, fashionable without gravity. She could anticipate the crowd: executives seeking anonymity, cultural intermediaries, people who wished to be seen without committing to the consequences of being known.

The choice fit him.

Mara rose and moved toward her console, activating the apartment's environmental settings for the night. The lights dimmed another fraction. Exterior blinds adjusted to soften glare while preserving view.

She paused before sending any response. In fact, she did not send one at all.

The packet had not requested acknowledgement.

That, too, fit him.

Later, lying in bed, she found sleep reluctant to comply. The ceiling above her displayed a slowly shifting pattern meant to encourage rest, though she chose not to alter it. Familiarity, even now, seemed preferable to optimization.

She thought of Keene Tower, of its curved upper floors catching salt light, the inefficiency that might soon be converted into someone else's asset. She thought of the auditor's careful phrasing, of consensus masquerading as impartial judgment.

And, despite herself, she thought of Elias Calder stepping back onto Reach soil, his movements no doubt unchanged in essence if not in context.

Contract completed. Return vector logged.

Mara turned onto her side and watched the pattern shift faintly above her.

If he had expected her to be surprised, he would be disappointed. If he had expected her to rush, he would be mistaken.

She closed her eyes and allowed the city's distant rhythms to settle into something approaching quiet.

Tomorrow would come, as it always did, with or without her consent.

She intended to meet it prepared.

A Controlled Retreat

The decision did not arrive as a decision.

It arrived instead as a sequence of acknowledgments: notifications routed to the appropriate queues, polite requests for availability, a suggestion that timing would be advantageous if certain conversations occurred sooner rather than later. Nothing bore the weight of finality. Nothing declared itself irreversible.

That, Mara recognized, was how displacement was managed now.

She stood in the eastern gallery of Keene Tower with her father's aide, a quiet woman named Lisette whose tenure with the family had survived two restructurings and one near-merger. Lisette held a slim console against her forearm, its surface displaying a floor-by-floor schematic of the building as it currently existed and as it was projected to exist under shared stewardship.

"Of course," Lisette was saying, tone respectful and utterly neutral, "the upper residential levels would remain under Keene occupation. That portion of the agreement has been emphasized."

Mara nodded, eyes tracing the diagram.

The shading told the real story. Entire sections of the tower—communal lounges, auxiliary workspaces, even one of the curved observation decks—had already been retagged in provisional hues, signaling anticipated reassignment. The system was careful not to mark them as lost. Loss implied resistance. These were simply... transitioning.

"And the lower levels?" Mara asked.

"Multi-use conversion," Lisette replied smoothly. "The operators require transit-adjacent access and flexible load capacity. The tower's infrastructure makes it an excellent fit."

Excellent fit. Another phrase designed to sound like fortune.

Mara crossed to the window at the end of the gallery. From this height, the Reach appeared orderly, its layout almost graceful. Transit lines curved through the space between towers with practiced precision. Farther out, the seawall held the tide in obedience to algorithms recalibrating minute by minute.

"This space was designed for continuity," Mara said, more to herself than to Lisette.

Lisette inclined her head. "Continuity can take many forms."

The gallery itself bore no personal marks. Keene Tower had never indulged in overt displays of sentiment. Its elegance had been architectural, not decorative. Still, Mara could not look at the room without remembering afternoons spent here years ago, studying in silence while her mother reviewed correspondence nearby. The light had always been best in this corner, filtered cleanly through the glass curvature.

"When will we need to vacate the shared levels?" Mara asked.

Lisette consulted her console. "Initial transfer windows open in three weeks. There will be overlapping presence for some time, of course. The transition is designed to feel... gradual."

Mara turned back from the window.

"Gradual changes," she said mildly, "are rarely unnoticed."

Lisette did not disagree. She never did.

The formal meeting was scheduled for the next morning, though the conclusions had effectively been reached already. Mara attended out of obligation rather than expectation, seated beside her father at the long table in the central conference suite while representatives from Allocation and Stewardship spoke in careful succession.

Her father listened with an expression she had learned to read long ago: composed, alert, resentful beneath courtesy. He asked questions that reflected diligence rather than doubt. He conceded points that could not be contested. The performance was impeccable.

Mara contributed when required, offering operational clarifications, confirming timelines, smoothing procedural seams. No one thanked her directly. Thanks would have implied that the labor mattered.

When the session ended, the lead steward summarized crisply.

"In effect," he said, "this arrangement allows Keene Holdings to preserve its positional integrity while freeing capital tied to high-maintenance structures. A sensible optimization."

Her father smiled faintly. "We've always believed in responsible adjustment."

Adjustment. Another word that resisted the admission of surrender.

The stewards departed with satisfied efficiency. Allocation followed. The conference suite seemed to relax once they were gone, as if relieved of its obligation to witness.

Her father remained standing for a moment, hands resting on the back of his chair.

"Well," he said finally. "That was civil."

"Yes," Mara replied.

"They've no interest in inconveniencing us. Not really."

"No," she agreed again. "Only in reassigning space."

He turned then and regarded her directly.

"You understand," he said, not quite a question, "that this is not a reflection on us."

Mara met his gaze without hesitation.

"I understand how the system frames it," she said.

He exhaled, the tension in his shoulders easing slightly.

"I'm glad you'll be handling the practicalities," he said. "I've never had much patience for logistics."

You've never had to, she thought, but did not say it aloud.

Instead, she said, "I'll ensure the move is efficient."

He hesitated, then corrected gently, "Not a move. A consolidation."

Of course.

That afternoon, Mara began the inventory.

It was not strictly required—most of Keene Tower's contents were categorized and digitized—but she had found that systems often overlooked the intangible value of presence. Walking each floor forced the reality of the change into manageable proportions.

The upper residential levels would remain theirs, for now. Everything below the seventy-second floor, however, fell under review. She moved through those spaces with practiced attention, pausing occasionally to make manual notes where the automated logs were insufficient.

The west lounge had been underused for years, its seating modular and nearly timeless. From its windows, the tide appeared closer than elsewhere, the city's boundary with the water made visibly fragile by perspective alone. She stood there longer than necessary, remembering gatherings that had once felt inevitable and now seemed improbable.

The library followed, still maintained out of tradition rather than demand. Physical volumes lined the walls, their spines arranged according to an order her mother had insisted on preserving. Digital equivalents existed elsewhere, accessed far more often, but the library had never been intended as a practical resource.

She suspected it would not survive the stewardship transition.

By the time she returned to her own apartment, evening had settled fully over the Reach. Lights shimmered against the glass, blurring the line between interior and exterior.

She activated her console and began the process the meeting had politely avoided naming: relocation planning.

It was not her own residence that concerned her first, but her father's. His quarters occupied the uppermost tier of the tower, designed to impress without excess. The thought of moving him elsewhere—even temporarily—required careful calibration.

She reviewed possible alternatives with professional detachment. Midway offered privacy without prestige. Azure Quarter offered visibility but demanded performance. Neither would please him.

The system proposed several optimized housing solutions, each accompanied by reassuring language about comfort and continuity. Mara dismissed them without much consideration. Her father's needs were not ones algorithms had ever understood particularly well.

She would find another way.

Her wrist interface chimed softly. Not an alert this time, but a message routed through her personal channel rather than professional priority.

Elias Calder.

There was no text. Only a location tag, identical to the one she had already seen, and a short addition beneath it.

If convenient.

She stared at the words longer than their brevity warranted.

Convenience, she thought, had never been his concern.

She did not reply.

Instead, she closed the message and returned to the console, forcing her attention back to floor plans and logistics. Boxes would need labeling. Access permissions adjusted. Staff reassigned delicately, without exposing the hierarchy of whose services would remain valued and whose would not.

The work was absorbing in the way only necessary work could be. It quieted the mind by occupying it completely.

Still, when her eyes strayed toward the windows again, the Reach seemed subtly altered, as if someone had adjusted the scale without her noticing. The tower remained where it had always been, yet its future felt less secure, its dominance softened by sharing.

A controlled retreat, she thought, was still a retreat.

She straightened, saved her progress, and stood.

Tomorrow would bring more confirmations. More polite assurances. Perhaps more messages she would have to decide whether to answer.

For now, she allowed herself one small acknowledgment of loss, unexpressed and unresolved, before setting it aside.

Rationality, after all, required sacrifice.

The announcement came three days later, though "announcement" was too generous a word for what amounted to a carefully timed informational release.

Mara learned of it not through her father, nor through Allocation, but through the subtle realignment of her access privileges. The main transit bank still recognized her without hesitation, but a secondary corridor—one leading toward the tower's lower shared levels—requested confirmation where it never had before. The pause lasted less than a second. Long enough to register. Short enough to be dismissed as coincidence by anyone inclined to trust the system.

She did not dismiss it.

Later that morning, Lisette sent her a message marked *procedural*, attaching a revised occupancy schedule and a set of talking points. The language was precise, intentionally bland.

Stewardship transition to begin Phase One.

Keene Holdings to retain principal residential and executive tiers.

Operational consolidation projected to improve fiscal resilience.

Fiscal resilience. The phrase had an almost physical weight to it, dense with assumption.

Mara acknowledged receipt and requested a brief meeting.

They walked the seventy-third floor together, where the ceilings rose into a shallow arch and the lighting followed daylight cycles rather than commercial schedules. The lift chimed softly behind them as it descended, carrying staff downward with items already being sorted into transitional storage.

"They're moving faster than projected," Mara observed.

Lisette nodded. "Interest was strong."

"Strong interest favors momentum," Mara said.

"Yes."

Neither of them slowed as they moved through the space. Slowing suggested hesitation.

"Have the operators been identified?" Mara asked.

"Formally?" Lisette hesitated. "Not yet. Informally, I believe two entities have submitted parallel proposals. Both are rated highly. One, in particular, has broad frontier experience."

That narrowed it considerably.

Mara said nothing, though the connection slotted itself neatly into place. The Reach was many things, but coincidence was rarely one of them.

They reached the observation curve at the far end of the floor. Below, the city's lower reaches stirred with mid-morning traffic, carriers moving between levels like disciplined insects. The water beyond the seawall shimmered under rising light.

"My father will ask about permanence," Mara said.

"He already has," Lisette replied. "The reassurance package is prepared."

Mara closed her eyes briefly.

"Does it include occupancy duration?"

"Language around review cycles," Lisette said. "Annual reassessment. Rolling options."

Always rolling. Always provisional.

"Thank you," Mara said.

Lisette inclined her head and withdrew without comment, leaving Mara alone with the view.

She allowed herself exactly one minute.

One minute to register the fact that the tower was no longer solely theirs. That its corridors would soon echo with unfamiliar footfalls, its access points calibrated to recognize other identities as equivalent. That the architecture her grandfather had insisted would assert Keene presence long after individual relevance faded would instead be monetized for its utility.

Then she straightened and turned back inside.

The minute had expired.

That evening, her father invited her to dinner.

The request came not as an order but as a suggestion routed through domestic channels, accompanied by the polite phrasing he reserved for matters that still unsettled him. Mara arrived punctually, the lift rising without pause to the topmost tier.

The dining room retained its original configuration: a broad table beneath a floating light panel calibrated to complement rather than dominate. Her father sat already, a tablet aligned neatly beside his place setting.

"They've begun," he said, not looking up.

"Yes."

He sighed. "Earlier than promised."

"Earlier than projected," Mara corrected gently.

He looked at her then, frustration flickering beneath control.

"I don't like being hurried," he said.

"No one does."

"There was a time," he went on, "when we set the pace."

Mara took her seat across from him.

"There was," she agreed.

They ate in near silence, the rhythm of the meal familiar enough to dull the tension. When the plates were cleared, her father pushed his tablet aside and folded his hands, mirroring her habitual posture without quite realizing it.

"You know," he said slowly, "I never thought we would be discussing alternatives."

Mara waited.

"Your mother would have disliked this," he added. "Sharing the tower. She believed in lineage as something indivisible."

"She understood adaptation," Mara said carefully. "She adapted often."

He smiled faintly at that. "Only when she could control the terms."

There it was.

"Will we need to move?" he asked at last.

"Not immediately," Mara replied. "Your quarters remain unaffected for now. Mine as well."

"For now," he repeated.

"I'm exploring contingency arrangements," she said. "Discrete ones."

"I trust your judgment."

It was not reassurance. It was abdication.

She accepted it nonetheless.

By the end of the week, the tower began to change in ways subtle enough that no announcement was required.

New security personnel appeared at lower checkpoints, their uniforms unbranded but unmistakably not Keene staff. Infrastructure teams ran diagnostics at irregular hours. Certain doors no longer responded to her authorization without secondary confirmation, though they opened eventually, always accompanied by a polite delay message apologizing for inconvenience.

Mara adjusted. She always did.

She rerouted routines. Learned which lifts were least affected by recalibration cycles. Made notes where the system interface offered none. The work absorbed her days, though not enough to distract her from the persistent awareness of displacement unfolding increment by increment.

When she passed through shared corridors, she kept her expression neutral, neither defensive nor proprietary. Ownership communicated itself poorly when performed aloud.

Late one afternoon, as she crossed an observation bridge connecting two administrative wings, she encountered the first of the incoming operators.

He stood near the railing, jacket open, gaze directed outward rather than toward the display panel glowing softly at his side. He did not turn immediately when she approached, which suggested either distraction or confidence.

Mara slowed slightly, preparing to pass without acknowledgment.

He turned then, eyes sharpening as they registered her presence.

For a split second, neither of them spoke.

It was not Elias Calder.

Relief and disappointment arrived together, canceling each other out before either could settle.

"Apologies," he said, stepping aside. His voice carried the faint rasp of someone accustomed to open air rather than conditioned corridors. "I wasn't watching my clearance zone."

"It's undergoing adjustment," Mara replied. "It's easy to miss."

He smiled at that, brief and observant. "So I've been told."

They stood there a moment longer than strictly necessary.

"I'm Rowan Hale," he said finally. "Frontier logistics."

"Mara Keene," she replied.

Recognition flickered across his features, quickly moderated.

"Ah," he said. "Then I imagine this hasn't been an easy week."

She considered him for a moment before responding.

"Change rarely announces itself as easy," she said.

"No," he agreed. "But often as beneficial."

The phrasing echoed too many meetings to be accidental.

"Welcome to the tower," she said.

"Thank you." He hesitated, then added, "If it helps at all — we've been instructed to keep our presence unobtrusive. Respectful."

She nodded. "I'm sure."

They parted with mutual courtesy, neither lingering long enough to suggest conflict.

Yet as Mara continued across the bridge, she felt the shape of the encounter settle uncomfortably in her mind. Respectful presence still occupied space. Obtrusion was not required for displacement to occur.

That night, she did not go to the Lower Reach.

Instead, she remained in her apartment, sorting through physical items she had not touched in years. Not because they would need to be moved—her residence remained nominally secure—but because postponement felt dishonest.

She began with the storage alcove near the entryway, its contents neatly catalogued yet rarely consulted. Old tablets. Memory wafers encrypted with obsolete protocols. A set of architectural plans rolled carefully into a cylinder she did not remember saving.

She unsealed the container and spread the plans out across the table.

Keene Tower, original construction.

The curves were more dramatic than she remembered, the proportions unapologetically aspirational. Notes in the margins bore her grandfather's handwriting, annotating choices that prioritized presence over efficiency. He had believed architecture could compel respect.

Perhaps it had, for a time.

She rolled the plans back up and returned them to their container, fingers lingering on the seal before finally closing it.

Her wrist interface chimed softly.

Elias again.

This time, a message.

I hear the tower's changing hands.

Not what you planned.

Mara read the words twice.

There was no accusation in them. No apology either. Just observation, offered with the ease of someone accustomed to commenting on events from the outside.

She drafted a reply, then deleted it.

Drafted another.

Deleted that as well.

Finally, she sent only this:

Change rarely announces intent.

The response indicator appeared almost immediately.

Still. I'd rather hear it from you.

She closed the message without replying.

The Reach extended patience unevenly. Some things could be delayed indefinitely. Others acquired momentum simply by being acknowledged.

She turned the interface face-down and returned to the window.

Below, the tower glowed with its usual confidence, its facade unchanged, its silhouette still unmistakably Keene. Anyone looking from a distance would see no difference at all.

Only those inside knew how space could be surrendered without ever appearing lost.

Mara rested her forehead briefly against the glass, then straightened.

Controlled retreat, she thought, required vigilance.

And vigilance, she knew from long experience, carried its own cost.

The New Tenants

The first sign came from the lobby.

Mara noticed it early one morning as she crossed the atrium on her way to a coordination meeting, her route chosen deliberately to intersect one of the newly shared access points. The space itself looked unchanged—same stone composite flooring, same column spacing, same restrained lighting calibrated to suggest permanence rather than welcome—but the cadence of movement had shifted.

People walked differently.

They did not hurry in the way Crestline traffic hurried, each step measured against obligation or advantage. Nor did they perform ease, that studied nonchalance common among those who wished to be seen without admitting effort. Instead, the newcomers moved with a practicality that suggested long familiarity with environments less forgiving than this one.

They adjusted their path without apology. They nodded to others instinctively. They took in details without appearing to catalogue them.

The contrast was unsettling in its calmness.

Two of them stood near the central display map, jackets worn rather than styled, speaking in low tones as they compared the annotated layout to the physical space around them. One gestured upward, tracing a route through the tower's mid-level service corridors. The other listened, then shook his head, smiling faintly, and suggested an alternative that bypassed a congestion point Mara knew well.

They were right.

She slowed, just enough to observe without intruding.

Neither noticed her at first.

When they did—when one finally turned and caught her watching—they did not stiffen or perform recognition. The taller of the two inclined his head politely, expression open, inquisitive rather than guarded.

"Morning," he said.

"Good morning," Mara replied, surprised by the directness of the exchange.

They stepped aside without being asked, clearing her path through the atrium even though she had not signaled any intention to pass between them. The act was unremarkable. That was what made it unusual.

"New routes take a little getting used to," the other added, glancing toward the slowly shifting floor map.

"They do," Mara agreed. "The building wasn't designed for modular use."

"No," the first man said, with a soft note of appreciation. "It was built to impress."

Mara almost smiled.

She moved on, conscious of the faint easing in her chest as she entered the lift. Relinquishing space felt different when those occupying it did not behave as though it were owed.

The formal introduction occurred that afternoon.

Infrastructure Allocation requested that a Keene representative attend a welcome session for incoming operators, part of the stewardship protocol meant to reassure both parties that coexistence would be civil and efficient. Mara accepted without hesitation; delaying acknowledgment would have ceded influence unnecessarily.

The meeting space had been selected with care. Not one of the tower's premier chambers, nor one of its purely functional rooms, but a mid-tier conference suite overlooking the Reach at an angle that softened its dominance. The table was round. Chairs were spaced with deliberate generosity.

Mara arrived early, as she often did, and stood by the window until the others filtered in.

They came in small groups rather than as a uniform delegation, some familiar with one another, others clearly meeting for the first time. Their clothing was practical, unadorned by recent fashions or brand signifiers. A few bore faint marks of exposure—calloused hands, sunlines at the eyes—details rarely seen among Crestline's long-term residents.

When they spoke, their accents varied slightly, their cadence shaped by communication delays and environmental noise rather than deliberative refinement.

The steward assigned to facilitate the session introduced them without flourish.

"Frontier Operations Collective," he said. "Long-term contracts specializing in off-world infrastructure stabilization and transit corridor security."

That explained the movement, Mara thought. People accustomed to instability tended to carry it with them differently.

"I'm Mara Keene," she said when it was her turn. "I oversee operational coordination for Keene Holdings."

The collective's representative—a woman slightly shorter than Mara, with cropped silver-streaked hair—smiled and extended her hand instead of offering a nod.

"Alina Torres," she said. "We appreciate you being here."

Her grip was firm but brief. No assertion. No test.

"Welcome," Mara replied. "I hope the tower proves comfortable enough for your purposes."

Torres's smile widened, just a little.

"We're adaptable," she said. "Comfort is secondary."

Several of the others murmured agreement.

The steward outlined logistics: shared facilities, access windows, maintenance redundancies. The language was dry enough that Mara could have recited much of it alongside him. What interested her more was the way the operators received the information.

They asked questions only where clarity mattered. They did not nitpick. They did not argue for exceptions preemptively. When told that certain amenities would remain prioritized for Keene use, one of them nodded and remarked that such boundaries were sensible.

It was disarming.

When the session concluded, conversation did not collapse immediately as it often did during Crestline briefings. People lingered, exchanging observations, offering to coordinate schedules to avoid interference. Torres approached Mara once more, this time with a tablet angled casually at her side.

"I hope we're not causing undue inconvenience," she said.

"Inconvenience is a matter of framing," Mara replied. "Adjustment, perhaps, is more accurate."

Torres considered that. "That's usually the better word."

"You've worked in shared structures before?" Mara asked.

Torres laughed softly. "We've worked in structures that didn't expect to survive the season. This is comparatively luxurious."

Mara found herself warming to her despite herself.

"If difficulties arise," she said, "I'd prefer to address them directly rather than through protocol escalation."

Torres inclined her head. "Agreed. Direct tends to preserve energy."

Another unfamiliar concept, in this context.

News of the new tenants spread quickly, though the Reach made no overt show of it.

Invitation patterns shifted subtly. Messages circulated with altered assumptions. Names unfamiliar to Crestline lists began appearing on access schedules and catering orders. Some residents reacted with visible discomfort, their carefully maintained expressions faltering as they navigated corridors no longer exclusively theirs.

Others pretended not to notice.

Mara observed it all with professional detachment, though she could not deny the sense of relief that accompanied many of the changes. The tower felt... steadier, in some indefinable way. Less performative. Less brittle.

One evening, returning late from Azure Quarter, she encountered Torres again in the south elevator bank.

"Long day?" Torres asked, reading the fatigue in Mara's posture without comment.

"Yes," Mara admitted. "Yours?"

"Always," Torres replied cheerfully.

They rode in companionable silence for several floors, the city slipping by outside in streaks of refracted light.

"You grew up here," Torres said eventually, phrasing it as an observation rather than a question.

"I did."

"Hard thing, watching a place redefine itself."

Mara glanced at her then, surprised by the gentleness of the remark.

"It can be," she said.

Torres nodded. "If it helps at all—we intend to be good neighbors."

Mara smiled, genuinely this time.

"I think," she said, "that will make more difference than you realize."

The lift arrived at Mara's floor. She stepped out, then paused and turned back.

"For what it's worth," she added, "the tower could use a little redefinition."

Torres's expression softened.

"We're rather good at that," she said.

As the doors closed, Mara found herself thinking—not for the first time—that the Reach's judgments were rarely aligned with its virtues.

And that, perhaps, this change—however imposed—was not without its quiet compensations.

The first dinner invitation arrived less than a week after the welcome session.

It came not from the tower administration, nor from any Crestline neighbor attempting to reclaim familiarity, but from Alina Torres herself. The message was brief, almost austere in its wording, and sent directly rather than routed through the customary layers of intermediary scheduling.

We're hosting a small gathering this evening.

Unstructured. No agenda.

You'd be welcome.

There was no reference to obligation, no apology for informality. It read less like an invitation than a statement of open space.

Mara hesitated longer than she intended.

Accepting would not be improper—the stewardship framework encouraged "social integration"—but etiquette in the Reach rarely rewarded spontaneity. Appearances mattered, especially when boundaries were newly redrawn. Declining, however, felt like an unnecessary fortification, the kind easily misread as resentment.

She accepted.

The gathering was held in one of the reassigned mid-level lounges, a space that had once hosted formal receptions and charity reviews. The furniture arrangement had been altered subtly rather than replaced: seating clustered informally, table surfaces cleared of decorative redundancy. The light levels were lower than Crestline standard, softened further by the evening haze casting gentle diffusion through the curved glass.

The effect was unexpectedly convivial.

Mara paused just inside the threshold, allowing herself a moment to absorb the scene. Conversations overlapped without crowding. Laughter appeared without first seeking approval. People stood when they wished and sat when they tired. Drinks were poured communally rather than allotted.

Someone had brought food that did not conform to dietary optimization profiles. The scent alone felt faintly rebellious.

Torres spotted her from across the room and crossed over, glass in hand.

"I'm glad you came," she said. "I worried we'd sent the wrong signal."

"What signal was that?" Mara asked.

"That we might expect you to perform."

Mara smiled. "That would require advance notice."

Torres laughed softly and gestured toward the center of the room. "Please. Help yourself. No protocols."

Mara accepted a drink—something dark, bitter, unfamiliar—and leaned against the low railing that separated the lounge from its panoramic view. The Reach shone beyond, a balanced geometry of light and shadow, indifferent to social realignment.

One of the operators joined her, introducing himself as Tomas. He spoke with a relaxed cadence that betrayed years of communicating through static and delay.

"You've lived in this tower your whole life?" he asked.

"Yes."

"Then you know its moods better than most," he said. "It has moods."

"It does," she agreed. "They're easy to ignore if you're not looking for them."

He nodded. "Structures always tell you what they need, eventually."

It was said without irony.

As the evening progressed, Mara found herself drawn into conversations she would not have encountered elsewhere in Crestline: stories of salvage missions that relied as much on intuition as data, of transit corridors stabilized not by algorithm but by human judgment under pressure. The operators spoke freely of failure, of recalibration through experience rather than optimization.

"No plan survives contact with reality," Tomas observed at one point. "But some people are better at adapting on the fly."

"Adaptation isn't a skill often celebrated here," Mara said.

"Then perhaps that's the problem," he replied, without malice.

The implicit critique landed more keenly than any overt challenge could have done.

The change in atmosphere did not go unnoticed.

Within days, subtle resistance began to surface among the tower's long-standing residents. Complaints were lodged—not formally, but through suggestion and tone—about noise levels that technically did not exceed acceptable thresholds, about unfamiliar faces appearing in shared transit cars, about the erosion of certain unspoken privileges.

Mara fielded these concerns with practiced diplomacy, reassuring, redirecting, contextualizing.

"It's temporary," one acquaintance insisted, voice edged with forced brightness. "Surely this arrangement can't last indefinitely."

"All arrangements are subject to review," Mara replied evenly.

The acquaintance frowned, dissatisfied. Permanence had always been assumed rather than negotiated in Crestline circles.

Her father, for his part, took refuge in dignified withdrawal. He attended fewer gatherings, citing prior engagements, and confined his movements largely to the upper tiers. When he did encounter the new tenants, he greeted them with cordial reserve, offering neither criticism nor warmth.

"They're... serviceable," he remarked one evening, after sharing a lift with two operators laden with equipment cases. "Not the sort we usually associate with."

"Usually associate with whom?" Mara asked.

"Us," he said, faintly irritated.

She let the remark pass.

The implicit contrast sharpened further with time.

One afternoon, a systems fault disrupted water pressure across several mid-level residential floors. The disruption was minor by technical standards, but Crestline residents reacted with disproportionate alarm, requests flooding management channels within minutes.

Before protocols could escalate, the operators intervened.

Mara observed the response from a monitoring station, watching as Torres and her team coordinated directly with maintenance crews, rerouting supply lines manually while bypassing two layers of approval. The issue was resolved within the hour.

No report was filed.

The absence of formal recognition disturbed several administrators more than the disruption itself.

"They acted without clearance," one steward protested during a follow-up briefing. "It sets a precedent."

"They restored essential service efficiently," Mara countered. "Is that not the intended outcome?"

"That depends on process compliance," the steward insisted.

Mara inclined her head. "Process exists to support outcomes, not to supersede them."

The steward had no ready reply.

That evening, Torres sent a simple message.

Hope we didn't overstep.

Old habits.

Mara responded without hesitation.

You solved a problem.

The reply came back almost instantly.

That's how we define it.

The presence of the operators began to influence the tower in ways more difficult to quantify.

Shared spaces were used more organically. Equipment was borrowed and returned without incident. People lingered in transitional areas longer, conversations forming without invitation or hierarchy. The tower felt less brittle, as though some unseen tension had eased.

Not everyone approved.

At a Crestline mixer hosted in an adjacent building, Mara overheard a remark phrased carefully enough to be attributed to concern rather than prejudice.

"They're competent, of course," someone said. "But competence alone doesn't entitle one to proximity."

Proximity, Mara thought, was rarely earned through entitlement.

She did not intervene.

Late one night, Mara encountered Torres again, this time on the upper observation deck—the portion still officially reserved for Keene use.

"I hope I'm not intruding," Torres said, noticing her hesitation at the deck entrance.

"You're not," Mara replied. "We share this space now, after all."

Torres smiled at that and moved to join her at the railing.

The city below seemed quieter at this hour, its movements reduced to essential flows. The tide was low, exposing the older bones of the Reach along the seawall's edge.

"Do you resent this?" Torres asked suddenly.

The question was gentle, almost careful.

Mara considered it.

"I resent the framing," she said finally. "Not the people."

Torres nodded. "That's fair."

"We were taught to believe continuity meant exclusion," Mara added. "That maintaining position required controlling access."

"And now?"

"And now I'm not entirely convinced," she said.

Torres leaned her forearms against the glass. "Where we come from, continuity means survival. You share space because you have to. Or you don't last."

The words carried no accusation. They did not need to.

Mara felt the quiet satisfaction of a truth articulated cleanly.

Below them, the tower's lights pulsed steadily, indifferent to philosophical alignment.

The first official social recalibration occurred the following week, when a long-standing Crestline benefactor declined to renew their contribution pledge after learning of the tower's shared occupancy.

The withdrawal was framed discreetly. Explanations centered on shifting priorities and strategic realignment. No names were attached.

Mara received the notice during a routine review session. She read it without visible reaction.

Later that day, Tomas approached her in the atrium.

"Heard you lost a patron," he said, not unkindly.

"Yes."

"Hard pill."

"Predictable," Mara replied. "Visibility invites opinion."

He nodded. "If it helps, we gained three requests for collaboration since moving in."

She met his gaze, surprised.

"From where?"

"Mostly transit authorities. Some municipal groups. They like our proximity."

Mara considered that quietly.

Change, she thought, never moved in a single direction.

That evening, as she reviewed the day's reports, a new notification appeared, flagged as low-priority but unusual.

Incoming inquiry: Azure Quarter Logistics Forum

Requesting consultation regarding multi-sector integration strategies.

She did not yet know what it would lead to.

But she knew, with growing certainty, that the presence of the new tenants had done more than occupy space.

They had reframed value.

And in doing so, they had exposed the fragility of prestige that relied entirely on exclusion to sustain itself.

As Mara stood by the window once more, watching the Reach adapt beneath her, she felt something like cautious optimism settle alongside her lingering unease.

Not all change, she was learning, arrived as loss.

Some arrived as contrast.

And contrast, once seen, could not easily be ignored.

The Ghost Contract

There were records Mara never accessed directly.

They existed, archived in redundant systems no longer prioritized for retrieval, preserved out of regulatory obligation rather than relevance. Most people trusted such records the way they trusted old locks on sealed doors—comforted by the idea of protection without any intention of testing it.

Mara knew exactly where hers were stored.

She accessed them late, the night after the tower's first shared social recalibration triggered its discreet withdrawal of capital. The apartment lights were dimmed to functional low, window blinds adjusted to let in only the faint shimmer of the Reach beyond. The city's rhythms filtered upward, softened by distance and glass.

She sat at her console, posture precise, fingers still.

The interface recognized her credentials at once. Of course it did. There were things lineage still protected.

She navigated past fiscal archives, past environmental assessments, past dozens of structural agreements bearing her grandfather's name and her father's. None of those held her attention for long. She was not interested in inherited certainty.

She was looking for a contract that had never been fully executed.

The search queries were clipped, unemotional:

Calder, Elias

Agreement Type: Personal Association

Status: Terminated — Pre-Registration

The file appeared almost immediately.

She did not open it.

Instead, she leaned back and closed her eyes, letting memory rise at its own pace.

Eight years earlier, Keene Tower had not yet begun its quiet decline.

Its corridors still carried the confidence of exclusivity. Invitations arrived without delay. The Index had glowed with no visible warnings, no softened lines tracing incremental drift away from its peak.

Mara had believed, at the time, that permanence was simply the default state of things.

She met Elias Calder through a logistics review committee—an unbelievably dull assignment administered under the guise of cross-sector collaboration. He had been newly arrived from the frontier corridors, his clearance provisional but unusually broad for someone without Crestline affiliations.

His first remark had not been clever.

"These numbers don't tell you where the failures cluster," he had said, browsing a projection others had accepted uncritically.

Several committee members bristled. One had politely explained the system's predictive accuracy.

Elias had listened, then nodded once.

"Accuracy isn't the same as understanding," he replied.

Later, when Mara encountered him alone in the process corridor, she surprised herself by speaking first.

"What would you change?" she had asked.

He smiled then—not broadly, not performatively, but with an ease that suggested he rarely felt compelled to impress the room.

"I'd walk the corridors before recommending how to reinforce them," he said. "You feel stress patterns better when you're standing in them."

She found herself intrigued by the simplicity of the idea.

They spoke infrequently at first, encounters spaced by scheduling chance rather than intent. When they did speak, the conversations moved easily, unburdened by hierarchy. Elias did not inquire after her lineage. She did not volunteer it.

Only later did she realize how rare that had been.

The contract—such as it was—had come several months into their acquaintance.

Not a romantic declaration, not a promise spoken aloud. In the Reach, institutional recognition carried weight greater than sentiment. Access privileges indicated affiliation more definitively than words ever could.

Elias had opened the proposal cautiously, as though uncertain whether it belonged in the space between them.

"I wasn't sure this was appropriate," he said. "Given where I am."

Mara had reviewed it carefully, heart steady despite the implications. It was not extravagant. It did not promise permanence. It offered legitimacy—a shared registry designation that acknowledged personal association under certain legal frameworks.

A stepping stone, not an endpoint.

"You're planning to stay," she said, tracing the parameters with her gaze.

"For now," Elias replied. "Until the next contract pulls me outward."

That had not sounded threatening then.

She had filed the documentation with her own credentials, pending family endorsement. The system accepted it provisionally, marking it as *in review*, awaiting final authorization.

That authorization never arrived.

Mara opened her eyes and turned back to the console.

The contract file waited, unchanged.

She accessed it at last.

The interface resolved into a clean layout: names, dates, legal identifiers. Her own designation appeared alongside Elias's, connected by a dotted line rather than a continuous one. *Pre-Registration*, the status read. *Terminated.*

The termination timestamp glowed faintly.

Her father's authorization key was embedded alongside it.

She remembered the conversation with aching clarity.

He had not shouted. He had not forbidden. That would have been easier to defy.

Instead, he had explained.

"We are already under observation," he had said, pacing the eastern gallery, hands clasped behind his back. "Any instability will be magnified."

"He isn't unstable," Mara replied. "He's unestablished."

"A distinction creditors do not make."

"He's capable. Proven."

"Temporarily," her father countered. "And beyond that?"

Mara had hesitated then, just for a moment. That moment had been enough.

"You are needed here," he continued, voice steady but strained. "The Index has begun to shift. We cannot afford associations that signal uncertainty."

It had not been framed as instruction.

It had been framed as necessity.

"You'll recover," her aunt had added later, more gently. "Time favors sensible choices."

Mara wondered now, as she stared at the record of that decision encoded in indifferent light, whether time ever favored anything at all.

Elias had not argued when she told him.

That was what struck her most, even now.

They met at Dock Nine, a public platform near the edge of Crestline, one of the last places not yet curated beyond recognition. The tide was low that evening, exposing structural ribs beneath the seawall.

Mara remembered the salt in the air, the way it caught at her throat.

"I can't proceed," she had said. "Not yet."

He had listened without interrupting.

"Because of timing," he asked.

"Yes."

"And stability."

"Yes."

Elias had nodded slowly, weighing her words.

"Is this what you want?" he asked.

She did not answer immediately.

The truth—that she did not know—felt insufficiently decisive.

"I need to be responsible," she said instead.

He had smiled faintly, though something in his eyes dimmed almost imperceptibly.

"Responsibility has a way of narrowing choices," he said. "I respect that."

He did not wait for her to reconsider.

The next contract he accepted took him further outward, beyond reliable communication windows. She received updates sporadically at first. Then, only through public channels.

Eventually, even those ceased.

Mara closed the contract file.

Her apartment felt smaller now, as though the walls had shifted without her noticing.

She rose and crossed to the window, resting her fingertips lightly against the glass. Below, the Reach glimmered with composed indifference. The seawall lights reflected back at her, cheering nothing, promising nothing.

Her wrist interface chimed softly.

Not a message this time, but a system alert.

Operator Authorization: Extended Access

Designation: Frontier Collective

Elias Calder's authorization key appeared among the listed credentials.

The Ghost Contract, she thought, had never truly expired.

It had only waited.

And now, with the tower reshaped, its boundaries softened, its certainties surrendered piece by piece, the past had found its way back through cracks she had once believed sealed.

She exhaled, steadying herself.

The regret, once diffuse, had crystallized.

And with it came gravity.

The morning after she accessed the contract, the city behaved as though nothing had changed.

Transit ran on schedule. The haze held steady above the seawall. Notifications arrived with their usual measured insistence, each one framed to suggest that delay was impractical but never urgent. Mara moved through her routines with practiced control, until she reached the shared operations corridor and found herself slowing without conscious intention.

A temporary authorization panel glowed beside the access door.

It displayed a list of names and clearance codes, rotating at intervals designed to discourage focus. She scanned it before she could stop herself.

Calder, Elias.

The name appeared between two others, unadorned, its presence neither emphasized nor concealed. It was simply... there. Integrated.

Mara entered the corridor before the system could time out.

The space beyond smelled faintly of metal and ozone, the scent of equipment recently unsealed. Crates lined the wall in tidy rows, labeled with destination tags and load limits rather than ownership marks. Someone had taken care to leave the central passage clear.

Voices carried softly from farther down the corridor.

"—if the pressure curve spikes again, reroute through the secondary intake. It'll hold."

"That'll stress the southern supports."

"Not past tolerance. We've tested worse."

Mara recognized Elias's voice immediately.

It had not changed as much as she had expected. The cadence remained familiar, shaped by conviction rather than performance. He spoke now with the same ease he once had in committee rooms and transit bays, as if the world were something to be addressed directly, not mediated.

She stopped.

For a moment, she considered retreating—allowing the encounter to be postponed, formalized, made manageable by protocol. The impulse passed almost as quickly as it arose. Eight years had taught her that delay altered nothing of consequence. It only allowed shape to harden.

She continued forward.

Elias stood near an open crate, sleeves rolled back, a diagnostic unit tucked loosely under one arm. He was turned slightly away from her, attention focused on the readout hovering above the crate's rim. Torres stood opposite him, leaning against the wall, arms crossed loosely.

Elias noticed her first.

He did not react immediately.

That, too, was familiar.

He finished the sentence he was speaking, handed the diagnostic unit to one of the technicians, and turned with deliberate composure.

"Mara," he said.

Her name sounded unchanged in his voice. Neither softened nor sharpened by time.

"Elias," she replied.

Torres's gaze shifted between them, curiosity held carefully in check. She did not ask questions. She did not excuse herself. She simply waited.

"I saw your authorization come through," Elias said. "I wasn't certain if we'd cross paths this quickly."

"The building has a way of compressing distance," Mara said.

He smiled faintly at that, the gesture restrained, almost cautious.

"So it does."

For several seconds, none of them spoke.

Torres cleared her throat lightly. "I'll leave you to it," she said, and stepped away without ceremony.

The corridor felt suddenly quieter.

"I didn't know if you'd received my message," Elias said.

"I did."

"And?"

"And what?"

He studied her then, more openly. His eyes were the same shade she remembered—dark, reflective, not easily surrendering their contents.

"I wasn't sure if this would be... welcome," he said.

Mara considered the word.

"Welcome is a generous concept," she replied. "But it isn't unwelcome."

"That's something," he said.

They stood there, the distance between them neither excessive nor intimate. Around them, the corridor continued its quiet business, technicians passing without staring, the building already adjusting to this new configuration of presence.

"You should have been informed," Mara said after a moment. "About the tower."

"I was informed," Elias replied. "I assumed you knew."

She nodded.

"I also assumed you knew."

Assumptions had been fatal to them before.

"I heard about the stewardship review through Allocation," he continued. "Before the Collective finalized the placement."

"And?" she asked.

"And I didn't intervene."

"I wouldn't have expected you to."

"Good," he said. "Because I wouldn't have."

There was no defensiveness in the statement. Only clarity.

They moved then, stepping aside as a group passed, the interruption oddly grounding. When they resumed their positions, Mara noticed the faint line at Elias's temple, the new angles to his posture. Time had done its work with nuance rather than cruelty.

"You left the city quickly," she said.

"Yes."

"Far?"

"Far enough that returning took effort."

She did not ask what kind. Some questions demanded trust rather than answers.

"I wondered," Elias said carefully, "if you might have heard before this."

"I hadn't," Mara replied. "Only afterward."

He nodded. "That's fair."

They fell silent again.

The past hovered between them, no longer diffuse but sharply outlined. The Ghost Contract lay unspoken beneath every word, its dotted line pulsing quietly beneath their restraint.

"I didn't come back because of the tower," Elias said eventually. "Or the Reach itself."

She had known that already.

"I came back because my contract window closed," he went on. "And because I realized I'd been carrying unresolved vectors longer than was advisable."

Mara almost smiled.

"Typical you," she said softly, "to phrase it that way."

His mouth curved upward at the edges, brief but genuine.

"I've gotten more careful," he said. "That's not the same thing as wiser."

"No," she agreed. "It isn't."

"May I ask," he said, tone even, "whether you regret it?"

The question landed cleanly. He had always been direct when it mattered.

She did not answer at once.

They moved again, drifting instinctively toward the observation curve at the end of the corridor. The Reach spread silently below them, a familiar sprawl of light and structure.

"I regret," Mara said finally, choosing each word with care, "confusing responsibility with certainty."

He watched her, unreadable.

"And you?"

"I regret," he replied, "believing distance would resolve what I refused to confront."

She turned then, meeting his gaze fully.

"That wasn't something you were taught to do," she said.

"No," he agreed. "But I learned eventually."

The admission carried more weight than any apology could have.

They stood side by side, not touching, but closer than protocol required. The building around them hummed softly, systems recalibrating, boundaries shifting.

"I won't pretend nothing's changed," Elias said. "I won't ask you to."

"I wouldn't trust a request like that," Mara replied.

"Good," he said again.

A message chimed on his interface. He glanced at it, then dismissed it without reading.

"You said Azure Quarter," she noted.

"Yes."

"You chose visibility."

"I chose neutral ground."

She considered that. "There's no such thing as neutral ground anymore."

He smiled at that, faintly rueful. "No. There isn't."

When they parted moments later, it was without ceremony. No promises. No rehearsed restraint. Just recognition, and the shared understanding that postponement was no longer benign.

As Mara walked back toward her apartment, the tower felt different again—not because space had been reassigned, but because memory now occupied it deliberately, rather than by accident.

The Ghost Contract had never truly waited.

It had simply refused to disappear.

And now, standing once more within proximity of the life she had chosen away from, Mara sensed with absolute clarity that responsibility, once invoked, did not absolve one from consequence.

It only delayed the reckoning.

—

Azure Quarter arrived before she did.

That was how Mara experienced it — the district's curated atmosphere pressing forward to meet her before she had fully decided to enter it. The promenade along Dock Six was lit in the particular way that made evening feel chosen rather than inevitable, its surfaces reflective without being declarative. Restaurants and exchange lounges occupied the ground level in careful rotation, their patrons visible without being examined, their conversations carrying just far enough to suggest sophistication rather than reveal it.

She was seven minutes early.

She did not adjust her pace.

The dock itself occupied the outer edge of the promenade, where the Azure Quarter's refinement softened against older infrastructure — mooring pylons worn smooth by salt and use, transit berths still functional beneath their cosmetic updates. It was, as Elias had chosen, neither Crestline nor Lower Reach. A place that acknowledged both without belonging to either.

He was already there.

She registered him from a distance before her mind fully assembled the fact: a figure leaning against the outer rail, jacket open to the evening air, attention directed toward the water rather than the approach. He had not dressed for the setting. That was either carelessness or statement, and she had known him long enough to suspect the latter.

When he heard her footsteps he turned, and the eight years collapsed without announcing themselves.

"You came," he said.

"You sent coordinates," she replied.

A pause that held more history than either of them had agreed to carry. He smiled faintly — not the broad performance of reunion, but something quieter, as if the expression had been waiting a long time to be accurate.

"I wasn't sure," Elias said, "whether the wafer was too much."

"It was sufficient," Mara replied. "No more."

He accepted the calibration without deflection.

She joined him at the rail. Not close enough to suggest resolution, not far enough to suggest refusal. The water below caught the promenade lights and distributed them imprecisely, the reflections less interested in accuracy than motion. A transit vessel moved through the lower berth, its running lights unhurried.

For a moment neither of them spoke.

The city filled the space with its usual indifference — sound without opinion, movement without judgment. It was the same city it had always been. That had once felt like stability. Tonight it felt like a witness.

"How long have you been back?" she asked.

"Long enough to understand I should have sent a message sooner," Elias replied. "Not long enough to know what to say."

"That's honest."

"I've been practicing."

She glanced at him, surprised enough to let it show. He was looking at the water still, his profile unchanged in its essential structure, though time had added what time always added — not diminishment, but density.

"You look established," she said.

"I look older," he replied.

"Those aren't opposites."

He turned then, the humor in his expression shading into something less easy to manage. He studied her the way she had occasionally caught herself studying the city from height — not possessively, but carefully, as if trying to understand how something had endured in his absence when endurance had seemed unlikely.

"You stayed," he said.

"Yes."

"Even when the tower began to change."

"Especially then," Mara replied. "Leaving would have been interpretation."

He nodded slowly.

"The Collective's placement," he began.

"I know," she said. "I saw your authorization key."

"I wasn't certain whether to—"

"You didn't need to," she said. "The system handled it."

"That's not what I meant."

She turned to face him fully then. The promenade moved behind him, its steady traffic of people navigating the evening with the practiced ease of those who had decided in advance how the night would go. Neither of them had decided anything.

That, she realized, was why this was difficult.

"What did you mean?" she asked.

Elias exhaled. It was not impatience — it was the sound of someone releasing a breath held too long.

"I meant," he said, "that I wanted to ask you. Before the system placed me. Before the Collective formalized anything. I wanted it to be a choice that you knew about."

Mara was quiet.

"And instead," he continued, "it arrived through infrastructure. Like everything else."

"That's how the Reach works," she said.

"I know," Elias replied. "I was hoping to work differently."

The admission landed without apology, which was what made it land at all. He had always understood that sincerity without self-pity was the only register she trusted. That, at least, had not changed.

"Why Dock Six?" she asked.

"Equal distance," he said. "From everything that has a claim on either of us."

She looked around — the worn pylons, the curated light, the water that did not care whose name appeared on any access panel. He was right, technically. No single interest owned this stretch of rail.

"There is no equal distance anymore," she said.

"No," he agreed. "But there's this."

She did not answer immediately.

A couple passed behind them, their conversation audible for two steps and then gone, absorbed back into the promenade's ambient hum. The transit vessel had disappeared into the lower channel. The water stilled briefly, then resumed its small negotiations with the dock.

"I don't know what this is," Mara said at last.

"Neither do I," Elias replied. "I only know that pretending it isn't anything would be inaccurate."

She almost smiled.

"Typical you," she said quietly, "to frame it that way."

He did smile then — the same brief curve she had seen in the corridor, genuine and unguarded.

"I've had eight years to practice the phrasing," he said. "I still haven't improved on accuracy."

They stood there a little longer, neither pressing, neither retreating. The rail was cool beneath her hands. The city glowed steadily around them, patient and without advice.

When she finally turned to leave, she paused just long enough.

"I'm glad you came back," she said.

He did not respond immediately. When he did, his voice was level, the words chosen without excess.

"I came back because distance stopped being an answer," he said. "I should have said that first."

Mara nodded once.

"You said it now," she replied.

She walked back into the promenade without looking behind her, the Azure Quarter's careful light closing around her as she moved. The meeting had not resolved anything. It had not needed to.

What it had done was simpler, and more durable.

It had confirmed that the weight she had been carrying was not imagined.

And that he had been carrying it too.

Peripheral Residence

The relocation was introduced as temporary.

Mara heard that word often in the days following the Dock Six meeting, offered by various members of Allocation and reinforced by her father's insistence that the arrangement was merely *interim*. Temporary solutions, he liked to say, preserved flexibility. They imposed no judgment on the past and no admission about the future.

Still, temporary required a location.

Mara agreed to the Midway proposal after reviewing the alternatives more carefully than anyone expected her to. Azure Quarter was dismissed almost immediately—too visible, too curated, too likely to invite interpretation. The Lower Reach was genuinely impractical for her assignments and would have appeared performative, a gesture of virtue that comforted no one.

The modular residences along the Midway edge offered something else: proximity without prestige.

They were designed to house professionals whose incomes fluctuated with contracts—engineers between postings, consultants on rotational service, families transitioning between phases of better fortune. The buildings lacked the visual authority of Crestline towers but compensated with warmth, sound, and a faintly disordered sense of life continuing irrespective of scrutiny.

Mara approved the lease herself.

Her father barely noticed the distinction.

"You'll be close enough," he said, scanning another briefing display while she stood beside him in the eastern gallery. "And it avoids unnecessary optics."

"Yes," she replied. *That*, at least, was true.

The unit assigned to her sat on the seventeenth level of a mid-rise composite block overlooking a transit greenway. The building curved slightly inward, its exterior clad in salt-worn polymer panels that bore marks of repeated repair. Nothing about it announced permanence. Nothing resisted adaptation.

Inside, the layout was sensible and compact. Living and working spaces blended without pretense, separated by sliding partitions that invited reconfiguration rather than discouraging it. The windows admitted more sound than she was accustomed to: voices from the greenway below, the whine of personal transit units passing too close to regulatory thresholds, the occasional laugh that carried upward before dissolving into ambient noise.

Her arrival went largely unnoticed.

A neighbor two doors down nodded politely but did not ask her name. Another held the door open without comment, balancing a crate of perishable supplies against one hip. The building's systems registered her presence, updated her profile, and receded into the background.

It felt unsettling.

Not threatening—just unfiltered.

That evening, she unpacked neatly, arranging the few personal items she had brought with her into the provided storage slots. She had chosen not to transport anything unstably symbolic. No architectural plans. No heirloom devices. Only functional records and the essentials required to maintain her work.

She left the rest behind in Keene Tower, preserved where they belonged, untouched by this quieter displacement.

At nineteen hundred hours, the unit's ambient display notified her of a building-wide maintenance cycle. The message was apologized for twice before requested compliance. She smiled faintly at the redundancy and acknowledged it.

Minutes later, a chime sounded at her door.

Mara hesitated.

Visitor announcements were unusual here; most residents preferred informal signaling. She opened the door to find a woman roughly her own age holding a tablet and a data stylus, expression alert but unguarded.

"Hi," the woman said. "Sorry to disturb. I'm Lina. Floor coordinator."

"Of course," Mara replied, stepping aside. "Go ahead."

Lina entered without ceremony, her gaze flicking over the unit with efficient curiosity.

"New arrival," she said, not a question.

"Yes."

"Lease flagged as transitional," Lina continued. "Not my business, but it helps me anticipate turnover."

"I understand."

Lina smiled, appreciative rather than apologetic.

"There's a communal meal on Thursdays," she added. "No obligation. But we do like to know who's around."

"I'll keep that in mind."

"Good," Lina said. "The system often misses context."

Then, as if thinking better of it, she extended the tablet slightly.

"If you experience any issues—noise conflicts, climate inconsistency, transit lag—I tend to respond faster than central support."

Mara accepted the contact request.

"Thank you."

Lina inclined her head and turned to leave. At the threshold, she paused.

"Oh—and if you need quiet, aim for the early morning hours. After that, people forget themselves."

"I'll remember," Mara said.

Once the door closed, the unit seemed to sigh—a barely perceptible shift in airflow as the system recalibrated to her presence.

She sat at the workspace and opened her queue, half-expecting to find some delayed reaction from her father or Allocation. There was nothing urgent. Only the altered rhythms of her notification density reflected the change.

Here, fewer messages competed for priority.

It felt inefficient.

—

The next morning, Mara woke earlier than required.

The sounds of the building reached her before the ambient light cycle activated. Footsteps overhead. Someone arguing amiably with a digital assistant. A burst of laughter from the greenway below.

She lay still for a moment longer than she needed to, acclimating.

Then she rose and set about preparing for the day.

The transit ride to Keene Tower took twelve minutes longer than before, though the distance itself had scarcely changed. The extra time came from crossings and recalibration nodes rather than linear displacement. Mara used it to review overnight updates from Infrastructure Allocation, her focus steady despite the unfamiliar jostling of fellow commuters.

She noticed how often people spoke near her without lowering their voices.

It was not discourteous. It simply did not occur to them that anyone might mind.

At Keene Tower, the contrast was immediate.

The lobby had regained its polished silence, now more conspicuous for having been broken recently. The operators moved through it with casual efficiency, their presence still faintly novel but already integrated. Crestline residents kept to their established clusters, conversations muting as needed, expressions carefully neutral.

Mara passed between them with the ease of practiced mediation.

She spent the morning resolving schedule conflicts between shared maintenance crews and executive access windows, her role once again clear: smooth, manage, absorb. Several issues resolved themselves more quickly now, thanks to the operators' willingness to act without ceremony.

She noted the efficiency.

By midday, she felt the accumulated fatigue of transition settle into her shoulders.

Instead of lunching at her usual Crestline café, she returned to Midway.

The greenway below her building hosted a small produce market at midday, stalls arranged loosely around a shaded pedestrian crossing. Vendors brought items not yet folded into supply optimization chains, some grown or fabricated locally, others acquired through informal networks that bypassed the primary distributors.

Mara navigated the space cautiously at first, unused to transactions conducted without standard interfaces. A vendor noticed her hesitation and smiled.

"First time here?" he asked.

"Yes."

He gestured toward a tray of fruit whose origin she could not place.

"Try this. No commitment."

Mara accepted a sample and tasted something bright, sharp, and unfamiliar.

"Thank you," she said.

He nodded. "Comes from upriver. Tastes better than it looks."

She bought two pieces, feeling faintly conspicuous but no longer unwelcome.

As she turned away, she heard her name spoken—not called out, but asked.

"Mara?"

She turned to find Lina approaching, basket balanced against her hip.

"We were just talking about you," Lina said cheerfully.

"I hope favorably."

"Curiously," Lina replied. "Which lasts longer."

They walked together without discussing trajectories, conversation flowing easily despite its lack of direction. Lina spoke about the building, about her role coordinating residents who seldom agreed on anything except their dislike of centralized intervention. She complained mildly about the maintenance cycles and the transit noise, praised the view in early rain.

Mara listened.

She was asked, several times, about her work. Each time, her explanation was met with nods rather than awe.

"That sounds useful," Lina concluded at last.

Mara smiled. "It tends to be."

The understated approval landed more solidly than she expected.

As they parted and Mara returned to her unit, she felt a peculiar blend of dislocation and ease.

Here, she was not invisible—but she was not exceptional either.

The community did not orbit prestige. It absorbed utility, noise, presence.

The discomfort lay in that anonymity.

The belonging, she suspected, lay there too.

By the end of the first week, Mara had learned the building's patterns.

They were not fixed in the way Keene Tower's had been, optimized into predictability and enforced by silent agreement. Instead, they shifted in response to small variables: weather changes, transit congestion, the arrival or departure of residents whose schedules did not align long enough to stabilize. The modular block breathed with its occupants rather than containing them.

It was louder than she preferred.

Not constantly—there were hours of near-stillness in the early morning, when the greenway below lay muted under fog and the transit lines thinned to necessity—but unpredictably. Noise arrived in bursts: a door slammed too hard, laughter rose suddenly and dissipated, music slipped through shared walls before being cut off mid-note.

The first time it startled her, she reminded herself that nothing was wrong.

The second time, she found herself adjusting her posture, alert for cues she could not yet interpret.

The third, she exhaled and let it pass.

That, she decided, might be the adjustment Lina had meant.

—

The building began to make use of her.

Not formally.

There were no requests routed through professional channels, no acknowledgment that her expertise exceeded the modest scope of a temporary tenant. Instead, small problems appeared in her vicinity and lingered just long enough to suggest invitation.

The first involved a systems delay in the shared laundry tier—nothing catastrophic, merely an intermittent failure in load recognition that caused machines to stall mid-cycle. Complaints had gone unanswered long enough to irritate the evening residents, and Mara happened upon a knot of them gathered around a blocked interface as she returned from work.

"It's been doing this all week," someone said, exasperated. "Support keeps cycling us."

Mara slowed, observing.

The interface display blinked, its prompts repeating in apologetic cadence. A familiar fault pattern emerged under her scrutiny.

"May I?" she asked.

There was a pause, then one resident stepped back, uncertain but hopeful.

Mara accessed the override, bypassing the automated queue, and adjusted the load calibration manually. The system accepted the change with immediate relief. Within seconds, the machines resumed operation.

No one cheered. No one thanked her extravagantly.

A man nodded once. "That did it."

"Yes," she replied. "The timing threshold was misaligned."

"Figures," another muttered, already losing interest now that the problem had resolved.

Mara moved on without comment.

Twenty minutes later, Lina tapped at her door.

"Word travels," Lina said, amused. "We could probably use you at the maintenance desk if you ever tire of whatever it is you do now."

Mara smiled. "I'll keep that in mind."

—

Similar incidents followed.

A transit schedule hiccup during a rainstorm that left commuters stranded one platform too far from cover. A misrouted power allocation that dimmed lights along the eastern corridor but spared the western wing entirely. A scheduling conflict between two families who had both assumed the rooftop garden was reserved for them that evening.

Mara resolved each quietly, efficiently, with minimal explanation.

She did not correct anyone when they assumed it was her responsibility.

The building, for its part, adapted quickly. Her visits to communal spaces were met with casual nods rather than scrutiny. Doors opened fractionally faster when she approached. Conversations paused—not in deference, but in expectation that she might listen.

It was a subtler position than authority.

At Keene Tower, she had been recognized.

Here, she was relied upon.

—

The Thursday meal proved more crowded than she had anticipated.

Mara arrived late, having underestimated transit delays and overestimated her own inclination to linger alone. When she entered the common hall, the air was dense with sound and motion, tables crowded with mismatched dishes and people shifting to accommodate additional seats.

No one asked her name.

Someone pointed her toward an empty chair.

She sat, accepting a portion of something warm and spiced handed to her without inquiry. The person beside her—a woman with tired eyes and a quick smile—began speaking as though they had already been mid-conversation.

"—and of course I know it's ridiculous, but I don't trust any system that apologizes before it fails."

Mara nodded. "Apologies tend to lag behavior."

The woman laughed, delighted. "Exactly."

The conversation flowed on without pause, branching in unexpected directions, circling loosely around shared irritations and minor satisfactions. Someone else leaned in, adding a story about a stalled permit. Another countered with a suggestion that ignored protocol entirely.

Mara found herself listening more than she spoke, contributing only when clarity was needed.

Her silence was not misinterpreted.

If anything, it invited others to fill the space.

She noticed, as the evening progressed, that her contributions were accepted without scrutiny, though rarely credited. When she suggested a workaround, someone else repeated it later as their own observation, and the table nodded in agreement.

The realization surprised her—not with irritation, but with recognition.

This was a different economy.

Value circulated here without requiring attribution.

—

Later, as the crowd thinned and residents drifted back toward their units, Lina appeared at her shoulder with two cups of tea.

"You did all right," Lina said, handing her one.

"I sat and ate," Mara replied. "I didn't disrupt anyone."

"That's an achievement," Lina said dryly.

They leaned against the railing overlooking the greenway, watching lights pass beneath them.

"I've been curious," Lina said after a moment. "And you don't have to answer."

Mara waited.

"You don't look like someone who belongs here," Lina continued. "But you don't look uncomfortable either."

The observation was sharp without being unkind.

"I belong... temporarily," Mara said.

Lina snorted softly. "Everyone does."

Mara smiled at that.

"What made you choose Midway?" Lina asked.

"The absence of performance," Mara replied honestly. "And proximity that didn't come with commentary."

Lina nodded. "That tracks."

They stood together in companionable silence, the late evening sounds of the building settling around them.

"You know," Lina added, "people here don't care where you come from. But they notice who solves what."

Mara inclined her head. "Then I'll do my best not to disappoint."

—

The following Monday, a message arrived from Infrastructure Allocation requesting confirmation that Mara could be reassigned to a primarily remote coordination role "during this transitional phase."

She read it twice.

The phrasing was neutral. The implication was not.

Remote roles preserved presence without proximity. They were offered to those whose physical location no longer aided institutional signaling.

Mara forwarded the message to her father with minimal commentary.

He responded hours later with a brief acknowledgment and no opinion.

She did not reply.

—

That evening, returning from Keene Tower, Mara encountered a cluster of residents gathered near the greenway entrance. Their postures suggested mild agitation rather than alarm.

"What's going on?" she asked, approaching.

"Transit grid glitched," someone replied. "Delayed everything northbound."

A resident sighed. "Support says twenty minutes."

Mara studied the transit display, reading between the indicators.

"Fifteen," she said. "If someone manually resets the feeder node."

She turned toward the control kiosk.

A man stepped forward. "I can climb it."

Mara paused. "Wait."

She accessed the kiosk, overriding the automated cycle, and input a recalibration sequence that rebalanced the load just enough to restore partial service. The display flickered, then updated.

The delay estimate dropped.

Someone let out a cheer. Another clapped once, reflexive.

Mara stepped back.

"Thanks," the first man said. "Didn't expect that to be fixed so quickly."

She nodded. "It wasn't complicated."

"Still," he said. "Good to have someone who knows how to talk to the system."

The phrase stayed with her as she returned upstairs.

Good to have someone.

—

Later, alone in her unit, Mara replayed the day with uncharacteristic restlessness.

She had not lost status here.

She had shed it.

The difference was subtle but profound. No one deferred automatically. No one framed their interactions around her presumed value. Her usefulness was not amplified—it was simply taken for granted.

That absence of ceremony unsettled her.

At Keene Tower, recognition had always preceded contribution. Here, contribution preceded recognition, and recognition—when it arrived at all—was unremarkable.

She wondered, dimly, whether this was how Elias had always experienced the Reach before his departure. Unmarked, effective, transient.

The thought pulled her toward the interface on her desk. She did not activate it. Instead, she moved to the window, watching the greenway quiet as night deepened.

Below, someone practiced an instrument badly but earnestly. A laugh followed the missed notes.

Life, she thought, continued here in a way that resisted optimization.

She did not know yet whether she would come to prefer it.

But for the first time since leaving Keene Tower, the discomfort of displacement carried something like texture—an uneven but living surface she could not smooth over with process.

Belonging, she suspected, required a willingness to be necessary without being exceptional.

The realization sat heavily and quietly.

Tomorrow, the building would need her again.
Not because of her name.
But because she would be there.

Ambient Noise

Mara first encountered the Serrin sisters on a morning when the Midway block seemed determined to produce interruption.

She had descended to the greenway earlier than usual, intending to reach Keene Tower before transit congestion reasserted itself. Rain misted the air lightly, enough to blur the edges of light without issuing a clear warning. She was adjusting her sleeve interface when a burst of sound cut across the walkway—laughter, sharp and unrestrained, followed by the unmistakable whine of personal lift-boosts powering down.

Two young women skidded to a stop near the curb, boots splashing shallow runoff onto the polished surface. One nearly collided with Mara, arresting her momentum at the last moment with a quick spin and a hand flung out to balance.

"Oh—sorry!" the woman said, wide-eyed but grinning. "Didn't see you."

"No harm done," Mara replied, stepping aside.

The second woman powered down her boost and removed her visor with theatrical flourish, dark hair clinging damply to her cheek.

"You're up early," she observed, as if it were an accusation.

"So are you," Mara said.

The woman laughed. "That wasn't early. That was *after*."

Mara let that pass.

"I'm Dax," the visor-wearer said, extending a hand gloved in weatherproof polymer. "This is Kira."

Kira—who had nearly collided with her—offered a curt nod. Her gaze had already shifted elsewhere, tracking something moving across her interface.

"Mara," she said, returning the handshake briefly.

"Right," Dax said. "You're the one everyone keeps borrowing."

Mara raised a brow. "Borrowing?"

"Fixing stuff," Kira said absently. "Doors. Systems. Scheduling glitches. Lina mentioned you."

"That explains it," Mara said.

Dax tilted her head, studying her openly in a way that Crestline etiquette would have considered blatant.

"You don't *look* like a systems fixer," she said. "No offense."

"None taken," Mara replied. "Appearances are unreliable."

Dax seemed delighted by that. "I like her."

Kira glanced up long enough to assess Mara with sharper attention.

"She's older," she said flatly.

Mara felt the words register—not painfully, but unmistakably.

"Thanks for the update," she said mildly.

Kira shrugged. "Just saying. You didn't react like you'd been late for something."

"I allowed for contingencies," Mara replied.

Dax snorted. "That's definitely older."

The sisters exchanged a look of shared amusement, and Mara understood immediately that she had been categorized.

They liked her.

But not because they resembled her.

—

The Serrins occupied Unit 1708, three doors down from Mara, though she did not learn that until later. Their presence announced itself by volume rather than formality. Music leaked intermittently from their unit, rhythms spiking and vanishing without warning. Their door rarely remained fully closed; someone was always coming or going, boots tracked with debris from places Mara never heard them naming twice the same way.

They were, she soon learned, feed sophisticates.

Their attention moved constantly between the lived and the projected, fingers scrolling reflexively between status streams displaying contract races, pilot rankings, and adrenaline sports that combined competition with spectacle. Mara passed their living space one evening to find both sisters leaning over a floating projection of a hovercourse run, arguing loudly over maneuver choice.

"She should've broken earlier," Kira insisted.

"No—she waited because she knew the wake window would widen," Dax countered. "That was confidence."

"That was stupidity that worked," Kira said.

Mara paused just long enough to observe the projection: a pilot skimming dangerously close to infrastructure barriers, crowd reactions pulsing in the metadata overlay.

"You're both right," Mara said, surprising herself by speaking. "Timing made it succeed. Without the crowd input delaying enforcement, it wouldn't have held."

The sisters froze.

They turned slowly, identical expressions of skepticism giving way to interest.

"You follow runs?" Dax asked.

"I analyze feedback patterns," Mara replied. "Occasionally."

Kira stared at her as though recalibrating.

"Can you explain why the eastern loop always overcompensates?" she asked.

Mara did.

Not passionately. Not with jargon. Simply, clearly.

By the time she finished, the sisters were leaned in, feeds forgotten for the moment.

"Oh," Dax said at last. "You're dangerous."

Kira nodded. "In a boring way."

Mara smiled despite herself.

—

They began including her after that.

Not intentionally—not with invitations or ceremony—but by proximity. If Mara sat on the greenway benches during her evening review cycles, the sisters hovered nearby, arguing over feeds or sharing clips without asking if she was interested. If she paused at the transit kiosks, they appeared, breathless and excited, recounting some near-miss or rumor pulsing through pilot forums.

She listened, mostly.

They spoke of things she had long ago stopped tracking closely: front-rank operators gaining traction, sponsorships gained and lost in hours, dangerous contracts accepted for visibility rather than necessity. Their enthusiasm was untempered by consequence.

"It's all about momentum," Dax explained one evening, pacing while her feed projected behind her. "You don't wait until you're ready. You move until someone notices."

“And then?” Mara asked.

“Then,” Kira said, grinning, “you don’t stop.”

Mara considered that.

“That assumes stopping is optional,” she said.

The sisters looked at her blankly.

“Of course it is,” Dax said.

Kira nodded. “You just pivot.”

Mara did not point out how rarely pivots were available once resources were spent. She suspected the lesson would not hold until its cost arrived.

—

Their assessment of her settled into a comfortable dismissiveness.

“She’s nice,” Dax told Lina loudly one afternoon, as Mara passed with a data slate tucked under her arm. “Just... steady.”

Kira made a face. “She’s already done whatever she’s going to do.”

Mara paused.

“Is that so?” she asked.

Neither sister seemed embarrassed to be overheard.

“Well,” Dax hedged, “you’re not into feeds.”

“Or races,” Kira added. “Or contract betting.”

“Or boosts,” Dax said.

“Or drama,” Kira concluded.

Mara regarded them calmly.

“Perhaps,” she said, “I’ve already had enough excitement to be selective.”

They exchanged a look—confused, then vaguely amused.

“That sounds exhausting,” Dax said.

“It was,” Mara replied.

This, she realized, was how age manifested here—not as diminishment, but as an accumulation invisible to those who had not yet felt its weight.

—

The Serrins did not mean to undervalue her.

Their world simply orbited motion, visibility, noise. They thrived on escalation, on the rush of attention and rapid consequence. In contrast, Mara’s steadiness registered as absence rather than presence—she filled gaps but did not intrude, smoothed systems without announcing success.

In Keene Tower, that quiet efficacy had been expected.

In Midway, it was… overlooked.

She did not resent it.

But she noticed.

One evening, returning from a late coordination session with the Frontier Collective, Mara found the greenway alive with energy. A pop-up projection had attracted an impromptu crowd—someone streaming a live pilot trial not yet sanctioned. The Serrin sisters stood front and center, Dax perched on a railing, Kira manipulating her interface with feverish focus.

"You're in the wrong spot," Dax called when she saw Mara lingering at the edge. "You won't see anything from there."

"I'm not watching," Mara said.

"Then why stop?" Kira asked.

Mara looked at the faces turned upward, the charged anticipation vibrating in the air.

"Because this will collapse," she said quietly.

Both sisters stared at her.

"Not in a clean way," Mara added. "Someone didn't account for crowd latency."

As if on cue, the projection stuttered. Shouts rippled through the gathering. The feed cut abruptly, replaced by a generic error display.

Groans followed.

Kira glanced at Mara, expression sharpened with something new.

"You called that."

Mara shrugged. "It was likely."

Dax squinted at her. "Why don't you tell people these things sooner?"

"Because," Mara said, "they don't ask."

Neither sister laughed.

The moment hung between them, awkward and unresolved.

Then the crowd dispersed, excitement bleeding away into minor irritation, and the sisters turned back to each other, already dissecting the failure.

Mara moved on.

The contrast followed her—youthful chaos swirling, mature stillness holding.

And for the first time since her relocation, she felt not displaced, but distinctly separate.

Not outside.

Just... beyond.

The Serrin sisters did not slow down.

If anything, the interruption of the failed feed sharpened their appetite for immediacy. Within days, new projections appeared in their shared space, half-formed ideas chased across displays with little regard for viability. Their conversations grew louder, more insistent, as if volume itself could accelerate outcomes.

Mara observed the shift without intervening.

She had learned early that momentum fed on resistance as much as encouragement. To caution without invitation only sharpened defiance; to predict without authority made one sound small.

So she listened.

One evening, returning late from a coordination call, she found the sisters sprawled across the greenway bench, interfaces floating before them like restless insects.

"There's a pilot transfer window opening," Dax said as Mara passed, turning her display outward without being asked. "High-visibility contract. Short duration. Risky."

"Very risky," Kira added, eyes alight. "No safety buffer on the northern arc."

Mara paused.

"Who's offering?" she asked.

"Independent syndicate," Dax replied. "They're pushing for speed. No time for secondary review."

Mara studied the projection, parsing the overlaid data. The crowd metrics pulsed aggressively, artificially inflated by pre-seeded commentary. She frowned.

"This feed is amplified," she said. "The interest curve doesn't reflect real engagement."

"So?" Kira shot back. "Visibility still counts."

"It counts until enforcement intervenes," Mara said. "Or until someone miscalculates."

Dax waved a hand. "They always say that."

"Until it happens," Mara replied quietly.

Neither sister responded. Their attention had already shifted back to the projection, fingers tracing hypothetical paths through digital air.

Mara moved on.

—

The recklessness crested two days later.

It happened in the early evening, when the greenway dipped into shadow and sound carried farther than usual. A crowd gathered with the same suddenness Mara had begun to associate with unsanctioned events—people drawn by rumor more than confirmation, eager to witness something unmediated.

The Serrin sisters stood at the edge of it, facing a hastily projected course layout that hovered unstable and over-bright above the crowd. Dax paced, anxious energy humming beneath her skin. Kira hunched over her interface, recalculating in sharp movements.

"You can't reroute now," Dax said. "You'll lose the window."

"The wind shifted," Kira snapped. "Someone's running interference upstream."

Mara arrived in time to hear the exchange.

She took in the scene quickly: the overtaxed projector, the crowd swelling without containment, the flicker in the enforcement radius indicator that suggested delayed response rather than absence. It was not a catastrophe yet.

But it was trending.

"You should shut this down," Mara said, stepping closer.

Dax spun, irritation flaring. "It's not ours to shut down."

"It's yours to disengage from," Mara replied.

Kira glanced up, eyes sharp. "You don't get it. This is the kind of run that makes someone."

"It's also the kind that breaks them," Mara said.

The sisters exchanged a look, caught between defiance and something else—uncertainty, perhaps.

Before either could respond, the projection stuttered.

Not fully—just enough to cause a ripple of confusion among the onlookers. A murmur passed through the crowd. Someone laughed, too loudly.

Mara felt the shift happen.

"Step back," she said, more firmly.

Dax hesitated. Kira did not.

She kept typing, jaw set.

The enforcement radius blinked again, closer now. Someone at the rear of the crowd shouted. Movement surged forward in reflexive anticipation, compressing space faster than the infrastructure liked.

Mara dropped her bag and moved.

She took hold of the greenway's edge-control interface and forced a manual override, dampening the projection's output and narrowing its visual dominance. The image dimmed, its allure reduced. Groans rose from the crowd, followed by scattered complaints.

A thrill-seeker attempted to restart the feed through a secondary channel. Mara locked it out before the request could propagate.

"This isn't your decision!" someone shouted.

"It's the building's," Mara replied evenly.

She accessed a second control, expanding the enforcement radius just enough to trigger procedural dispersal without full intervention. The crowd instinctively obeyed, stepping back as the system issued calm, unreadable prompts.

Within minutes, the gathering dissolved into grumbling fragments of disappointment.

The sisters stared at her.

"You killed it," Dax said, incredulous.

"I prevented it from killing someone," Mara replied.

Kira's face flushed. "You didn't have the authority."

Mara met her gaze steadily. "I had the access."

For a moment, it seemed one of them might argue further. Then Lina appeared at Mara's side, expression tight but relieved.

"What happened?" Lina asked.

"Nothing," Mara said. "Which is the point."

Lina looked between them, reading the tension, then nodded once.

"Good," she said.

—

The resentment took longer to disperse.

The Serrin sisters did not avoid Mara, exactly—but they changed the quality of their attention. Where once their curiosity had been casual and dismissive, now it carried an edge of challenge.

"You enjoy being right," Dax accused one afternoon, not quite seriously.

"I enjoy systems holding," Mara replied.

“That’s not an answer.”

“It’s not intended to be,” Mara said.

Kira watched her with more scrutiny than before.

“You didn’t hesitate,” she said. “You saw the problem, and you shut it down without asking.”

Mara folded her arms loosely. “Asking would have prolonged the risk.”

“And if we wanted to take that risk?”

Mara considered her carefully.

“Then you should understand its cost,” she said.

Kira frowned, bristling. “You think we don’t?”

“I think,” Mara replied, choosing her words with care, “that risk feels different when consequences are hypothetical.”

Silence followed.

This time, neither sister laughed.

—

Two nights later, Dax knocked on Mara’s door.

Mara opened it without hesitation.

Dax stood there, restless energy dimmed but not extinguished, her interface dark for once.

“You embarrassed us,” she said, flatly.

Mara inclined her head. “That wasn’t my intention.”

“It still happened.”

“Yes.”

Dax hesitated, then exhaled sharply.

“Kira’s furious,” she said. “She thinks you undercut us.”

“Did I?” Mara asked gently.

Dax looked away. “You made us feel... inexperienced.”

Mara let the silence stretch.

“Experience accumulates,” she said at last. “It doesn’t announce itself.”

Dax frowned. “You think we’re naive.”

“I think,” Mara replied, “you’re operating under the illusion that momentum forgives miscalculation.”

Dax’s sharpness faded, replaced by something more uncertain.

“We can’t just wait,” she said. “Nothing happens if you wait.”

Mara studied her—the restless posture, the tension coiled beneath bravado.

“Waiting,” she said, “isn’t the same as stagnation.”

Dax scoffed weakly. “That sounds like something someone past their peak would say.”

The words struck true enough to sting.

“Perhaps,” Mara said calmly. “Or perhaps it sounds like someone who’s survived theirs.”

Dax said nothing, but her expression shifted.

“What did you want?” Mara asked.

Dax swallowed. “Kira’s considering taking a run anyway. Private. No feeds.”

Mara stiffened.

“That’s worse,” she said.

“I know,” Dax replied. “That’s why I’m here.”

For several seconds, neither spoke.

“Tell her,” Mara said finally, “that if she insists, she should at least route the support correctly.”

Dax’s eyes widened. “You’d help?”

“I won’t endorse it,” Mara said. “But I won’t let her do it blindly.”

Dax nodded, relief breaking through her tension.

“Thank you,” she said. “She won’t say it.”

“I know,” Mara replied.

—

The next evening, Mara sat with Kira in the Serrins’ unit, both leaning over a quieter projection—less spectacle, more data.

Kira rejected half of Mara’s suggestions without comment. Accepted the other half with tight-lipped focus.

“You always like to be right?” Kira asked abruptly.

“I like systems to endure,” Mara replied.

Kira nodded slowly.

When the run ended without incident—small, contained, unseen—Kira leaned back and exhaled.

“That felt... different,” she admitted.

“Yes,” Mara said. “It was managed.”

Kira grimaced. “That’s not exciting.”

“No,” Mara agreed. “But it’s sustainable.”

They sat in silence for a moment.

“You really think we’re young,” Kira said.

"You are," Mara replied. "And that's not an insult."

Kira tilted her head. "What is it, then?"

"A privilege," Mara said. "One that spends quickly."

Kira absorbed that.

For the first time, she did not argue.

—

The building quieted over the following days.

Not completely—the Serrins were still Serrins, still loud, still restless—but something in their rhythm had recalibrated. The ambient noise softened, its spikes more deliberate, less reckless.

Mara noticed another change, too.

When problems arose now, the sisters looked to her first.

Not to praise her.

Not to elevate her.

But to check.

She did not correct their assessment.

She did not reject it either.

In the shifting balance between youthful chaos and mature stillness, something steadier had begun to form—not authority, but trust.

And in that unremarkable exchange, Mara sensed the shape of influence that did not require recognition to persist.

It required only presence.

And endurance.

Return Vector

The first announcement came by way of ambient correction rather than declaration.

Mara noticed it in the transit upgrades scheduled for Keene Tower—an expanded access buffer marked *temporary*, a bandwidth allotment adjusted upward without explanation, a discreet advisory noting increased operator traffic through the tower's primary nodes. None of it named a person. None of it needed to.

Return vectors always rippled before they landed.

She was reviewing the update from Midway when Lina leaned against the doorframe of her unit, arms crossed loosely, expression attuned to curiosity rather than concern.

"You seeing this?" Lina asked, nodding toward Mara's open interface.

"Yes," Mara said. "It's not subtle."

"Not for people who know what to look for," Lina replied. "Word is, someone big's coming through. Frontier big."

Mara stilled.

"Big how?" she asked.

"High contract density," Lina said. "Long horizon, short windows. The kind that draws attention even if you're trying not to."

Mara closed the interface.

"Do we know the operator?" she asked.

Lina shook her head. "Just a name floating. Calder."

The word settled between them with an audible finality.

Mara did not trust herself to respond immediately.

"Calder," Lina repeated. "Apparently he's already cleared at multiple sites. Keene Tower included."

Mara nodded once, motion contained.

"That would be consistent," she said.

"With what?" Lina asked.

"With return," Mara replied.

Lina studied her more carefully now, reading the posture rather than the words.

"History?" Lina asked gently.

"Yes," Mara said.

Lina did not press.

By noon, the feed confirmed it.

Not in an official release—those would lag behind necessity—but in the elevation of one name across procurement dashboards and transit clearances. Calder's identifier appeared in contexts that invited speculation: tier-one docking privileges, accelerated customs clearance, a temporary residence block assignment that spanned both Crestline and Midway thresholds.

The Serrin sisters noticed immediately.

Kira found Mara in the greenway, her interface blazing with overlays.

"Have you seen this?" she demanded, waving a projection inches from Mara's line of sight. "E. Calder. Frontier Collective lead operator."

"Yes," Mara said.

"Do you know him?" Dax asked, leaning over Kira's shoulder, eyes bright with interest.

Mara hesitated, then nodded.

"From before."

Dax's interest intensified. "Before *what*?"

"Before his contract density spiked," Mara said.

Kira flicked her feed into expanded view, scanning the summary with rapid precision.

"Look at these numbers," she said. "Revenue capture alone puts him in the top tier. And his autonomy index—he negotiates his own windows."

"Which means no oversight," Dax added admiringly.

"It means trust," Mara said quietly.

The sisters glanced at her, surprised by the tone.

"Is he dangerous?" Dax asked.

"Only to poorly designed systems," Mara replied.

They exchanged a look.

"That's not reassuring," Kira said, smiling.

The formal return took place at Keene Tower the next evening.

Mara did not attend by obligation. She attended because absence would have been interpretation. The event—if it could be called that—was framed as an operational reception, a convergence of stewardship stakeholders and contract collaborators under the guise of efficiency.

The main hall had been restored to presentation standards for the occasion. Lights calibrated higher. Environmental buffers adjusted to suppress extraneous sound. Crestline residents arrived early, their movements synchronized by expectation rather than invitation.

Mara entered just as the hall's attention shifted.

It was not the volume of voices that fell—but their pitch. A subtle recalibration of direction, bodies angling toward a shared focal point.

Elias Calder stood near the center of the hall, jacket open, posture relaxed in a way that suggested he neither feared nor sought the attention he now received. He was not surrounded, precisely; rather, people arranged themselves at conversational distances, waiting for openings they pretended not to anticipate.

He looked... established.

Not polished in the Crestline sense—his clothing bore signs of function rather than refinement—but unmistakably successful. His reputation traveled ahead of him now, clearing space he did not ask for.

When he laughed, heads turned.

When he spoke, others listened without prompting.

Mara stopped several paces from the edge of the gathering, her presence unnoticed at first. She took in the scene with professional detachment, cataloguing reactions the way she always did when something systemically significant unfolded.

Crestline benefactors smiled too carefully. Stewards leaned forward, seeking proximity. Operators from the Collective held themselves with quiet pride, as though Elias's success validated more than individual outcome.

She did not look at him yet.

She knew better than to meet something head-on without preparation.

Torres spotted her first.

"Ah," she said, weaving through the crowd with purpose. "I was hoping you'd come."

Mara inclined her head. "It would have been impractical not to."

Torres smiled, recognition flickering. "He's drawing quite the cross-section."

"He always did," Mara said.

Torres studied her. "You were right about him, you know."

Mara did not ask what she meant.

Before Torres could elaborate, Elias turned as if pulled by alignment rather than sound.

He saw Mara instantly.

The shift was slight—visible only to those watching closely—but real. His posture adjusted, attention re-focused, the room receding without effort as his gaze locked onto hers.

There it was.

The unresolved heat did not announce itself with drama. It arrived as pressure, tightening the air between them even as they stood apart.

Mara met his eyes and held them.

He did not smile.

Nor did she.

They moved toward one another without haste, the crowd parting instinctively in acknowledgment of something unarticulated but palpable.

"Mara," Elias said when they were close enough to speak privately.

"Elias."

"I wondered if you'd come."

"I wondered if you'd be noticed," she replied.

A ghost of amusement crossed his expression. "So did I."

They stood within the accepted bounds of greeting, neither breaching protocol nor retreating into formality. Those around them pretended not to listen. No one succeeded.

"You've done well," Mara said.

"You've done what was necessary," Elias replied.

The words carried weight neither pretended not to feel.

Around them, conversation resumed cautiously, orbiting their exchange without intruding. Elias gestured slightly toward a quieter alcove, an offer rather than a request.

"May we?" he asked.

Mara nodded.

The alcove overlooked the Reach through angled glass, the lights of transit lanes threading through water-reflected glow below. From here, the hall's energy softened, its hum reduced to distant texture.

"You're—" Elias began, then stopped himself.

"Changed?" Mara supplied.

"No," he said. "Placed."

She regarded him. "So are you."

He smiled faintly. "Placement comes with returns."

"And costs."

"Yes."

They fell into a silence that was no longer awkward, shaped by awareness rather than uncertainty.

"I didn't expect to arrive like this," Elias said quietly. "But momentum accumulates."

"I've been watching it," Mara said. "From public channels."

He acknowledged that with a nod.

"I didn't reach out sooner," he added.

"You did," Mara replied. "Just not directly."

His eyes sharpened. "Did you want me to?"

Another careful pause.

"I wanted you to be deliberate," she said.

"I wasn't ready for deliberate," he admitted. "Not then."

"Nor was I," she said.

A beat passed—longer than conversation justified, shorter than memory demanded.

"I'll be here for a while," Elias said at last. "The contracts allow it."

Mara absorbed that without comment.

"That would alter several assumptions," she said.

"Does it?" he asked.

"For me," she replied.

Another shift—subtle, unmistakable.

Elias studied her with the same attentiveness he once brought to instability metrics and structural stress. He had always looked at systems the way he now looked at her: not to evaluate worth, but to understand capacity.

"Then perhaps," he said softly, "we should assume less."

Mara did not answer.

Around them, the reception continued, its rhythms undisturbed by the quiet convergence at its edge. The Reach pulsed below, indifferent as ever.

Shock gave way to tension.

Tension to something sharper.

The return vector had completed its arc—and nothing, Mara knew with absolute certainty, would proceed as before.

Elias Calder's return did not remain confined to Keene Tower.

Within forty-eight hours, his name threaded its way through Midway with the ease of something already anticipated. Feeds recalibrated around him, surfacing fragments of earlier contracts, rumors of payouts, speculation about the lengths of his various engagements and the kind of autonomy that allowed such flexibility. None of it was precise, but precision was rarely the point.

Momentum was.

Mara encountered the effects first through absence.

Her transit ride home one evening encountered a minor delay, nothing worth reporting, but the platform was crowded beyond its usual density. Conversations converged around a single axis, voices pitching higher as names and figures repeated with contagious enthusiasm.

"That's him—Calder."

"No oversight. Negotiates directly."

"Did you see the run he stabilized off-orbit last cycle?"

Mara stood among them, unnoticed, her presence dissolved into the press of bodies drawn by admiration rather than necessity.

It felt strange, watching a name she once spoke only in private now take up public weight.

When she reached the greenway, the Serrin sisters were already there.

They had reshaped their living space into a feed hub, multiple projections angled to capture different content streams simultaneously. Dax paced, energized. Kira sat cross-legged in front of a glowing display, eyes darting as she cross-referenced data at speed.

"Tell me you know him," Dax said the moment she spotted Mara.

"I told you," Mara replied. "From before."

"Before *this*," Kira said, gesturing broadly. "Look at this—contract density across five zones. Who does that?"

"Someone trusted to self-regulate," Mara said.

"That's obscene," Dax breathed. "I didn't even know that level of autonomy was still granted."

"It isn't," Kira amended. "Usually."

They both turned fully toward Mara then, interest sharpened into something more evaluative.

"Is he... like he looks?" Dax asked.

Mara hesitated.

"Competent," she said carefully. "Capable."

"That's not an answer," Kira said. "Is he *formidable*?"

Mara considered the shape of the word.

"He always was," she said.

Dax grinned. "I need to meet him."

Kira nodded, already plotting. "Same."

Mara said nothing.

The Collective adjusted around Elias's presence without ceremony.

Tasks shifted into more efficient configurations. Decision chains shortened. Requests that once bounced between committees resolved within single exchanges. The operators' shared spaces no longer felt provisional; they hummed with purpose, as if the building itself had accepted a new gravitational center.

Torres observed the change with quiet satisfaction.

"He steadies the group," she remarked one afternoon, as she and Mara reviewed revised coordination logs. "People trust him instinctively."

"Trust isn't instinct," Mara said. "It's accumulated evidence."

Torres smiled. "Then I suppose he's been busy."

Mara did not disagree.

She watched Elias from a distance over the following days, noting his movements less for content than pattern. He spoke little, but efficiently. When he entered a space, it quieted—not out of deference, but attention. People oriented toward him naturally, eager for direction even when none was issued.

Admiration followed him like wake.

At Midway, he was novelty.

At Keene Tower, he was confirmation.

Both reactions unsettled Mara equally.

Their next meaningful conversation occurred unexpectedly, and without audience.

She was returning from the Serrins' unit late one evening, her path interrupted by the soft pulse of the tower's internal shift lighting. The corridor near the shared observation curve stood temporarily empty, its glass angled to catch only the muted glow of transit lanes.

Elias leaned against the railing, hands loosely clasped, gaze directed outward. He did not startle when she approached.

"I had a feeling you'd pass through here," he said.

"You know the building well already," Mara replied.

He smiled faintly. "Better than I expected."

She joined him at the railing, maintaining the careful distance they had not yet crossed.

"You're becoming quite the presence," she said.

"So I've been told."

"Does that trouble you?"

"No," he said honestly. "It complicates things."

"For you?"

"For others," he corrected. "I've learned to navigate complexity."

"And yet," Mara said quietly, "you didn't anticipate this return unfolding so publicly."

His mouth curved. "You noticed."

"I observe systems," she said.

"Then you'll understand this," Elias replied. "Once momentum brews, restraint appears like withdrawal."

She absorbed that in silence.

"You're admired," she said at last.

"Yes."

"And that admiration carries expectation."

"It always does."

"For some," Mara continued, "expectation becomes pressure."

"And for others," Elias said, turning his gaze fully back to her now, "it becomes validation."

There it was—the difference exposed gently, without accusation.

"You never sought validation," Mara said.

"I never had time to," he replied. "I was too busy surviving the consequences of not having it."

The past slid closer, no longer content to remain adjourned.

Mara regarded him carefully. "Do you believe that's changed now?"

Elias did not answer immediately. He watched a transit cluster glide beneath them, lights threading water and steel into brief cohesion.

"I believe," he said slowly, "that the Reach rewards visibility until visibility collapses into demand."

"And then?" she asked.

"Then," he said, meeting her eyes, "you discover which demands are worth answering."

The quiet between them stretched, no longer fragile.

"I noticed," Mara said, "that you've been assigned provisional residence access."

"Yes," Elias replied. "Here."

"You intend to stay."

"For as long as the vectors allow," he said. "And for reasons beyond efficiency."

Mara nodded.

"That will invite interpretation."

"Everything does," he said.

She hesitated, then asked what had been forming since the reception.

"Are you careful now?"

Elias considered.

"I'm... deliberate," he said. "There's a difference."

She smiled faintly. "You've learned a new language."

"I've learned to listen to boundaries," he replied. "Even when I don't like them."

The acknowledgment landed cleanly.

"Midway is adjusting to you," Mara said. "So are the Serrin sisters."

He laughed quietly. "Yes. They made that obvious."

"They admire risk," she added.

"They mistake velocity for mastery," Elias said. "I've made that error."

She felt something settle, not as reassurance, but as alignment.

"Do you resent the admiration?" she asked.

"No," he said. "I resent the distortion."

"Admiration distorts," Mara agreed.

They stood there until the corridor lights shifted to signal cycle rollover.

"I'm having dinner with Torres tomorrow," Elias said. "And a few others."

"Inclusion," Mara said neutrally.

"Choice," he replied. "You're welcome."

She considered the offer.

"I might come," she said. "If it remains unstructured."

His smile deepened, just slightly. “I’ve learned that structure follows presence, not the other way around.”

In that moment, surrounded by quiet glass and motion far below, the unresolved heat between them sharpened—not into longing, but into something more precise.

Recognition.

As Mara left the observation curve and made her way back toward Midway, she felt the Reach recalibrating in her wake. Elias Calder had returned with gravity, and the city had reorganized itself accordingly.

So had she.

The future, once deferred, now pressed closer with undeniable insistence.

And proximity, she knew, would test restraint in ways distance never could.

Altered Recognition

Mara realized she was no longer readable to Elias Calder in a room full of people.

The realization did not arrive abruptly. It took shape gradually, settling into something precise and unyielding, the way discomfort does when it has time to organize itself.

The gathering was informal by Crestline standards and structured by Midway's looser conventions—a negotiated space that aimed for balance without fully succeeding. Torres had chosen one of the lower terraces overlooking the Reach, its glass panels angled to diffuse attention rather than display it outright. Operators mingled easily with a handful of Crestline associates who pretended adaptation came naturally to them.

Mara arrived on time.

That, she noticed immediately, placed her at a disadvantage.

Elias had already been speaking with a small knot of people gathered near the railing, their bodies angled subtly inward, attention orbiting him with practiced ease. His voice carried through the ambient sound, confident but unforced. He looked at home in the role he now occupied, his presence anchoring the group without visible effort.

She paused just inside the terrace boundary and waited for the moment when presence would realign recognition.

It took longer than she expected.

When Elias finally turned and saw her, his expression shifted—not dramatically, not coldly—but enough. Enough that she understood something essential had moved out of alignment.

"Ah," he said, stepping forward. "You're here."

The words were neutral. Too neutral.

"Yes," Mara replied. "You invited me."

"So I did." He smiled faintly, then gestured toward the others. "You've met Torres, of course. And this is Hale, from transit oversight. And—"

Introductions flowed around her, brisk and efficient, framed by Elias without ornament. She nodded, exchanged greetings, absorbed the polite interest directed her way.

She was being placed.

The realization sharpened as the conversation continued.

Elias spoke easily about current contracts, about the challenges of frontier stabilization and the peculiarities of off-world infrastructure. He fielded questions with practiced assurance, his responses measured to convey competence without arrogance.

Mara listened.

Once, she offered a brief observation—an adjustment to a contingency model intersecting water pressure and transit routing. Elias acknowledged it with a nod and incorporated it into his response without looking at her directly.

The others glanced her way, registering contribution and moving on.

It was not dismissal.

It was absorption.

Something about that unsettled her more deeply.

She had been absorbed before—quietly effective, woven into outcomes without recognition—but never by him.

As the conversation drifted toward future projections, Elias turned slightly away from her, attention pulled toward Hale's inquiries. Mara found herself edged outward, not physically, but conversationally, her presence no longer required to sustain the exchange.

She stepped back.

No one noticed immediately.

From her new vantage, she could observe the group with greater clarity. Elias animated, responding to curiosity and admiration with restraint that only increased both. The Serrin sisters hovered nearby, not yet incorporated but watching with naked fascination.

Dax caught Mara's eye briefly, eyebrows lifting in an unspoken *this is who you meant* before turning back with renewed interest.

Mara felt the first quiet prick of mortification then—not because Elias was admired, but because she was apparently no longer necessary to him in the same way.

It was not that he ignored her.

It was that he did not *need* her.

The distinction settled heavily.

She moved toward the edge of the terrace, resting her hands on the railing and looking out over the Reach. The city sprawled below in composed brilliance, light threading water and steel into something briefly legible. From here, it was possible to pretend that distance equalized perspective.

Behind her, she heard Elias laugh.

The sound carried easily, unburdened.

"You've known him a long time?" Hale asked, through the blur of conversation.

A beat passed before Elias answered.

"We've known each other," he said. "In a different context."

The phrasing landed with unexpected force.

Different context.

Mara closed her eyes briefly.

She wondered whether that was how he now framed it—a former alignment rendered obsolete by movement, location, success. She wondered whether he saw her as unchanged or unchangeable, the distinction between them having widened quietly over years of divergence.

When she rejoined the group, it was with deliberate composure.

"I'm heading back," she said, addressing Torres first. "Thank you for the evening."

"Already?" Torres asked. "We were hoping you'd stay."

"I have work early," Mara replied. Not untrue.

She turned toward Elias.

"I'll let you get back to it," she said.

"To—" He hesitated, then recovered, glancing around as if the space itself had pressed a pause. "Of course. Thank you for coming."

His tone was courteous. Professional.

It pierced her more cleanly than open disregard would have.

As she moved past him, he added, "We should speak sometime. When things are quieter."

She paused.

"When?" she asked.

A small silence followed.

"I'll reach out," he said.

The answer, once sufficient, now rang hollow.

She nodded and left without looking back.

—

The walk back to Midway was longer than usual.

Mara took routes she rarely chose, extending the distance without conscious intention. The city's noise pressed in around her, the ambient chaos of commuters, vendors, and shifting light flowing without regard to her internal recalibration.

She replayed the moment again and again—not as accusation, but analysis.

Had she misread his earlier attentiveness? Had return and recognition reordered his values in ways she failed to anticipate? Or had she simply overestimated the constancy of something that had existed in a narrower, more fragile frame than she had allowed herself to believe?

At Midway, the greenway sounded louder than it had in days.

Music spilled from somewhere nearby. Voices overlapped. The Serrin sisters stood near their usual bench, Dax animatedly recounting something to a cluster of neighbors whose attention flickered between her and their feeds.

Kira noticed Mara first.

"There you are," she called. "We were wondering if you'd show."

Mara stopped, forcing her attention to settle.

"I stopped by," she said. "I won't stay."

"You okay?" Dax asked, peering at her with frank curiosity.

Mara considered deflecting.

Instead, she said, "Fine."

Kira frowned slightly. "That's not an answer."

Mara smiled faintly. "It's sufficient."

Dax exchanged a look with her sister.

"He's impressive," Dax said, tone reverent. "Calder."

"Yes," Mara replied.

"Kind of hard to picture you in the same room before all this," Kira added. "No offense."

"None taken," Mara said lightly.

And yet.

She continued past them without lingering, unlocking her unit and closing the door behind her with more force than necessary.

Inside, the room felt unfamiliar—too quiet now that her internal noise had sharpened. She moved through the space without purpose, pausing near the window, then the desk, then the door again before finally sitting.

She did not open her interface.

There were messages she might have received. There were patterns she could examine to justify what she had felt.

She did not do either.

Instead, she allowed the mortification its moment—not indulged, not dramatized, simply acknowledged.

She had been changed.

And so, disturbingly, had Elias.

Whatever they had once been to one another, that shape had not survived translation into this new context intact. He had returned successful, admired, autonomous.

And she—competent, steady, quietly indispensable—had become... background.

The realization hurt not because it diminished her worth, but because it altered her visibility in his eyes.

She rested her forehead briefly against the cool glass.

Outside, the Reach continued, untroubled.

Stoic endurance, she reminded herself, was not ignorance of pain. It was the decision not to perform it.

Tomorrow, she would return to work. To coordination. To usefulness that did not seek applause.

And perhaps, she told herself carefully, she would learn to read him anew.

Even if he no longer read her at all.

The misunderstanding did not announce itself.

It revealed itself slowly, accumulating weight through absence rather than confrontation, through small fractures in expectation that Mara noted and Elias, she suspected, never fully perceived.

He did not reach out the next day.

Nor the one after that.

Mara did not expect immediacy. She had learned long ago not to mistake prominence for availability. Still, the silence reconfigured her understanding of the previous evening with uncomfortable efficiency.

Each hour that passed without a message recalibrated the meaning of his parting assurance, transforming *I'll reach out* from intent into contingency.

She adjusted accordingly.

Work offered refuge.

Infrastructure Allocation passed along a fuller remote reassignment proposal midweek, framed as a flexible optimization rather than retraction. Mara accepted most of its terms without objection, negotiating only the sections that would have removed her from on-site coordination entirely. If she was to be peripheral, she would choose the edge thoughtfully.

At Keene Tower, Elias's gravity continued to reorient space.

His presence accelerated decisions. Stewards deferred more readily. Crestline associates leaned in eagerly, mirroring his confidence in smaller, less convincing ways. Their admiration came packaged with interpretation: assumptions about alignment, speculation about preference, quiet recalculations of status that no one admitted to making.

Mara watched from a distance.

On one occasion, while crossing the lobby with Torres, she overheard a man remark, "Calder's nostalgia phase is charming. But obviously transitory."

Another replied, laughing, "Yes, one assumes."

They did not look at her.

She wondered, briefly, whether Elias would have corrected them.

She did not wonder whether she should.

—

The Serrin sisters took matters less delicately.

"Why didn't you stay the other night?" Dax demanded one evening as Mara passed through the greenway, arms wrapped around a warm beverage rather than her usual data slate.

"I had work," Mara said.

Dax snorted. "We all did. That didn't stop us."

Kira watched her more closely this time, head tilted.

"He didn't follow," Kira said.

It was not phrased as accusation. It was observation.

"No," Mara replied.

"That's..." Dax hesitated. "Odd."

"For whom?" Mara asked.

"For him," Dax said. "You don't usually let someone like that drift."

Mara met her gaze calmly.

"Usually," she said, "assumes pattern."

Kira nodded slowly. "So what are you assuming now?"

Mara took a sip of her drink, buying herself a moment.

"That if clarity is required," she said at last, "it won't come from speculation."

Dax frowned. "That sounds exhausting."

"It often is," Mara agreed.

—

The misunderstanding crystallized a few days later, in a space not meant to hold emotional weight.

Mara was reviewing updated transit integrations at a shared console near the Collective's operations wing when Elias approached from behind, his reflection appearing faintly in the glass before she heard his footsteps.

"You've been reassigning routing parameters," he said.

"Yes," Mara replied without turning. "They were misaligned with the building's new load profile."

"Efficient," he said approvingly. "Torres mentioned it."

Mara inclined her head.

"I hadn't realized you were going fully remote," he continued, tone light, conversational.

"I'm not," she said. "Selectively present."

He smiled. "That suits you."

Something about the casual confidence of the statement unsettled her.

"Does it?" she asked, finally turning to face him.

Elias noted the shift immediately—her stillness, the way she squared herself as though entering a formal exchange rather than continuing an informal one.

"I meant," he said carefully, "that you've always worked best with flexibility."

"That's an interpretation," Mara replied.

He studied her now, brow faintly furrowed.

"Is something wrong?" he asked.

There it was—the gap.

She understood then that he had not perceived the injury at all, let alone contributed to it. In his read of the situation, her quiet withdrawal had registered not as mortification but as equilibrium, a steady adaptation fully in character.

She had been misinterpreted by virtue of her restraint.

"No," she said evenly. "Nothing's wrong."

Relief crossed his face—brief and genuine.

"Good," he said. "I was concerned I might have misstepped."

Mara almost laughed, not with humor, but recognition.

"You haven't," she said—and this time, the answer carried more truth than comfort.

He nodded, satisfied, and gestured toward the console.

"There's a dinner tonight," he said. "One of those necessary engagements. Crestline-adjacent. I suspect attendance will be... theatrical."

Mara waited.

"I thought you might decline," Elias continued, "but felt I should mention it regardless."

She met his gaze.

"You thought I would decline," she repeated.

"Yes."

"Why?"

He hesitated. "You prefer quieter contexts."

The words landed with surgical precision.

"I prefer contexts," Mara said softly, "that do not require translation."

Elias's expression shifted—not defensively, but with dawning awareness.

"I see," he said.

Do you? Mara thought.

"I won't attend," she said aloud. "But thank you for mentioning it."

"Of course," he replied. "Another time, perhaps."

She nodded once.

"That would require clarity," she said.

He did not answer immediately this time.

—

The following evening, Mara encountered the consequences of that exchange from a distance.

The Crestline dinner unfolded much as Elias had predicted—loud with implication, rich with admiration, full of conversation that praised his restraint while rewarding his prominence. Feeds documented fragments filtered through flattering angles, commentary framed around his return as vindication rather than complication.

In several instances, his presence was paired with speculation about alignment.

Not hers.

Mara watched one clip in which someone gestured animatedly and remarked, "Calder's adaptability is remarkable—he's cut himself loose from everything that might limit him."

The clip cut away before context could intrude.

She closed the feed.

At Midway, things were quieter.

The Serrin sisters sat on the stairwell between floors, arguing amiably about a recent pilot transfer gone wrong.

"You can't rely on hype," Kira insisted.

"You can if you know when to exit," Dax countered.

Mara paused nearby.

"Exit strategies," she said, "are only useful if you're permitted to leave."

Both sisters turned toward her.

"You're in a mood," Dax observed.

"No," Mara replied. "I'm in alignment."

Kira studied her thoughtfully.

"He didn't see it," she said.

Mara stilled.

"See what?" Dax asked.

"That she was hurt," Kira continued. "He thought she was... unaffected."

Mara smiled faintly. "That's a generous reading."

Kira shrugged. "It's what happens when you don't perform pain."

"Or ask for resolution," Dax added.

Mara regarded them both.

"Resolution," she said, "requires recognition."

They fell silent.

For the first time, the Serrin sisters did not rush to fill the space with noise.

—

Later that night, alone in her unit, Mara replayed the exchange at the console with Elias—his casual assumption, her refusal to correct it more forcefully.

She understood now that his altered recognition had not diminished her value in his eyes so much as fixed it too rigidly. He saw her as constant: capable, composed, functionally unshakeable. That perception, once a kind of admiration, now shielded him from perceiving her vulnerability.

She had become unreadable to him not because she had faded, but because she had hardened into something he assumed required no interpretation.

The thought carried a peculiar ache.

She did not reach out.

Instead, she refocused on the rhythms of Midway, on problems that presented themselves honestly and without pretense. She resolved a misalignment in shared energy draws, mediated a dispute between two residents over access scheduling, and helped Lina draft a revised building notice that replaced apology with clarity.

Each action steadied her.

In usefulness without spectacle, she recovered a sense of self that did not rely on being read by someone else.

And yet—

When her interface chimed late that night, she glanced at it instinctively.

Elias's name did not appear.

She let the moment pass.

Stoic endurance, she reminded herself again, was not sacrifice. It was choice.

And if clarity were to come, it would be because both of them were willing to re-see what had been misrecognized.

For now, the gap remained.

Quiet.

Sharp.

Unmistakable.

Market Value

Mara understood what was happening before she understood why it unsettled her.

The pattern was familiar. She had seen it before in different configurations—capital chased momentum, momentum attracted attention, attention recalibrated desire. The mechanism itself was impersonal. What changed was the scale.

Elias Calder had become an asset.

Not formally—not to Allocation or the Collective, not to any ledger that could be audited without resistance—but socially, unmistakably so. His presence now carried implied value that others sought proximity to, eager to be reflected in whatever authority his success conferred.

The first signs appeared at Midway.

The Serrin sisters were no longer content to watch from the margins. Dax adjusted her schedules without consulting anyone, engineering coincidental overlaps in shared spaces. Kira curated her feeds carefully, amplifying only those moments that displayed Elias surrounded by interest, admiration, velocity.

"He *belongs* here," Dax announced one afternoon as Mara reviewed a transit monitor beside them. "At Midway. Not stuck in Crestline performance loops."

"He belongs wherever leverage is," Mara said evenly.

Kira glanced at her sharply. "You sound unimpressed."

"I sound accurate," Mara replied.

Kira smiled thinly. "Same thing to you, maybe."

They had begun speaking to Mara differently—less as a stabilizer, more as someone oddly adjacent to relevance.

The shift was subtle. That did not make it imaginary.

—

Elias did not discourage the attention.

Nor did he overtly invite it.

That, too, was familiar.

He fielded admiration with practiced neutrality, allowing others to orbit while he remained ostensibly detached. The effect was magnetic. People mistook restraint for selectivity, selectivity for discernment, discernment for invitation.

Younger women noticed first.

They were not careless about it. Their interest was calculated, socially legible, framed as curiosity rather than pursuit. They positioned themselves near him during gatherings, asked questions that allowed him to speak about his work without appearing to boast, laughed at remarks that were not particularly witty but carried the right kind of authority.

Mara observed this from a distance that no longer protected her.

At a shared Midway planning forum, she watched Dax lean casually against the central display while Elias explained a logistics contingency he had already resolved an hour earlier. Dax listened with rapt attention, nodding at intervals designed to confirm engagement rather than comprehension.

"That's impressive," Dax said. "You must have learned that the hard way."

"Experience compounds," Elias replied. "If you last long enough."

Dax smiled. "I plan to."

Mara did not intervene.

Kira was subtler.

She engaged Elias on technical grounds, framing curiosity in the language of competence. She asked precise questions—how autonomy thresholds were negotiated, how contract risk was hedged without institutional backing. Elias responded thoughtfully, clearly pleased to encounter someone who understood the architecture beneath his success.

"You could do this," he told her once, gesturing toward a projection of competitive contract pathways. "With the right patience."

"Patience," Kira echoed, amused. "That's not my strongest asset."

"It's learnable," he replied.

Mara caught the exchange from across the room.

Something tight settled beneath her sternum.

—

The misinterpretation arrived quietly, seeded by these interactions and reinforced by Mara's own restraint.

Elias assumed she was indifferent.

Not hostile. Not withdrawn. Simply untroubled.

He watched her adapt seamlessly to the new dynamics, her expression unaltered by shifts that would have unnerved others. He noted her absence from optional gatherings and attributed it to preference rather than injury. When she offered no commentary on the admiration directed his way, he read the silence as confirmation that it held no personal consequence.

He was wrong.

But from his perspective, the error was reasonable.

Mara did not perform jealousy.

She did not angle for attention. She did not signal possession or claim history in contexts that rewarded neither. Her history with him existed, but it did not insist upon recognition.

That, in this social economy, read as detachment.

—

The Serrin sisters confronted the issue with less restraint.

"You could say something," Dax said one evening, arms crossed as they stood near the greenway railing. "You know. Remind him."

"Remind him of what?" Mara asked.

"That you're not... neutral."

"Am I not?" Mara replied.

Kira frowned. "Don't do that."

"Do what?"

"Pretend you don't know how this reads," Kira said sharply. "People think you don't care."

Mara considered her.

"And what do you think?"

Kira hesitated, confidence faltering.

"I think," she said slowly, "you care enough not to interfere."

The observation struck closer to truth than Mara expected.

"Interference," Mara said, "would require permission."

Dax looked between them, clearly frustrated.

"You're letting him be *marketable*," she said. "That's dangerous."

Mara almost smiled.

"All value is contextual," she said. "The danger lies in mistaking it for permanence."

Dax scoffed. "You sound like my mother."

"And yet," Mara replied, "you listen."

Dax fell silent.

—

The comparison sharpened when Elias attended a high-profile coordination review accompanied by two younger operators whose presence was clearly not required.

They arrived together at Keene Tower, their entrance drawing attention for reasons unrelated to logistics. One trailed half a step behind Elias, the other flanked him with practiced ease, laughing at something he murmured as they crossed the lobby.

Crestline associates noticed.

So did Mara.

She stood near the perimeter, reviewing schedule adjustments, her position granting her both cover and clarity. She noted the way Elias's companions mirrored his pace, adjusted his angles, absorbed attention he did not need to manage himself.

They made him look even more valuable.

Torres leaned toward Mara.

"Am I wrong," she murmured, "or have you been rendered strategically invisible?"

Mara didn't look away from the display.

"You're not wrong," she said.

"And yet," Torres added, watching Elias greet a cluster of stewards, "you don't appear concerned."

Mara closed the display.

"That," she said quietly, "would be another misinterpretation."

Torres studied her expression longer this time.

"Do you mind if I speak plainly?" she asked.

"Please."

"He assumes you're untroubled," Torres said. "And everyone else assumes that means you're disengaged."

Mara exhaled slowly.

"Yes."

"That serves him," Torres continued. "But it doesn't serve you."

Mara met her gaze.

"I'm aware."

"Then why let it persist?"

Mara paused.

"Because correction," she said, "would be read as competition."

Torres blinked. "And?"

"And I'm not competing," Mara said.

Torres nodded slowly. "Then what are you?"

The question lingered.

Before Mara could answer, Elias approached them, smile easy, posture relaxed.

"There you are," he said, to Torres, then to Mara. "We'll begin shortly. Allocation insists on punctuality when image is at stake."

"Of course," Torres replied.

Elias turned fully toward Mara.

"You're well," he observed. "Midway suits you."

"It's functional," Mara said.

He smiled, satisfied. "I thought so."

And there it was again—that assumption of alignment without verification.

The oversight did not wound because it was cruel.

It wounded because it was careless.

—

Later that evening, as Mara returned to Midway alone, her restraint began to feel increasingly misread as indifference by those least entitled to judge it.

On the greenway, she overheard a passing remark:

"She never seemed invested," someone said. "Calder moves on quickly."

The words lodged.

Mara did not stop them. She let them pass like ambient noise, absorbed into the city's background hum.

Inside her unit, she stood by the window and considered the Reach.

Market value, she thought, rewarded visibility, not constancy. Admiration shifted easily, attaching itself to spectacle and momentum rather than endurance. Elias now operated in a system that celebrated replaceability as flexibility and novelty as proof of success.

And she—quiet, unperformative, unreadable—had become the omission in his narrative.

Not because she lacked value.

But because she refused to announce it.

Frustration settled beneath her composure, controlled but persistent. Jealousy followed—not loud, not corrosive, but edged with clarity. She recognized it for what it was and refused to let it direct her actions.

Still.

As she prepared for bed, her interface chimed—a message from Allocation requesting her input on a scheduling conflict involving Elias's expanded commitments.

She stared at the request for several seconds before responding.

Yes, she would resolve it.

Of course she would.

She always did.

But tonight, the realization pressed closer than before:

Being indispensable did not prevent one from being overlooked.

And restraint, once misinterpreted, became its own kind of concealment.

The misdirection hardened into habit.

By the end of the week, it had become natural to see Elias Calder accompanied. Rarely alone, never unobserved. Attention clustered around him in ways that required no effort on his part to sustain—an economy of admiration that fed itself, moving faster the more it was indulged.

Mara learned this not from proximity, but from pattern.

Her coordination requests began arriving with altered assumptions embedded in them. Availability timelines phrased as if Elias's presence implied capacity beyond logistics. Invitations copied to her as courtesy rather than necessity. Decisions routed around her unless explicitly required.

She remained essential.

She was no longer central.

At Keene Tower, she arrived one evening to find a small group gathered near the atrium—two younger operators laughing openly as Elias explained something with animated restraint. He was relaxed in a way she had not seen since his return, the ease of being admired without having to manage the admiration itself.

One of them—Elise, she thought vaguely—leaned closer as he spoke, her attention careful, deliberate. She laughed at his concluding remark, reached out and touched his sleeve briefly as if to anchor the moment.

Elias did not discourage it.

Nor did he reciprocate.

The subtlety mattered. It always did.

Mara paused just long enough to register the configuration before moving on.

She felt the now-familiar tightening beneath her composure—not sharp, but persistent. A low-grade irritation sharpened by the knowledge that her silence had been interpreted as acquiescence not only by others, but by Elias himself.

Later, Torres found her reviewing a logistics conflict in a quiet side corridor.

"I don't like this," Torres said without preamble.

"Which part?" Mara asked.

"The orbit," Torres replied. "It's narrowing."

Mara nodded. "That happens when perceived value rises."

"And when no one challenges the narrative," Torres added pointedly.

Mara looked up.

"You believe I should," she said.

Torres hesitated. "I believe you could."

The difference mattered.

"I won't," Mara said.

Torres regarded her carefully. "That's a decision."

"Yes," Mara agreed. "It is."

—

The Serrin sisters, meanwhile, treated the situation with less restraint and more impatience.

Kira confronted her first.

"You're letting this go too far," she said bluntly, cornering Mara near the stairwell between floors. "People are starting to rewrite things."

"People rewrite constantly," Mara replied.

"Not like this," Kira insisted. "They're assuming you were never... significant."

Mara met her gaze evenly.

"Significance," she said, "that requires constant reinforcement is unstable."

Kira scoffed. "That's easy to say when you don't want the reinforcements."

"Or when you don't need them," Mara replied.

Dax joined them, less confrontational but no less agitated.

"He's being reckless," Dax said. "Not operationally. Socially. That's worse."

Mara studied her with faint curiosity.

"You seem invested," she said.

Dax shrugged, flustered. "I don't like when people don't see what's right in front of them."

Mara softened slightly.

"Neither do I," she said.

Dax glanced away.

—

The fault line revealed itself at a forum Mara had not intended to attend.

Allocation had requested a consolidated review of cross-sector engagement, and despite her remote reassignment, her presence was deemed "contextually useful." Mara accepted without comment, arriving early enough to choose a seat that offered neither prominence nor concealment.

Elias arrived late.

Not tardy—simply unconcerned with being first. He entered with composed assurance, two operators flanking him, conversation breaking around his arrival as attention shifted instinctively in his direction.

When he caught sight of Mara, his expression registered mild relief rather than anticipation.

You're here, it seemed to say. Good. Things are as expected.

The meeting progressed efficiently. Elias spoke often, fielding questions and outlining strategies that aligned neatly with plans Mara had helped draft weeks earlier. He referenced her work more than once, credit delivered smoothly but without emphasis.

"And this adjustment," he said at one point, "was handled by Mara Keene. She has an eye for these overlaps."

Several stewards nodded approvingly.

No one looked at her.

As the session closed, an Allocation representative thanked Elias profusely for his flexibility and vision, praising his willingness to remain autonomous while supporting institutional goals.

"You've managed to detach cleanly from older obligations," the representative remarked. "That can't have been easy."

The room murmured approval.

Detachment.

Mara felt something inside her still.

Elias smiled, polite and accepting.

"Yes," he said. "It was necessary."

Necessary.

The word echoed too loudly.

Mara stood before the session could fracture further, collecting her materials with deliberate calm. She did not look at Elias as she passed him, though she felt his attention flick briefly in her direction, reassessing something he did not yet understand had shifted.

Outside the forum hall, she encountered Torres again.

"That was..." Torres began.

"I know," Mara said.

"They assume it ended cleanly," Torres continued. "Whatever it was."

Mara nodded.

"They assume many things," she said.

"Do you intend to correct them?"

Mara considered the question carefully.

"No," she said. "Not publicly."

Torres watched her for several seconds.

"And privately?"

Mara did not answer.

—

The misdirection tipped toward imprudence when Kira acted on her admiration rather than her restraint.

It happened at Midway, predictably.

A spontaneous gathering formed near the greenway—smaller than the earlier incidents, more contained. Kira positioned herself beside Elias with deliberate ease, drawing him into a technical debate visible enough to attract attention. Dax hovered nearby, tension threaded through her enthusiasm.

Mara watched from the edge.

She recognized the maneuver immediately: attention marshaled through competence, admiration framed as collaboration. Elias responded obligingly, engaging without reserve, evidently pleased by the exchange.

When Kira suggested a hypothetical joint bid—speculative, informal—the crowd leaned in.

"That's interesting," Elias said. "It could work with the right support."

Kira's eyes lit.

"We'd learn fast," she said. "We wouldn't hesitate."

Elias smiled. "Hesitation isn't always weakness."

"Sometimes it is," Kira countered.

Mara stepped forward then—not intruding, not claiming space—simply present in a way that shifted alignment.

"Hesitation," she said evenly, "is often the only thing standing between foresight and consequence."

The crowd stilled.

Elias turned, surprise flickering across his expression.

"Mara," he said. "I didn't see you."

"That," she replied, "has been happening."

The words landed softer than accusation, harder than explanation.

Kira stiffened.

Elias studied Mara now—really studied her—with the same analytical focus he brought to unstable systems.

"I thought," he began, then stopped.

The pause stretched.

"Thought what?" Mara asked calmly.

"That you were... fine," he said. "With all this."

Mara inclined her head. "I am composed."

"And doesn't that mean the same thing?" Kira demanded, unable to stay silent.

Mara looked at her briefly.

"No," she said. "It doesn't."

The distinction hung between them, unadorned and uncomfortable.

Elias exhaled slowly.

"I may have mistaken silence for indifference," he said at last.

Mara met his gaze.

"You may have," she agreed.

Around them, the greenway's ambient noise softened as people instinctively withdrew, sensing a convergence they were not meant to witness.

"I didn't intend to invite misinterpretation," Elias continued.

“Intention,” Mara said, “rarely prevents impact.”

Dax shifted uneasily. Kira looked away, chastened.

Elias straightened, composure reasserting itself with visible effort.

“When would it suit you to talk?” he asked.

Mara considered the request.

“When readability returns,” she said. “For both of us.”

He nodded slowly, accepting the boundary without protest.

As she turned away, Elias did not follow.

That, too, was instructive.

—

Back in her unit, Mara sat in the dim quiet and allowed herself a long exhale.

The frustration had not dissipated.

Nor had the jealousy.

But beneath them, she felt something solidifying into resolve.

She had been misread because she had allowed herself to be. Not out of passivity, but out of principle. Now, she recognized the cost of that choice.

Market value, she thought, distorted affection just as efficiently as distance once had. It rewarded visibility, punished endurance, and mistook restraint for irrelevance.

She would not compete in that economy.

But neither would she erase herself to accommodate it.

The misunderstanding had been allowed to grow. The misdirection had been tolerated too long. Correction would come—not through display, not through rivalry, but through clarity that did not ask permission.

For now, she held to her composure.

But she no longer mistook silence for dignity.

And when the time came to be seen again, she would not rely on anyone else to do the reading for her.

The Unchosen Path

The alternative arrived without spectacle.

Mara first noticed Rowan Hale not because of his entrance but because of his *absence* from the attention economy that now governed so much of Midway and Crestline alike. He moved through shared spaces without drawing eyes, spoke when necessary, and departed without leaving behind conversational wake. It was a skill she recognized immediately.

He was stable.

The realization surprised her with its immediacy.

Rowan occupied a narrow band of influence—transit oversight liaison, mid-level authority whose jurisdiction touched enough systems to matter without ever rising high enough to invite scrutiny. His presence was often felt rather than remarked upon, his work revealing itself through the absence of cascading problems rather than the presence of acclaim.

They encountered one another properly during a coordination overlap that neither of them had requested.

Mara was reviewing a set of transit resilience reports near the Midway operations desk when Rowan joined her, setting his tray down with careful deliberation.

"Keene," he said. "I hoped it was you."

She glanced up. "That's either reassurance or warning."

"Usually reassurance," he replied. "Today, both."

He gestured toward the display.

"They've adjusted flow priority again," he said. "Too tight this time. If we get a weather surge, the west lines will choke."

Mara studied the data for barely a second.

"Yes," she said. "They optimized for visibility metrics."

Rowan grimaced faintly. "That tracks."

They worked together for fifteen minutes, quietly, efficiently. No duplication of effort, no contest for authority. He deferred when she was faster; she accepted his assessments when they exceeded hers. The system responded to the refinement with immediate compliance.

When they finished, Rowan inclined his head.

"Thank you," he said. "That avoids three weeks of cascading complaints."

Mara smiled faintly. "You're welcome."

He hesitated, then added, "If you ever want to check these upstream before Allocation releases them, I'd appreciate it."

A request, not a presumption.

"I can do that," Mara said.

He nodded once and returned to his place without lingering.

The exchange should have been unremarkable.

Instead, it stayed with her.

—

Rowan's attentiveness sharpened over the following days.

Not toward her personally—there was no performative interest, no sudden influx of messages or manufactured coincidence—but toward her work. He routed issues her way only when they aligned genuinely with her capacity to resolve them, and he accepted her conclusions without modification when they proved sound.

Their conversations remained brief, contained, and precise. They did not drift toward the personal without reason. When they did, the commentary stayed grounded—observations rather than inquiries, respect rather than curiosity.

One evening, as they crossed paths on the greenway, Rowan gestured toward the horizon where the Reach's lights thinned into reflective haze.

"You've lived alongside this a long time," he said.

"Yes."

"It must be strange," he continued, "seeing it reconfigure without asking."

Mara considered the remark.

"It reconfigures because it doesn't ask," she replied.

He nodded. "That's what I thought."

He did not press further.

—

The Serrin sisters noticed him next.

They always did.

"This one's quieter," Dax observed one afternoon, watching Rowan pass through the greenway with a data slate tucked under his arm. "Too responsible to be interesting."

Kira frowned. "He's thorough."

"Thorough doesn't trend," Dax replied disdainfully.

"Neither does reckless," Mara said.

The sisters looked at her.

"That's not what the feeds say," Dax countered.

"No," Mara agreed. "It isn't."

Kira studied Rowan more closely as he disappeared into the transit hub. "He watches systems instead of people," she said slowly.

"That's a survival strategy," Mara said.

Kira glanced at her, startled. "Is it?"

"It is when people complicate faster than systems adapt."

Dax rolled her eyes. "You sound like you're defending him."

"Only clarifying," Mara replied.

But the distinction felt thinner than before.

—

It was Torres who named what Mara had been avoiding.

They were reviewing a stewardship report when Torres leaned back and said, "Hale is a good man."

Mara did not look up. "You make that sound like an anomaly."

"In this context," Torres replied, "it nearly is."

Mara paused, fingers stilling over the display.

"He's careful," Torres continued. "Ethical. He asks fewer favors than he's owed. That's rare."

"Yes," Mara said carefully.

Torres smiled, seeing too clearly as ever. "And he sees you."

Mara looked up then.

"He sees the work," she said.

Torres shook her head. "He sees the person doing it."

The words landed gently, and for that reason, deeply.

"He knows you won't make things louder than necessary," Torres added. "For people like him, that's not invisible. It's stabilizing."

Mara absorbed the observation without protest.

"Stability," she said, "is often mistaken for lack of passion."

Torres regarded her thoughtfully. "Not by those who crave it."

—

Rowan did not pursue her.

This, oddly, made him harder to dismiss.

He did not appear at social gatherings he had little reason to attend. He did not amplify signals, did not seek to align himself with Elias's orbit or compete within it. His value lay elsewhere—in continuity rather than acceleration, in trust built slowly rather than opportunity seized quickly.

When he invited her to coffee, it was framed as logistical convenience.

"I'll be near your office tomorrow," he said in passing. "If you're free, there's a place on the lower tier that keeps tolerable hours."

Mara considered.

"Yes," she said.

The café overlooked a lesser-used transit channel, its windows fogged enough to soften passersby into shape and movement rather than detail. Rowan arrived early and had already ordered when she joined him.

"No preferences?" she asked lightly.

"I noticed you tend toward bitterness without sweetening," he replied. "I took a risk."

She smiled. "Correctly."

They spoke of work at first, then of peripheral matters—transit labor shortages, the ethics of predictive routing, the difficulty of planning for systems that pretended neutrality while encoding preference.

Rowan listened attentively without interrupting. When he spoke, it was with consideration rather than assertion.

"You don't rush decisions," he observed at one point. "That frustrates people who profit from momentum."

"Yes," Mara said.

"But it allows correction before consequences solidify," he continued. "I respect that."

The respect was genuine, unembellished.

She found herself appreciating the absence of tension, the lack of undercurrent requiring navigation.

Afterward, they parted cleanly.

No prolonged farewell.

No implied continuation.

Just acknowledgment.

—

The clarity came to her later that night, unwelcome in its precision.

Rowan Hale represented the path that would not destabilize.

With him, there would be no misinterpretation of restraint as indifference. No admiration economies to navigate, no triangulation of affection with public valuation. He would not require her to explain silence or justify composure.

He would *understand*.

The thought carried a quiet sorrow.

Because understanding, she realized, was not enough.

She did not want ease.

She wanted recognition that challenged rather than settled, that pressed rather than soothed. She wanted a resonance that did not flatten her edges into comfort.

Rowan offered security.

Elias offered complication.

Neither was neutral.

The difference lay in cost.

—

The evening before her next scheduled coordination review, Rowan sent a message.

I'll be off-shift tomorrow. Still, if you need anything, I'll be nearby.

Simple. Available without expectation.

Mara stared at the message for several seconds before replying.

Thank you.

The truth of it weighed heavier than the word suggested.

She set the interface aside and looked out at the Reach.

Somewhere not far away, Elias Calder continued to be admired, courted as market value, treated as momentum embodied. His presence still drew her attention in ways she neither welcomed nor denied.

Rowan Hale, in contrast, stood quietly adjacent to her life, offering a future that would not require endurance.

And therein lay the problem.

Mara rested her hands against the glass.

Understanding was a gift.

But love, she knew with emerging clarity, was not always aligned with what one *ought* to choose.

And so the unchosen path revealed itself—not as temptation, but as the certainty of what she would not take.

Not because it lacked worth.

But because it did not ask enough of her.

Mara did not sleep immediately.

She lay still in the darkness of her unit, listening to the Midway block settle into its nocturnal rhythms: the distant hum of transit lines switching load cycles, a door closing somewhere above her, the faint echo of laughter dissipating down the stairwell. None of it felt intrusive. None of it offered escape.

Her thoughts returned, with unwelcome persistence, to Rowan Hale.

Not as an image, but as an equation she could not dismiss.

He did not trouble her equilibrium. He did not unsettle her sense of self or force her into recalibration. Where Elias's presence bent space perceptibly, Rowan occupied it without distortion. With him, there were no misunderstandings to correct, no silences to interpret, no competing narratives to navigate.

He would be kind to her.

The simplicity of that promise tightened something in her chest.

In another version of her life—one framed by reduction rather than expansion—she might have chosen it gratefully.

The next few days passed without incident, which only sharpened the contrast.

Rowan continued as before: attentive without insistence, present without intrusion. He sent updates when they were useful, deferred when her analysis superseded his, and accepted recalibration without defensiveness. When they crossed paths, their exchanges remained efficient but warm, threaded through with an ease that required no adjustment.

"You look tired," he observed one afternoon as they reviewed a projected load shift near the transit hub.

"Temporarily," Mara replied.

He nodded. "That's usually recoverable."

The understated assurance lingered long after he left.

Elias, by contrast, threw the city's rhythms into sharper relief simply by moving through them.

Mara was keenly aware of his proximity even when she did not see him—of the subtle gravitational tug his reputation exerted on spaces she inhabited. Conversations skewed toward him. Schedules adjusted accordingly. Even problems seemed to arise with the expectation that his presence would matter in their resolution.

When she did encounter him, it was always within a context that diluted intimacy into performance: shared briefings, public crossings, settings where observation was inevitable.

They spoke politely. Sparingly.

As if an understanding hovered just beyond the acceptable boundaries of setting.

The confirmation came the evening Rowan invited her to walk.

Not a date. Not presented as such.

"There's an inspection route along the eastern greenway," he said, tone neutral. "The lighting adjustments have altered foot traffic. I thought it might be useful to observe before submitting revisions."

Mara considered, aware of the subtext even as she recognized its admirable restraint.

"Yes," she said. "That would be useful."

The walk unfolded quietly.

The greenway curved along a lowered transit artery, its edges lit by ambient panels recalibrated to reduce glare rather than highlight movement. People passed without remark, their trajectories crossing and diverging without friction.

Rowan walked beside her, hands unsheathed, posture unguarded.

"They tend to optimize for throughput," he said, indicating a cluster point forming near a junction. "But they underestimate hesitation. People pause when light changes, even when conditions don't demand it."

"They pause when outcomes aren't legible," Mara said.

"Exactly," Rowan replied. "Which means the system should adapt to uncertainty, not ignore it."

She studied him as he spoke—not assessing competence, but alignment.

"You think like a mediator," she said.

"I think like someone responsible for avoiding conflict," he replied. "There's a difference."

She smiled faintly. "Is there?"

"Yes," Rowan said. "Mediators stabilize after damage. I try to prevent the fracture."

The distinction was quietly profound.

They reached the end of the route and paused, leaning against the railing overlooking a water channel faintly illuminated from below. The city felt distant here, its pressure softened by physical separation.

"Mara," Rowan said, meeting her gaze steadily. "I'd like to ask something."

She inclined her head.

"I know you're... navigating something," he continued carefully. "I won't pretend ignorance."

She appreciated the honesty.

"And I won't ask you for certainty," he added. "But I want to be clear about my own position."

Her chest tightened.

"I like you," Rowan said simply. "Not because you're stabilizing. Not because you make things easier. But because you choose restraint deliberately."

Mara held his gaze.

"That restraint," he continued, "tends to be misread. I don't misread it."

There it was.

The understanding she had identified days earlier—offered now without condition or pressure.

"I'm not asking for an answer tonight," Rowan said. "Only that you know my regard isn't based on proximity or convenience."

Silence stretched between them, gentle and unbearable.

"Thank you," Mara said at last.

It was inadequate. She knew it. So did he.

"I suspected that might be your response," Rowan replied evenly. "For now."

She nodded, grateful for the mercy of that final phrase.

They walked back without speaking further.

At the intersection where they parted, Rowan paused.

"For what it's worth," he said, "if this path isn't yours, I hope you don't choose it out of obligation."

Mara met his gaze, eyes steady.

"I wouldn't," she said.

He smiled, relieved rather than disappointed.

"That's all I needed to know," he replied.

The sadness arrived later, unmoderated by the clarity that had preceded it.

Mara sat alone in her unit, the Reach spreading beyond her window in its familiar pattern of light and shadow. The city did not react to decisions not yet enacted. It did not anticipate regret.

Rowan Hale had offered her something rare: a future shaped by mutual comprehension rather than tension, by steadiness rather than escalation. He would be a partner who saw her fully without requiring translation, who did not mistake her composure for absence or her restraint for distance.

He would not ask her to endure misunderstanding.

And still—she knew she would not choose him.

Not because he lacked depth.

But because with him, she would not need to grow sharper, braver, more precise. The relationship would smooth her contours rather than test them, settle her into a version of herself that made sense without having to stretch.

She understood the danger of that comfort.

It would be a life of good decisions made well, of problems handled capably, of nights undisturbed by conflict or longing. It would be safe.

And safety, she realized with quiet sorrow, was not the same as fulfillment.

The following day, the contrast sharpened unexpectedly.

Mara encountered Elias in a narrow connector corridor where the hum of nearby systems muffled sound and reduced the likelihood of interruption. He looked up as she approached, surprise flickering before warming into recognition.

"Mara," he said. "I was hoping to see you."

"Yes?" she replied, guarded but composed.

"I owe you an acknowledgment," he said. "About the other night."

She waited.

"I've been... careless," Elias continued. "In assuming your silence equated to comfort."

"It was an easy assumption to make," Mara said.

"Perhaps," he replied. "But not an accurate one."

She studied him closely. There was no deflection in his expression now, no performance. Only the unsettled awareness of someone realizing he had misunderstood something essential.

He hesitated.

"I see now," he said slowly, "that your restraint isn't detachment. It's deliberation."

The words landed carefully, belated but sincere.

Mara felt the alignment—not comfort, but recognition.

"I'm still recalibrating," Elias added. "Success rearranges perception more than I expected."

"It always does," Mara replied.

A pause.

"I don't want to misread you again," Elias said.

She met his gaze steadily, weighing the cost of honesty against the habit of concealment.

"Then don't assume stillness means consent," she said. "Or absence of reaction."

His expression tightened with understanding.

"Understood," he said.

The air between them shifted, tension distilled into something quieter and more dangerous: possibility grounded in awareness.

Rowan's face rose briefly in her mind—his calm, his kindness, his readiness to accept what she could offer without demanding more.

Elias, by contrast, stood at the edge of recalibration, neither safe nor stable, but undeniably awake.

The choice, she realized, was already made.

Not aloud.

Not publicly.

But inwardly, unmistakably.

—

That night, Mara drafted a message to Rowan.

She read it twice before sending.

Thank you for your honesty. It matters more than you know. I don't want to mislead you by accepting what I can't truly return.

The reply came hours later.

I know. I hoped anyway. I don't regret it.

She closed the interface gently.

The sadness did not overwhelm her.

It clarified her boundaries.

She chose the unchosen path not with regret, but with moral certainty—aware of its worth, and resolute in her refusal to dilute either of them by pretending it was enough.

Some paths, she knew now, were illuminated precisely so one could recognize they were not meant to be taken.

And clarity, though costly, was kinder than comfort offered under false alignment.

As the Reach hummed quietly beyond her window, Mara rested her palm against the glass and let the ache settle without resistance.

Not every good thing, she reminded herself, was meant to be chosen.

But seeing it clearly mattered.

Always.

Threshold Collapse

The walk was Elias's idea.

He presented it as a necessary recalibration rather than an indulgence—an opportunity to assess repairs along the eastern skyway, where the seawall met the lower transit lattices and the city's infrastructure showed its age most clearly. The phrasing was familiar to Mara: efficiency framed as virtue, risk acknowledged only to be neutralized by decisiveness.

"You can't evaluate stress patterns from a console," Elias said, fastening his jacket as they prepared to leave the tower. "You have to feel the structure respond beneath your footing."

The words echoed something he had once said to her, years ago, in another corridor, another context.

She did not point that out.

Instead, she asked, "And the advisory flags?"

He waved a hand, casual. "Out of date. Overcorrective. They haven't factored in the last reinforcement cycle."

"You're certain."

"Yes."

She noted that he did not say *I've checked.*

They exited Keene Tower through a lower portal reserved for oversight access, bypassing the polished corridors for passages that smelled faintly of salt and metal. The air sharpened immediately as they stepped onto the skyway—cooler, damp with rising mist from below, carrying the steady thunder of water driven against barriers designed to outlast declarations of permanence.

The skyway stretched ahead of them in a long, graceful arc, its surface segmented into flex-plates that adjusted to load and movement. Seen from above, it was elegant. Up close, the seams were more apparent.

"You see?" Elias said, gesturing forward. "It's holding. Better than projected."

Mara felt it too—the subtle give underfoot, the way the structure breathed with weight and wind. She also felt the unevenness at the joints, the slow rhythmic pull that suggested pressure redistributed rather than removed.

"It's compensating," she said.

Elias smiled, pleased. "Exactly. Adaptive systems work best when they aren't constrained by fear."

Mara glanced at him.

"Or empathy," she said quietly.

He did not respond immediately.

They walked on, the city unfurling beneath them in layered planes of light and movement. Below the skyway, maintenance platforms clung to the seawall like barnacles, reinforced again and again in response to rising tides and the city's refusal to retreat. Sensor lights pulsed along the barrier in disciplined intervals, measuring stresses that could never be fully eliminated.

"This section here," Elias said, slowing. "Look at the angle. That reinforcement was installed three years ago. Everyone insisted it wouldn't hold without additional bracing."

"And?"

"And it did," he replied. "Because whoever authorized it trusted the materials instead of the projections."

Mara crouched slightly, resting her palm against the railing. It was cool, vibrating faintly.

"It held," she said, "because the conditions aligned long enough to allow it."

Elias straightened. "You always contextualize," he said, not unkindly. "At some point, decisions require firmness."

There it was—the word that had begun to trouble her more than any other since his return.

"Firmness," she said slowly, "is not the same as inflexibility."

"No," he agreed. "It's the willingness to act when hesitation increases risk."

"And empathy?" Mara asked. "Where does that fit in your equation?"

Elias frowned slightly, considering.

"Empathy informs design," he said. "But it can't dictate action."

Mara rose to her feet.

"That depends," she said, "on who bears the consequences."

He looked at her then, attention sharpening.

"You think I disregard consequence?"

"I think," she replied, measuring her words, "that you've grown accustomed to surviving outcomes personally. That makes external risk easier to abstract."

The wind picked up then, stronger off the water, pressing dampness against their coats. Elias turned toward the seawall, squinting into the haze.

"You're worried," he said, framing the observation with gentle certainty. "That's natural. These structures make most people uneasy."

Mara felt something tighten—not fear, exactly, but recognition of dismissal disguised as reassurance.

"I'm not uneasy," she said. "I'm attentive."

He exhaled, half a laugh.

"That's what caution sounds like to people who prefer motion."

They resumed walking, though the path narrowed perceptibly as the skyway curved toward a junction point where maintenance access met pedestrian flow. Here, the structure dipped slightly, its support pylons angled to distribute load toward the seawall's heavier buttresses.

The city's noise intensified—transit engines below, the low boom of waves striking reinforced stone, the constant hum of systems negotiating with forces larger than themselves.

Mara slowed.

"Here," she said. "Feel that."

Elias paused, shifting his weight deliberately. The flex-plates responded with a subtle lag, correcting themselves fractions of a second after demand.

"It's within tolerance," he said.

"It's approaching a threshold," Mara replied. "The margin is narrower than it appears."

"Margins exist to be used," Elias countered.

"And exceeded," Mara said.

He turned, studying her expression.

"You've always favored caution over action," he said. "That hasn't changed."

Her mouth tightened almost imperceptibly.

"I favor responsibility over impulse," she replied. "Those aren't opposites."

He held her gaze, something unreadable passing through his eyes.

"When I was working beyond the Reach," Elias said, tone shifting, "hesitation killed people. Crews froze waiting for perfect data that never arrived."

"And recklessness killed others," Mara said. "The ones whose stories don't circulate in debriefs."

A beat passed, taut as the cables beneath their feet.

"You're projecting," Elias said. "This structure isn't those conditions."

"No," Mara agreed. "It isn't."

She did not add: *That's what makes it dangerous.*

They reached the midpoint of the skyway, where the railing gave way to reinforced transparent panels, allowing an unfiltered view of the water below. The tide was higher than forecast, waves pressing insistently against the seawall's lower reaches, their force dissipated upward in fine mist.

Warning lights flickered once, then steadied.

Elias noticed.

"See?" he said. "Self-correcting."

Mara's eyes tracked the lights along the lower barrier.

"What's the error margin on those sensors?" she asked.

"Minimal."

"That's not a number."

He shrugged. "Enough."

The wind gusted again, stronger this time, and the skyway shuddered faintly—not alarmingly, but enough to register in the body. Mara felt the vibration travel through her boots, into her calves.

She stopped.

"We should turn back," she said.

Elias looked at her, surprised.

"It's fine," he said. "We're barely halfway."

"That's precisely the issue," she replied. "Conditions are escalating. The tide's rising faster than expected, and the wind vector isn't consistent with the last model."

"You're extrapolating from sensation."

"I'm extrapolating from pattern," she said.

He smiled, that familiar curve that once meant reassurance.

"You always trust patterns more than resolve," he said.

"And you trust resolve more than restraint," she countered.

Something brittle entered his expression.

"Fortune favors decisiveness," he said.

Mara felt the chill then—not from the wind, but from the philosophy underneath the words.

"Fortune," she said, "favors those who survive miscalculation."

Another warning light pulsed—this time redder, slower.

Elias glanced at it, then away.

"Temporary fluctuation," he said. "The system's sensitive."

Mara stepped closer to the railing, peering down at the structure below.

"A sensitive system," she said quietly, "isn't fragile. It's informative. It's telling us something."

He did not respond immediately.

The skyway creaked softly, a sound that might have been dismissed as ordinary if one were inclined to dismiss.

Mara was not.

"This isn't about bravery," she said, more firmly now. "Or control. It's about understanding that thresholds don't collapse loudly at first."

Elias turned back to her, a flicker of irritation surfacing.

"You're letting caution override capability," he said. "That's not who you are."

The words struck harder than the wind.

"This," Mara replied, each word deliberate, "is exactly who I am."

For a moment, only the city spoke—the churn of water, the hum of stressed metal, the whisper of air forced through joints engineered to bend rather than break.

Elias's gaze softened, then hardened again, as if some internal calculus had resolved in favor of motion.

"Let's continue," he said. "A few more meters won't make a difference."

Mara did not move.

Above them, distant thunder rolled—not a storm, but the sound of water striking deeper, older foundations.

The threshold, she knew, was nearer than either of them wanted to admit.

And decisiveness, wielded without empathy, was about to find its consequence.

For a moment, neither of them moved.

The skyway seemed to pause with them, held in uneasy equilibrium—a living structure balancing forces it had been designed to tolerate, but only just. The wind off the water surged again, carrying a tang of salt and iron that settled at the back of Mara's throat. Below, waves hammered the seawall with a rhythm that felt newly insistent, each impact sending a dull vibration up through the supports.

"Elias," she said, keeping her voice level. "Listen."

"To what?" he asked, irritation sharpening his words as another warning indicator flickered amber along the rail.

"To the delay," she replied. "The structure's response is lagging."

He shifted his stance, testing the flex-plates again, harder this time.

"It's compensating," he said. "You can feel it."

"I can feel it *struggling*," Mara said.

A low groan ran through the skyway—brief, almost apologetic, the sound of metal adjusting itself under asymmetric load. The transparent panels along the railing trembled, their internal reinforcement lines pulsing faintly as sensors updated in real time.

Elias's jaw tightened.

"You're assuming escalation," he said. "But systems like this are designed for worst-case scenarios."

"They're designed for modeled worst-cases," Mara replied. "Not for compounded variables arriving out of sequence."

Another gust slammed into them, harder than the last. The skyway dipped perceptibly—no more than a few centimeters—but enough that the horizon tilted for an instant. Mara instinctively reached out, fingers brushing the rail.

The warning lights deepened to red.

This time, they did not steady.

"Okay," Elias said sharply. "That's new."

Mara said nothing. She was already counting.

One, the wind vector.

Two, the tidal surge.

Three, the pedestrian load still behind them.

Thresholds, she thought, rarely failed because of one thing.

"Back," she said. "Now."

Elias hesitated, eyes flicking forward along the span, as though distance still tempted him.

"Elias," she said again, steady but urgent. "Decisiveness doesn't mean insisting. It means changing course when conditions do."

For a fraction of a second, pride and analysis warred openly across his expression.

Then the skyway answered for her.

A sharp crack echoed beneath their feet—not a break, but the unmistakable sound of a stressed joint snapping into a new alignment. The deck shuddered again, more violently this time, and a ripple ran outward along the flex-plates, sending a visible wave through the structure.

Alarms sounded—not blaring, but precise, layered tones issuing from embedded emitters along the rail.

Elias swore softly.

"That joint wasn't due for load redistribution," he said.

"No," Mara replied, gripping the rail firmly now. "Which means the predicted margins are no longer relevant."

He finally turned.

"All right," he said. "We're heading back."

They moved together, their steps measured, timed to the skyway's uneven rhythm. Behind them, the transparent panels flickered, projecting evacuation prompts that scrolled too quickly for casual reading.

The distance back felt longer than it should have been.

Halfway to the junction, another shudder ran through the deck. This time, it tilted subtly toward the seawall, gravity pulling laterally rather than down. Mara adjusted instinctively, shifting her weight inward.

Elias, a step behind, did not.

His boot slid on the dampened surface, traction lost for a split second as the deck flexed beneath him. He reached for balance, fingers grazing empty air.

Mara turned without thinking and caught his sleeve.

The impact jolted her shoulder as his momentum transferred, dragging her sideways. They collided with the railing together, the transparent panel bowing outward under the sudden combined force before rebounding with a hollow thud.

For an instant, the world reduced itself to sensation: the cold bite of glass against her palm, Elias's weight pressing against her shoulder, the roar of water surging far too close below.

She planted her feet, bracing.

"Hold on," she said through clenched teeth.

"I've got it," Elias gasped, scrambling for footing.

Another alarm chimed, this one lower, more insistent—a signal that the skyway's automated dampeners were diverting resources away from comfort and toward structural integrity.

Mara felt the panel beneath her hand warm slightly as embedded systems activated, stiffening the surface to resist further bowing.

"Don't fight it," she said. "Let the deck settle."

Elias forced himself to still, matching his weight to the skyway's slow, uneven sway. Gradually, the tilt lessened, and the flex-plates beneath them found a temporary equilibrium again.

They stood frozen for several seconds, the city's noise roaring up around them.

Finally, Elias laughed once—short, breathless, incredulous.

"All right," he said. "Point taken."

Mara did not release him immediately.

"Are you steady?" she asked.

"Yes," he replied more quietly. "You?"

She nodded and eased her grip.

They resumed walking, slower now, each step deliberate. The evacuation prompts ahead grew brighter as they neared the junction, and maintenance drones began to appear along the skyway's edge, their movements quick and purposeful.

When they reached solid ground, the contrast felt abrupt. The platform beneath their feet was rigid, unmoving, its stability suddenly conspicuous.

Mara stepped back and turned to face him fully for the first time since the incident.

"You could have gone over," she said.

Elias ran a hand through his hair, breath still uneven.

"Yes," he said. "I could have."

The wind gusted again, but here it felt distant, its force absorbed by bulk and mass rather than suspended design.

For a long moment, neither spoke.

"I misjudged the timing," Elias said finally. "And the margin."

"You misjudged the system," Mara replied. "And yourself in it."

He met her gaze, something raw flickering beneath the residual edge of adrenaline.

"I've survived worse," he said, almost reflexively.

"That's not a metric," Mara said sharply. "Survival doesn't validate the process."

His shoulders slumped slightly, the fight draining out of him.

"You're right," he admitted. "I was treating hesitation like weakness."

"And decisiveness like virtue," she finished. "Detached from impact."

He nodded, once.

"I didn't consider how hard I've leaned on my own tolerance," he said. "How that skews what I expect from structures... and people."

The admission cost him something. She could see it.

Maintenance lights flared brighter behind them as drones latched on beneath the skyway, assessing damage unseen from above. The alarms softened, shifting into a diagnostic cadence rather than warning.

"We were lucky," Elias added quietly.

"We were attentive," Mara replied.

He looked at her then—not as an abstract stabilizer, not as an unshakeable constant—but as someone who had intervened, decisively, when his certainty had outpaced reality.

"You didn't just caution me," he said. "You acted."

"Yes," she said. "Because the threshold had already begun to collapse."

A tremor passed through the skyway behind them—controlled this time, absorbed by reinforcements diverting load away from the compromised joint. The disaster had been arrested, not avoided.

Elias exhaled.

"I talk about firmness as if it's always clean," he said. "As if action without doubt is the ideal."

"And doubt," Mara replied, "is often the last signal before catastrophe."

He leaned against the railing of the junction platform, gaze fixed on the suspended arc of the skyway as drones traced its contours.

"I praised decisiveness because it saved me," he said. "Out there."

"And now?" she asked.

"Now," he said slowly, "I see how easily it becomes cruelty when it ignores what can't be endured."

The words settled between them, heavy with implication.

They stood there as the city continued its work—rerouting foot traffic, recalibrating sensors, absorbing the near-failure into its endless churn of adaptation.

Mara felt the residual shake in her hands only when she loosened her grip on the rail. She flexed her fingers once and stilled them.

"This won't be the last time," she said. "Thresholds don't announce themselves once. They deteriorate."

Elias nodded. "Then I'll need you to keep telling me when I'm wrong."

She regarded him carefully.

"I'll need you," she said, "to listen when I do."

He held her gaze and inclined his head in acceptance rather than agreement.

"I will," he said.

Above them, the emergency lamps dimmed, returning the junction to standard illumination. Behind them, the skyway remained cordoned, stable for now, its failure narrowly deferred.

Dread lingered—not because disaster had struck, but because it had come so close. Because ideology, once unexamined, had nearly proven fatal to infrastructure and trust alike.

As they left the platform together, Mara felt the shifting certainty that something essential had cracked—not the skyway this time, but Elias's philosophy of firmness without regard.

The collapse had begun.

It had simply not finished yet.

The Fall

The call came without panic.

That was what made it dangerous.

Mara was midway through a routine systems reconciliation when her interface chimed twice in rapid succession—an anomaly flag she rarely ignored. The alert header resolved into a civic safety cascade, not yet escalated, tagged across multiple subsystems with a confidence interval too wide to be reassuring.

Event Type: Uncontained failure

Location: Midway Sky Spur — Eastern Lattice

Status: Developing

She was on her feet before the second line populated.

From her window, the sky spur cut across the Reach like a delicate thought—an elevated pedestrian lattice threading between transit pylons and maintenance arrays. It had been partially reopened after the previous night's skyway cordoning, its access limited and its load monitors supposedly conservative.

Supposedly.

Her interface updated, this time with a live feed.

The camera angle juddered as a maintenance drone clipped its own stabilizer against a crossbrace, sparks spilling briefly before the feed corrected. Below, people scattered, their movements disorganized but not yet frantic. A crowd had gathered despite advisories—curiosity attracted to height and motion, the human tendency to witness risk as spectacle.

Mara recognized the cluster immediately.

The Serrin sisters stood near the spur's midpoint, Kira closer to the rail than regulations allowed, Dax half-turned toward her, laughing at something off-camera.

Mara did not wait for the system to finish thinking.

She routed commands manually, overriding the default escalation ladder.

"Turn back," she said aloud, though no one could hear her. "Clear the span."

The interface resisted, warning tags flickering. She downgraded the drone's autonomy, forcing it into hover while the spur's load-balancing protocols recalculated.

Too late.

A second drone—private, unsanctioned—entered frame from the upper right, its stabilizers misaligned, feed latched to a third-party channel that prioritized coverage over clearance. The two machines collided at the spur's seam.

Metal rang.

The camera lurched violently.

The image caught Kira at the rail, one hand raised reflexively, fingers hooking instinctively into the transparent barrier as a shockwave rippled through the lattice.

The rail bowed.

Mara's breath shortened.

"No," she said. "Not there."

The spur's flex-plates responded, redistributing load with admirable speed—fast enough that the structure did not fail, slow enough that the human body could not adjust.

Kira lost her footing.

There was no screaming. No dramatic plunge.

Just the sudden, physical fact of gravity taking precedence.

She pitched forward, her shoulder striking the rail as it rebounded, momentum carried sideways rather than down. The barrier held—barely—but the impact twisted her off-balance and sent her tumbling through the maintenance gap between panels.

She fell.

The feed cut for half a second.

When it returned, Kira lay sprawled on a lower service platform, body twisted at an angle that made Mara's stomach hollow. She was motionless, one arm pinned beneath her, hair plastered damply against her face.

The platform alarm began to wail.

Shock arrived exactly one beat later.

"Emergency access," Mara said, already moving. "All available responders to Midway Spur lower tier. Priority medical clearance."

The system hesitated, debating jurisdiction.

Mara overrode it.

"Now."

She grabbed her coat and was out the door before confirmation chimed.

Midway was chaos tempered by people who did not know yet how bad it was.

By the time Mara reached the lower tier, crowd-control prompts had begun to pulse through the air, projecting calm instructions that few obeyed cleanly. People clustered at sightlines, feeds raised, mouths moving in overlapping rumor.

She cut through them without breaking stride.

"Kira!" Dax's voice cracked over the din. "Kira can you hear me?"

Dax knelt at the platform edge, one hand reaching across a boundary line that pulsed yellow in warning. Her face was drained of color, fury and fear flickering indistinguishably.

Mara dropped beside her.

"Dax," she said firmly. "Look at me."

Dax's eyes snapped up.

"She fell," Dax said, breathlessly. "She fell and she's not—she's not moving."

"I know," Mara said. "Listen carefully."

She keyed her interface to local diagnostic view, pulling in med telemetry as it came online. The platform's sensors streamed data faster now, no longer conservative.

"Kira," Mara said, pitching her voice to carry through the alarms without competing with them. "Don't move if you can hear me."

There was no response.

Mara did not panic.

"She's breathing," she said to Dax. "Shallow, but present."

Dax let out a sound that was half sob, half laugh.

"She hit hard," Dax said. "She wouldn't stop talking about the angle—about how it would hold."

Mara's jaw tightened.

"Where does it hurt most?" she asked.

"I—I don't know," Dax stammered. "Her neck—her leg—"

"Okay," Mara said. "We're not guessing."

She leaned forward, careful not to cross the boundary until the platform acknowledged her presence. The yellow pulse softened to amber—conditional access.

"Kira," Mara said again. "I need you to squeeze my hand if you can hear me."

A beat.

Then—barely perceptible—Kira's fingers twitched.

Dax gasped.

"She heard you," Mara said. "That's good."

Mara switched channels, broadcasting to arriving responders with clipped efficiency.

"Possible cervical injury," she said. "Left femur or pelvic trauma. Consciousness intermittent. Do not reposition until immobilization is confirmed."

Voices answered in affirmation, professional and steady. Stretchers deployed. Drones reoriented to provide stabilization rather than spectacle.

Someone else arrived at her shoulder.

Elias.

He was pale, eyes fixed on the figure below them, his earlier confidence stripped down to raw focus.

"I should've—" he began.

"Not now," Mara said, without looking at him. "Later."

She felt him inhale sharply, then fall silent.

"Kira," Mara said softly. "You're doing well. Help is here."

Kira's eyes fluttered open, unfocused. Her lips parted, soundless.

Dax sobbed outright.

"I'm here," Dax said. "I'm right here."

Mara placed a steady hand on Dax's shoulder.

"She needs you calm," Mara said. "Be still with her."

Dax nodded shakily and fell silent, gripping Kira's fingers without pulling.

The responders reached the platform at last, their movements precise and unhurried despite the alarms. They worked around Kira with practiced choreography, stabilizing her neck, scanning for internal injury, securing her limbs.

Mara stepped back just enough to give them space.

The crowd noise dimmed as the perimeter expanded, feeds cut cleanly by enforced blackout protocols. The air felt suddenly quieter, heavier.

"She's stable," one medic said after a long minute. "For now. We're transferring."

"Where?" Dax asked.

"Trauma center, Lower Reach," the medic replied. "Direct line. No delay."

The stretcher lifted, smooth and controlled.

As they moved, Kira's eyes found Mara's.

Recognition flickered. Confusion. Pain.

Mara leaned in.

"You're safe," she said. "We've got you."

Kira's mouth moved again, a whisper barely audible.

"Told... you," she managed. "It'd work."

Mara closed her eyes for half a second.

"Rest," she said instead. "Save your strength."

The stretcher passed through the access gate and was gone.

Dax collapsed against Mara, shaking.

"She fell," Dax said, voice breaking. "I told her—we shouldn't—"

Mara held her upright.

"Later," she said again. "Right now, breathe."

Dax did, raggedly.

Across the platform, Elias stood very still.

He watched the responders depart, his hands clenched at his sides.

"She listened to me," he said, low. "I told her the structure would hold."

Mara turned to face him.

"It did," she said. "That wasn't the failure."

"No?" His voice wavered. "Then what was?"

"Hubris," Mara said gently. "Amplified by attention."

His eyes met hers, stricken.

"She tried to be firm," he said. "She thought—"

"She thought decisiveness would keep her safe," Mara finished. "That refusing caution would make her resilient."

Silence stretched between them, filled only by the hiss of receding alarms and the murmur of shaken onlookers dispersing.

"I should've intervened sooner," Elias said.

"Yes," Mara agreed.

He flinched, but she did not soften it.

"And I should have," she continued, "been louder when silence was misread."

They stood together in the aftermath, the city resuming its motion with uncanny speed, as though catastrophe were merely another variable absorbed by design.

The dynamics between them had shifted—not subtly, not gradually.

Something had broken.

Not reconciled.

Not healed.

But irrevocably realigned.

Mara looked down at the empty platform where Kira had fallen, now cordoned and quiet.

The cost of firmness without empathy lay exposed.

And everyone could see it now.

The aftermath arrived before anyone was ready to name it.

It settled into Midway with the peculiar violence of quiet—systems recalibrating, walkways rerouted, advisory tones dissolving back into neutral hum. The lower platform where Kira had fallen was sealed behind translucent barriers, its surface scrubbed clean within the hour, as if erasure might erase consequence.

It did not.

Mara remained until the responders withdrew and the last data stream confirmed Kira's transfer complete. Only then did she step back, allowing the weight she had been holding at bay to distribute itself more evenly through her body.

Dax sat on the edge of the greenway bench, hands locked together, staring at nothing.

"She didn't even hesitate," Dax said suddenly, voice flat with shock. "That's what everyone kept saying. That hesitation was fear."

Mara sat beside her.

"Hesitation can be information," she said. "And information ignored becomes consequence."

Dax swallowed hard. "She was right about other things."

"Yes," Mara replied. "Which is why this hurts."

They sat in silence for a while, Midway's usual noise subdued around them—not out of respect, but uncertainty. People moved more cautiously, as if calibrating what boldness might cost today.

Dax spoke again, quieter. "She thought she was proving something."

"To whom?" Mara asked gently.

Dax didn't answer. She didn't need to.

Kira underwent surgery that night.

The updates came in clipped phrases: fractured vertebra—stable; internal bleeding—controlled; femoral damage—significant; neurological response—positive, guarded.

Mara read each line without comment, processing probabilities and outcomes with the same steady precision she applied to infrastructure failures. It was easier to think in systems than in bodies, but she refused to let the abstraction lull her.

She forwarded pertinent data to Lina and the building council without commentary. Corrections would come later. Right now, the essential thing was that Kira lived.

Elias did not leave.

He stayed near the lower tier until the platform power cycled completely and the warning lights faded. He watched maintenance drones reinforce the damaged seam, silent, arms folded tightly as if holding something together only he could feel coming apart.

When Mara finally approached him, his voice came first.

"I taught her that," he said, staring at the closed gate. "Not directly. But enough."

Mara did not contradict him.

"You didn't push her," she said. "But you validated the philosophy."

He turned to her then, eyes rimmed red with something more than exhaustion.

"I admired her certainty," he said. "Because it mirrored my own."

"And ignored her vulnerability," Mara answered quietly. "Because it threatened it."

Elias's mouth tightened.

"I never meant for anyone else to bear my margins," he said.

"That's the danger of margins," Mara replied. "They look generous when you've lived inside them too long."

He nodded once, sharply.

The silence that followed was not awkward. It was reckoning.

By morning, the event had been absorbed into narrative.

The feeds softened the language almost immediately. *Structural incident. Isolated failure. Swift response prevented further harm.*

Images circulated of the spur intact, the skyway repaired, the city framed as resilient rather than fragile. The footage that showed Kira's fall was suppressed within hours, replaced by contextless stills of responders doing their work efficiently.

Success, reframed.

Mara tracked the language shifts dispassionately.

They minimized panic. They maximized confidence. They preserved forward motion.

They also erased accountability.

At the trauma center in the Lower Reach, accountability was unavoidable.

Mara arrived mid-morning, credentials clearing her through levels that smelled faintly of antiseptic and salt. The ward was quiet in the way only places accustomed to crisis could be—voices low, movements economical, every surface designed for repair rather than permanence.

Dax sat outside Kira's room, eyes raw from sleeplessness.

"She asked for you," Dax said when she saw Mara.

Mara nodded and entered.

Kira lay propped against reinforced supports, her neck braced, one leg suspended in immobilization scaffolding. Bruising bloomed vividly across her shoulder and ribs, pharmacological sedation dulled but did not erase awareness.

Her eyes opened when Mara approached.

"I messed up," Kira said hoarsely.

Mara sat beside her without hesitation.

"No," she said. "You believed something that wasn't tested under the right conditions."

Kira let out a weak laugh that turned into a grimace.

"I thought not hesitating made me strong."

"It made you loud," Mara said gently. "Strength is quieter."

Kira's gaze sharpened despite the haze of pain.

"You tried to warn us," she said. "Didn't you."

"Yes," Mara replied. "And I should have tried harder."

Kira looked away, jaw tightening.

"I didn't want to look..." She fought for the word. "Careful."

Mara reached out and rested her hand lightly on Kira's uninjured arm.

"Careful," she said, "is not the same as afraid."

Kira met her eyes again then, really seeing her for the first time without filters or momentum.

"I see it now," she said. "Everything holds—until it doesn't."

Mara nodded. "That's the part no one likes to hear."

"Will I walk?" Kira asked quietly.

"Yes," Mara said, without deflection. "But you'll remember this."

Kira swallowed. "Good."

Elias did not enter the room.

He stood outside, listening to voices that mattered more than his own just now. When Mara emerged, he straightened, searching her face.

"She'll recover," Mara said. "With time. And restraint."

He exhaled, shoulders sagging briefly before he mastered himself again.

"Thank you," he said. "For... everything."

She met his gaze steadily.

"This wasn't about thanks," she said.

"No," he agreed.

They left the trauma center together, the city pressing back into their awareness as they returned above ground.

The reset was not immediate.

People did not stop admiring decisiveness overnight. Momentum still glittered seductively in public discourse, and success continued to be mistaken for virtue by those who benefited from its reflection.

But something had shifted.

The Serrin sisters' feed quieted. Dax stopped performing certainty and started asking questions. Lina revised the building's advisory structures, reintroducing friction where speed had been overvalued.

And Elias—Elias recalibrated.

Mara watched it happen in small but unmistakable ways.

He asked before acting.

He deferred publicly.

He corrected others when they praised recklessness as strength.

At one coordination meeting, someone exclaimed, "You don't hesitate anymore, Calder," with admiration.

Elias responded evenly, "I hesitate all the time now. I'm just faster about deciding when to stop."

Mara looked up from her console and met his gaze across the room.

For the first time since his return, the look he gave her held no presumption.

Only recognition.

They spoke late that night, not by design but by residual gravity.

They stood on a quiet connector terrace overlooking the Reach, the water calm for once, reflecting the city's light without distortion.

"I thought firmness made me reliable," Elias said, resting his forearms on the rail. "But it made me predictable."

Mara stood beside him, her posture relaxed but attentive.

"Predictability feels like safety," she said. "Until it isn't."

"I built my survival around it," he continued. "Around acting before doubt could intervene."

"And now?" she asked.

"Now," he said, turning toward her, "I realize doubt is what kept you alive. And kept others safer around you."

The admission was not grand.

That was what made it matter.

"You took command today," Elias added. "Without drama. Without forcing relevance."

"I did what was required," Mara replied.

"And reset everything," he said. "Not structurally. Ethically."

She regarded him carefully.

"This wasn't a lesson," she said. "It was a cost."

"I know," he replied.

He hesitated, then said, "I won't praise decisiveness without asking who it endangers again."

Mara nodded. "That's a beginning."

They stood in silence, the Reach stretching below them, patient and indifferent as ever. Somewhere in the city, Kira slept under careful supervision, her future altered but intact.

Something had fallen.

Not just a body.

Not just a structure.

But an illusion—that resolve alone could outpace consequence.

In its place stood something harder, quieter, and far more durable: a recalibration of values, tested by gravity and survived.

As Mara turned to leave, she felt the dynamics between them settle into a new alignment—not resolved, not romanticized, but reset.

The midpoint had passed.

Nothing ahead could pretend to be untouched by what had happened here.

And for the first time, that knowledge felt like stability rather than loss.

Aftermath Authority

Authority did not arrive as recognition.

It arrived as need.

Mara discovered this within an hour of the fall, as the city settled into post-incident choreography and systems struggled to agree on who was responsible for what now. She had returned to Midway expecting to rest—expecting, perhaps, to feel the delayed tremor of fear she had deferred—but the building would not allow it.

A message came first from the trauma center, routed indirectly.

Requesting coordination support.

Patient transfer dependencies unresolved.

Then another, this time from Infrastructure Allocation.

Need confirmation on reroute permissions—conflicting advisories detected.

Then Lina, breathless through a voice channel that skipped protocol entirely.

"I'm sorry," Lina said. "I know it's late. But everything's snarling at once."

"I'm coming," Mara replied, already pulling on her coat.

She did not ask where she was needed.

The building would answer that itself.

The lower-tier coordination hub had been activated on emergency footing, its usual calm replaced by layered urgency that had not yet decided whether to escalate into panic. Displays flickered with overlapping priorities: casualty transport, structural diagnostics, public communication dampening, access control.

Three different teams issued partial commands to the same subsystems.

Mara stopped just inside the threshold.

She did not raise her voice.

She did not call attention to herself.

She stood still long enough for the room's competing rhythms to register her presence.

Then she began.

"Shut off nonessential alerts," she said to no one in particular, fingers already moving across her interface. "They're cascading and obscuring signal."

A junior coordinator hesitated. "But those are mandated—"

"I'll absorb the compliance trail," Mara replied evenly. "Mute them."

The alerts fell silent, replaced by a steadier hum.

"Medical transport is priority," Mara continued. "Nothing else overrides it for the next nineteen minutes. Where is the bottleneck?"

"Elevator banks," someone said. "Two are down for recalibration."

"Recalibration can wait," Mara said. "Bypass through freight shafts six and nine. Those supports were reinforced last quarter."

"But the clearance—"

"I've already issued it," she said.

No one argued.

They did not need to.

The systems obeyed.

Within ten minutes, order began to coalesce—not because chaos had been eliminated, but because it had been sorted. Problems found their lanes. Conflicts stopped competing and started sequencing.

Mara moved without pause, her awareness widening rather than narrowing under pressure. She listened to three channels at once, responding only to the one that mattered most at any given second.

When a medic's voice broke over comms—strained, uncertain—she slowed.

"Say it again," Mara said gently.

The medic repeated the concern: blood pressure instability during transfer, internal monitoring conflicting with transit vibration tolerances.

"Shorten the route," Mara said immediately. "Reduce vertical movement by one level. Reroute through the quiet corridor—we'll sacrifice speed for control."

The medic exhaled audibly. "That'll cost us six minutes."

"It will buy you stability," Mara replied. "Take it."

The line cleared.

Lina watched from the edge of the hub, hands clasped tightly, awe flickering unchecked for the first time.

"You do this like you've been waiting for it," she said quietly.

Mara did not look up. "I've practiced."

It was Elias who noticed first what was truly shifting.

He stood at the far end of the hub, no longer the center of anything, his presence reduced to its natural scale. No one deferred to him here. No feeds angled toward his reactions. He was simply another figure in a room that had found its axis elsewhere.

And he was watching Mara.

Not casually.

Not distantly.

He watched the way she triangulated priorities instead of crowning them, the way she stripped drama from crisis until only solvable components remained. He watched her speak with clarity that neither hurried nor softened, issuing instructions that carried trust simply because they made sense.

This was not decisiveness as performance.

This was competence as inevitability.

At one point, a systems analyst pushed back—a procedural objection grounded more in habit than logic.

Mara let them finish.

Then she said, "You're protecting the system. I'm protecting the outcome. Those are not opposed goals."

The analyst flushed, nodded, and complied.

Elias felt the realization settle—a recalibration as physical as the skyway's had been.

This was what he had failed to see.

By nightfall, the immediate crises had been narrowed to aftermath cases.

Kira remained stable. Transport lines had been rebalanced. Public feeds softened around language that now accurately reflected containment rather than triumph. The Midway spur remained closed, its reopening contingent upon review rather than confidence.

Mara finally stepped back from the console and rolled her shoulders, feeling fatigue surface at last.

"That's... most of it," Lina said, disbelief edging her voice. "We've never resolved a cascade that cleanly."

Mara nodded once. "Because no one tried to own it."

Lina frowned. "Isn't that a good thing?"

"For credit," Mara replied. "Not for action."

People began to disperse, conversations lowering, urgency subsiding into subdued relief. As they left, several paused—just long enough to look at Mara with something that bordered on gratitude.

Not awe.

Recognition.

"Can we talk?"

Elias's voice cut through the newly settled quiet.

Mara turned to him.

"Yes," she said.

They stepped out onto an adjacent service terrace, the air cooler, the Reach quieter than it had been all day. Below them, lights traced stabilized routes—proof, if any were needed, that the city responded to care as readily as it did to force.

"I didn't interrupt," Elias said. "I knew better."

She inclined her head. "Thank you."

He rubbed a hand along the rail, uncharacteristically restless.

"I thought leadership looked like standing forward," he said slowly. "Like being visible when things went wrong."

"And now?" Mara asked.

"Now," he admitted, "I realize it looks like disappearing into motion. Making others focus on the work instead of the person directing it."

She studied him quietly.

"You didn't disappear today," she said.

"No," he replied. "But I wasn't central."

"The difference matters," she said.

He nodded, absorbing it without resistance.

"I've been wrong about you," Elias said then. "About how you function under pressure."

Mara did not deflect.

"In what way?" she asked.

"I mistook your restraint for distance," he said. "Your silence for disengagement. I thought decisiveness meant acting fastest."

"And now?"

"I see that decisiveness," he said carefully, "means acting *last.* After everything unnecessary has been removed."

The words were not eloquent.

They were true.

Mara felt something loosen—not pride, but vindication.

"I don't seek authority," she said. "I accept it when it's required."

"That," Elias said quietly, "might be why it works."

They stood there as wind moved gently across the terrace, carrying the scent of water and metal that now felt familiar rather than ominous.

"I don't know how long I've overlooked that," Elias continued. "Years, maybe."

"Long enough," Mara said. "But not irretrievably."

He looked at her then, really looked—no projection, no assumption layered over observation.

"I see you," he said.

Not dramatically.

Not apologetically.

As a statement of fact.

Mara met his gaze, steady and unguarded.

"Good," she said.

Later that night, she returned to Midway alone.

The building greeted her with softened light and the subdued hush that followed shared shock. As she passed through the greenway, people nodded—some with relief, others with something like trust.

Dax waited near her unit, arms folded tightly around herself.

"They said Kira's stable," Dax said immediately.

"She is," Mara replied.

Dax exhaled, shaky. "You didn't have to stay all day."

"Yes," Mara said gently. "I did."

Dax hesitated, then said, "She kept saying your name before they sedated her."

Mara's chest tightened.

"She said you were the only one who didn't yell. The only one who made it feel… manageable."

Mara swallowed once.

"I'm glad," she said.

Dax nodded, eyes shining. "Me too."

They parted quietly.

Inside her unit, Mara finally sat, fatigue settling fully and without resistance. She leaned back, closed her eyes, and let the events of the day align into something resembling order.

For once, her value had not been inferred, or misread, or obscured by spectacle.

It had been undeniable.

And someone—not just anyone—had finally witnessed it without needing translation.

Respect, she realized, was not given when one demanded it.

It arrived when circumstances made it unavoidable.

Outside, the Reach continued its slow, resilient pulse.

Mara rested her palms against the cool glass and allowed herself one small, inward certainty:

She would not need to be louder.

She would not need to be faster.

She simply needed to be exactly who she already was.

The shift did not announce itself with a meeting or a message.

It announced itself in how people moved.

Mara noticed it the following morning, when she returned to the lower-tier coordination hub to review overnight diagnostics. Conversations adjusted as she entered—not halting, not deferential, but angled. Decisions that might once have waited for escalation were already organized, questions grouped by relevance rather than urgency.

When someone spoke, they looked at her without quite realizing they were doing it.

Authority, she understood, had settled.

She did not comment on it. She never did.

Instead, she listened.

"Transport alignment is stable," a coordinator said. "But we're seeing lag in eastbound freight since the spur closure."

Mara scanned the overlay. "It's bias, not lag," she replied. "Priority reassignment overcorrected. Restore two percent capacity and it will even out."

It did.

No one applauded.

They simply moved on.

At Keene Tower, the reverberations were quieter but no less pronounced.

Stewards sought her input earlier in deliberations than before, requests phrased not as assistance but as inclusion. Allocation rerouted a proposed oversight change through her channel first rather than last, an acknowledgment that evaluation now preceded validation.

Elias noticed this almost immediately.

He made no comment during the morning briefing, but afterward, as they walked through a connector corridor washed in filtered daylight, he slowed his pace deliberately to match hers.

"They're listening," he said.

"They're recalibrating," Mara replied. "Listening is a byproduct."

He smiled slightly. "You're allergic to credit."

"Credit encourages replication without understanding," she said. "I'd rather accuracy."

He nodded, not arguing.

That alone was new.

They visited the trauma center later that afternoon.

Kira was awake, pale but alert, her movements limited by braces and procedure rather than fear. When she saw them, something like embarrassment crossed her face.

"So," she said dryly. "I fell."

"Yes," Mara replied.

"And you caught everything else," Kira added. "Figures."

Mara pulled a chair closer and sat.

"How do you feel?" she asked.

Kira considered. "Like I learned a lesson the expensive way."

"That's how most real ones arrive," Mara said gently.

Elias stood back, giving space without retreating. When Kira looked at him, her gaze was steady, free of accusation but heavy with awareness.

"She didn't hesitate," Kira said, nodding at Mara. "Everyone else did. Even you."

Elias accepted this without flinching.

"She didn't need my permission," Kira continued. "That's what I thought firmness was."

"And now?" Mara asked.

Kira sighed. "Now I think it's knowing when to stop pretending momentum protects you."

Mara nodded.

"That's not defeat," she said. "That's judgment."

Kira's mouth twisted into a faint smile. "Hard-earned."

When they left, Elias walked beside Mara in thoughtful silence.

"She sees you," he said at last.

Mara glanced at him. "She always did. She just didn't know how to listen yet."

The Serrin sisters' dynamic shifted almost imperceptibly after that.

Dax still filled space with motion, but the motion had changed shape—less confrontational, more circumspect. Her commentary turned from proclamation to speculation, questions replacing declarations without announcement.

"You ever notice," she said one evening as they walked the greenway together, "that people talk about strength like it's volume?"

"Yes," Mara replied.

"And you didn't raise your voice once," Dax continued. "Not even when—" She stopped herself.

"Not raising one's voice," Mara said, "doesn't mean one isn't heard."

Dax absorbed that.

She nodded. "I think I get it now."

They continued walking.

Recognition gathered quietly.

A revised safety protocol circulated Midway two days later, its language unmistakably hers—clear, unembellished, intolerant of ambiguity. Someone had attached her name to it, officially.

She removed it before distribution.

Lina caught her in the corridor.

"They'll still know," Lina said.

"Yes," Mara replied. "That's enough."

Lina studied her with frank admiration.

"You could take more," Lina said. "People would let you."

"I don't want more," Mara answered. "I want fewer failures."

Lina smiled. "That tracks."

Elias's recalibration was visible to those who watched carefully.

He began deferring in public contexts—subtly, without announcement—redirecting questions to others who held more precise knowledge rather than fielding them himself. He ceded conversational ground without surrendering presence, allowing competence to surface where it actually belonged.

At one review session, an Allocation representative remarked, half-jokingly, "You've gone quiet, Calder."

Elias responded easily, "I've been listening to the right people."

His eyes found Mara briefly across the table.

She did not look away.

Their understanding did not require conversation to advance.

They worked alongside one another now—not orbiting, not colliding, but aligned. Elias learned to wait without interpreting delay as opposition; Mara learned that presence, when chosen rather than imposed, did not need to be defended.

One evening, late, they sat at the edge of the connector terrace, the Reach stretched wide beneath them, quiet with that rare, temporary calm that followed disruption.

"You were always capable of this," Elias said quietly. "I just didn't know how to see it over my own velocity."

Mara considered his words.

"I was always capable," she agreed. "But capability alone doesn't ensure visibility."

"And you never asked for it."

"No," she said. "I trusted necessity to reveal me."

He nodded, understanding the cost of that trust more clearly now.

"It almost didn't," he said.

She met his gaze. "But it did."

Later still, alone in her unit, Mara reflected on the trajectory that had brought her here—not upward, not dramatically forward, but into a place of unmistakable solidity.

Her competence had not been new.

Her clarity had not changed.

What had shifted was recognition—earned not through insistence, but through the unarguable weight of action under pressure.

Vindication did not feel like triumph.

It felt like quiet relief.

Outside her window, Midway moved with a steadier rhythm now, its systems adjusted, its people more attentive to the spaces between impulse and response. Somewhere across the city, Kira healed. Somewhere else, Rowan Hale continued his careful work, respectful distance intact, his path unchosen and honored for precisely that reason.

And beside her—no longer ahead of her, no longer orbiting elsewhere—Elias Calder stood within sight of who she had always been.

Not idealized.

Not misread.

Recognized.

Mara closed her eyes briefly and rested against the glass, the city's hum grounding rather than demanding.

Authority, she understood at last, was not something one acquired.

It was something one revealed—by holding still when others rushed, by speaking when consensus faltered, by remaining present when fear tempted spectacle.

She would remain that way.

And for the first time in a long while, she sensed that the city—and the man who mattered most within it—would finally move with her rather than around her.

Moral Recalibration

The recalibration did not occur all at once.

It revealed itself in hesitation.

Mara noticed it first in the way Elias Calder paused—just briefly—before answering questions that once would have prompted immediate response. The pause was almost imperceptible, a fraction of time most people would have read as thoughtfulness or professionalism. She read it as something else entirely.

Doubt.

Not the paralyzing kind he once despised, but the productive, destabilizing sort that forced reconsideration before motion. It crept into his posture, too—shoulders no longer angled forward by habit, gaze less inclined to lead and more inclined to scan.

They were seated at a coordination table in Keene Tower's mid-level review suite, a room chosen for function rather than prestige. The meeting concerned the eastern transit lattice, still under partial restriction following the Midway incident, and the discussion had reached its predictable impasse: speed versus caution, visibility versus patience.

A steward leaned forward, fingers steepled.

"If we delay reopening any longer," he said, "we invite speculation. The feeds are already restless."

Elias inhaled as though about to respond—then stopped.

Mara watched him out of the corner of her eye.

"What kind of speculation?" Elias asked instead.

The steward blinked. "Concern. Rumor. Doubt about structural confidence."

Elias nodded slowly.

"And if we rush?" he asked. "What kind of certainty do we invite?"

The steward opened his mouth, then closed it again.

Silence settled across the table.

"That's a different frame," Torres murmured, not quite smiling.

Elias leaned back, hands folded loosely now rather than set ready for emphasis.

"We can reopen when the structure tells us it's ready," he said. "Not when the audience gets bored."

The words would have sounded like rhetoric, once.

Now they sounded like reconsideration.

Mara felt something warm and cautious unfold in her chest.

They walked afterward, as they had so often begun to do, choosing a path along the inner galleries rather than the dramatic exterior spans. The city pressed close through the glass—present, insistent, alive—but no longer demanding performance.

"I would have answered that differently," Elias said at last.

"Yes," Mara replied.

"And not that long ago."

"No."

They slowed near a junction where the corridor curved gently, forcing them closer together without urgency.

"I used to believe decisiveness was the clearest signal of capability," Elias continued. "That hesitation meant weakness, or worse—fear."

"And now?" she asked.

"And now," he said, brow furrowing in thought, "I think decisiveness without context is just velocity."

She turned her head slightly, intrigued.

"Velocity," she repeated, "can be useful."

"When you know where you're going," he agreed. "But dangerous when you've mistaken motion for direction."

They walked on.

For a while, neither spoke.

The quiet between them was different than it had been before—less brittle, less charged with unspoken grievance. It carried weight instead: the pleasure of ideas meeting resistance and surviving the contact.

"I've been replaying that moment on the skyway," Elias admitted eventually. "Not the stumble—the assumption that preceded it."

"Which assumption?" Mara asked gently.

"That the structure's resilience validated my approach," he said. "That because something *had* held, it *would* hold. I built a philosophy around my own survivorship."

"And ignored," Mara said, "those who didn't survive to testify."

"Yes."

The word landed heavily, but not defensively.

"I think," Elias went on, "that dominance often disguises itself as confidence. We praise the ability to impose will on uncertainty, when sometimes the more difficult act is restraint."

Mara stopped walking.

He noticed immediately.

"That's not an easy conclusion to reach," she said.

"No," he replied. "It unsettles almost everything I've been rewarded for."

She studied him carefully now—the serious openness in his expression, the lack of self-congratulation. He was not performing contrition or soliciting reassurance.

He was thinking.

"This shift," she said, "will make some people uncomfortable."

"Good," Elias replied without reflex. "Comfort has been a poor diagnostic."

She smiled faintly.

"That's new."

"I'm learning," he said. "Belatedly."

They resumed walking.

The conversation deepened later, not by design but by gravity, drawn back together at the edge of a shared observation deck overlooking the Reach. The tide was low, exposing structures normally hidden here—older supports, layered reinforcements laid down over generations of incremental failure and stubborn survival.

Elias rested his hands on the rail.

"I used to admire systems that didn't bend," he said quietly. "I thought rigidity meant integrity."

"And now?" Mara asked.

"And now I see how often they break catastrophically," he replied. "While flexible ones absorb damage quietly and keep going."

She nodded.

"That," she said, "is why they're often overlooked. Survival without spectacle rarely earns applause."

He turned toward her then.

"I never applauded you," he said. "Not really."

She met his gaze calmly.

"No," she agreed. "You didn't."

The admission did not sting the way it once might have. It felt acknowledged, no longer lodged in silence.

"I admired outcomes," Elias continued. "But failed to credit the intelligence that made them resilient. I thought because you didn't demand space, you didn't need it."

Mara considered.

"I didn't need *space*," she said. "I needed accuracy."

"And I was imprecise," he said.

"Yes," she replied.

He exhaled, not regretful so much as clear-eyed.

"I think firmness appealed to me because it simplified things," Elias said. "Decision, action, result. It minimized ambiguity."

"And minimized accountability," Mara added softly.

He nodded.

"When things went wrong," he said, "I could attribute failure to insufficient resolve—my own or someone else's. It spared me from examining whether the choice itself was flawed."

"That's a powerful illusion," Mara said.

"And a dangerous one," Elias replied.

They stood there, the city stretching out beneath them—not distant now, not abstracted, but present as consequence made visible.

"I don't believe dominance is strength anymore," Elias said at last. "I believe it's... fear with better branding."

The words surprised even him.

Mara felt a flicker of something like hope—measured, cautious, but real.

"That realization," she said, "can unmoor people."

"It's unmoored me," he admitted. "But not adrift. I feel... recalibrated."

There was a faint smile in his voice now, not of satisfaction, but relief.

"I don't have to be first," he said. "Or loudest. Or always right."

"No," Mara agreed. "You have to be responsible."

"And open," he added, glancing at her. "To being wrong."

She returned the look steadily.

"That," she said, "is far rarer."

Their intellectual intimacy grew not from agreement, but from the way their disagreements had softened into inquiry rather than defense.

They spoke now of design ethics, of leadership models that valued distributed intelligence over centralized command, of cities that survived not because they were strong, but because they remembered their failures accurately.

At one point, Elias laughed softly.

"You know," he said, "this is the first time in years I've felt genuinely *corrected* without feeling diminished."

Mara considered that.

"Correction," she said, "shouldn't be humiliation. It's maintenance."

He nodded. "I've treated it like punishment."

"And avoided it accordingly," she said.

"Yes."

The admission carried no shame now, only adjustment.

As they parted that night, there was no declaration, no sudden emotional convergence. What bound them felt quieter and, for that reason, sturdier: the shared pleasure of thought sharpened by trust.

Elias paused just before stepping away.

"I hope," he said, carefully, "that any future decisions I make don't require you to absorb the consequences of my certainty again."

Mara met his gaze, something gentle and resolute passing between them.

"I won't," she said. "Not anymore."

He accepted that without protest.

As she returned to Midway alone, the city felt different—not safer, not calmer, but more legible. As though the lines between action and impact had been redrawn more honestly.

Moral recalibration, she knew, did not resolve all tension.

It created better ones.

Hope, she reflected, did not come from certainty.

It came from the willingness to remain teachable—especially after success.

And for the first time since Elias Calder had returned, she believed that the philosophy that once separated them was no longer immovable.

It was thinking.

And thinking, once begun, rarely stopped.

The test came sooner than Elias expected.

It arrived cloaked in necessity, framed as opportunity, and delivered with the confidence of people accustomed to being obeyed.

Allocation convened an emergency review three days after the Midway protocols were revised, citing "external pressure" and "confidence metrics trending downward." The session was closed to general observation, the invitation list curated to include only those whose assent could be presumed or persuaded.

Elias recognized the shape of it immediately.

They wanted spectacle.

The eastern transit lattice, still under controlled restriction, had become symbolic—a visible reminder that decisiveness had failed publicly, that restraint now demanded explanation. The feeds were restless, commentators speculating about weakness, about overcorrection, about leadership losing its edge.

Allocation wanted to reopen the spur.

Not conservatively.

Not incrementally.

They wanted a gesture.

"They're proposing a phased reopening with media presence," Torres said quietly as they took their seats at the long table. "Live confirmation of load tolerance."

Mara did not look up from the briefing slate she was skimming.

"They want a performance," she said.

"Yes," Torres agreed. "They do."

Across the table, the lead steward cleared his throat.

"We can't allow confidence to erode," he said. "Resilience is as much perception as engineering."

Elias felt the familiar pull—the instinct to respond quickly, to counter anxiety with assertion. He recognized the muscle memory of his former self flexing, prepared to reassure through confidence alone.

He let the urge pass.

"This reopening," Elias said instead, carefully, "would occur under what conditions?"

The steward blinked. "Standard post-incident thresholds. We'd broadcast live diagnostic overlays to demonstrate integrity."

"And if the structure isn't ready?" Elias asked.

"We believe it is," the steward replied. "The models suggest—"

"Elide belief," Elias said, surprised at his own firmness. "What does the structure say?"

A silence followed.

Mara shifted slightly beside him.

"That's not the usual order of questioning," Torres murmured, approval threading her voice.

The steward composed himself.

"The structure hasn't indicated impending failure," he said. "Which suggests readiness."

Mara finally looked up.

"Absence of failure," she said evenly, "is not evidence of resilience."

The steward frowned. "You're advocating indefinite delay?"

"No," she replied. "I'm advocating accurate timing."

Another steward leaned forward.

"With respect," he said, "timing must also consider morale. The city needs reassurance."

Elias inhaled.

Here it was.

The old invitation.

If he spoke now, they would listen. If he reassured, they would applaud. If he reclaimed dominance, the uncertainty would recede—temporarily.

And someone else would absorb the risk.

He thought of the skyway bending beneath his feet.

Of Kira falling.

Of Mara standing immovable when velocity failed.

"I understand morale," Elias said at last. "But I won't authorize a reopening designed to placate anxiety rather than address conditions."

The room froze, then stirred.

"That's a significant deviation," the lead steward said. "Your support carries weight here."

"I'm aware," Elias replied. "That's why I won't lend it lightly."

Mara felt the shift like pressure equalizing.

"You're saying no," Torres said softly.

"Yes," Elias said. "Until the structure demonstrates readiness under quiet conditions. No feeds. No audience."

The stewards exchanged looks.

"This could cost us public confidence," one warned.

Elias looked directly at him.

"It will cost us more if someone is injured proving they should have waited."

The words did not land dramatically.

They landed conclusively.

The fallout unfolded exactly as predicted.

Feed analysts pounced. Stories proliferated about hesitation at the top, about leadership paralyzed by fear, about the erosion of decisive command. Some speculated openly whether Elias Calder had "lost his edge."

The comments did not wound him the way they once would have.

He forwarded the speculation to Mara without commentary.

She responded with one line:

Noise increases when systems lose shortcuts.

He smiled.

At Midway, the recalibration rippled outward.

Dax confronted the shift with visible effort, resisting the temptation to frame it as betrayal or retreat.

"He didn't back down," she said one evening, paced frustration threading her voice. "He just... stopped pushing."

"Yes," Mara replied.

"That's harder than pushing," Dax admitted. "People don't know how to read it."

Mara nodded. "They eventually learn."

And they did—slowly, unevenly.

As days passed without incident, without spectacle, the absence of catastrophe began to speak for itself. The structure responded positively to measured stress testing. Feedback models recalibrated, reinforcing restraint rather than undermining it.

The city adapted.

Not because it had been reassured.

Because it had been allowed to stabilize.

Elias paid for his refusal in subtler ways.

Invitations thinned. Certain voices cooled. He found himself excluded from informal strategizing where momentum and projection were prized above integrity.

For the first time in years, his authority encountered friction.

He did not push back against it.

Instead, he asked questions where answers were thin. He invited dissent rather than acclaim. He redirected credit whenever possible, loosening the very myths that had elevated him.

One afternoon, a steward cornered him after a briefing.

"You're changing the rules," she said, not angry, but unsettled.

Elias nodded. "I am."

"And if the city doesn't follow?"

"Then I'll know the recalibration hasn't taken," he replied.

She studied him carefully. "You're willing to lose relevance over this."

"Yes," Elias said easily. "Because relevance that requires distortion isn't worth sustaining."

The words surprised even him.

Mara saw the cost most clearly.

She watched the subtle diminishment of Elias's gravitational pull—not reduced competence, not diminished respect, but a shedding of superficial admiration that had once clung automatically. The people who remained around him now did so with intention rather than incentive.

That, she knew, was the harder circle.

They met one evening on a quiet maintenance bridge crossing a lower canal, the water reflecting muted light below. No audience. No agenda.

"You lost ground today," Mara said, not unkindly.

Elias considered. "I shed ground."

She smiled faintly. "You're learning to frame it."

"It's strange," he admitted. "Letting go of momentum feels like erasure. Like stepping out of a story where I knew my role."

"And now?" she asked.

"And now," he said, "I'm not sure what replaces it."

She stopped walking and turned toward him.

"Responsibility," she said. "Care. Accuracy."

He nodded.

"It doesn't shine," he said.

"No," Mara agreed. "But it holds."

They stood together, the city accommodating their stillness without demand.

"I used to believe dominance was leadership," Elias said quietly. "Now I think it's just noise that mistakes itself for direction."

Mara studied him, something unmistakably tender in her gaze.

"That belief," she said, "is earned, not adopted."

He met her eyes.

"I earned it the hard way."

"Yes," she said. "But you earned it."

The reopening came without announcement.

No crowd.

No feed countdown.

No performance.

The spur eased back into service under ordinary load, its resilience affirmed by absence of incident rather than spectacle. Transit resumed, cautiously at first, then with growing confidence that required no reinforcement.

People noticed.

Not loudly, but with relief.

The feeds moved on.

And in their passing disinterest, the recalibration completed itself.

Later that night, Elias sent Mara a message.

Thank you for not confusing my hesitation with retreat.

She replied after a moment.

Thank you for letting recalibration cost you something.

They met again by default rather than design, their paths intersecting where they always now seemed to do—places of transition rather than emphasis.

"You know," Elias said thoughtfully, "I think firmness was never about certainty. It was about avoiding vulnerability."

"And prudence?" Mara asked.

"Accepting it," he replied.

She rested her hand briefly against the railing.

"Then this," she said, "is real change."

He smiled—quiet, grounded.

"It is," he said. "And I don't want to undo it."

Mara believed him.

Not because he promised.

But because he had already proven it—when it would have been easier, more rewarding, to do otherwise.

As they parted, hope did not feel fragile.

It felt deliberate.

Intellectual intimacy, she reflected, was not agreement.

It was the courage to rethink out loud, together, and to let that rethinking alter the shape of one's actions in the world.

Elias Calder was no longer dominant.

He was becoming responsible.

And for Mara, that transformation did not diminish him.

It finally made him equal.

Transitional Exile

The relocation was framed as practical.

Mara understood that immediately, the way she understood most institutional decisions—not by what was said, but by what was *smoothed over*. The message from Allocation arrived shortly after dawn, language careful and efficient, its tone pitched at inevitability rather than request.

Temporary reassignment to Core City liaison role recommended.

Presence requested for cross-sector harmonization.

Duration: provisional.

Provisional, she noted, was becoming a favored word.

She accepted the reassignment without objection. Not because she wished to go, but because refusal would have required an explanation she no longer had energy to provide. Midway was stabilizing. The crisis had passed into memory. Her remaining would have been interpreted as lingering rather than necessary.

Still, the thought of Core City sat heavily.

It was not that she had never been there. Everyone passed through it eventually—its polished transit halls, its dense concentration of influence and refinement. But to *live* there, even provisionally, was another matter. Core City demanded posture. It rewarded fluency in ritual. It asked for a kind of attentiveness different from hers.

She packed lightly.

Few things defined her by place alone. Work followed her. The rest remained reduced to essentials—clothing adaptable to formal and functional settings, personal devices, a small collection of physical notes she had not digitized for reasons she could no longer fully articulate.

Before leaving Midway, she walked the greenway one last time.

The atmosphere had shifted since the fall—subtly but unmistakably. People moved with greater awareness of edges and thresholds, conversations quieter when they passed beneath elevated structures. Dax waved from across the way, her smile tentative but real.

"They'll keep things steady," Dax called.

"Yes," Mara replied. "You will."

Dax nodded, perhaps understanding more than she let on.

Lina met her near the transit lift, arms folded tight around herself as though bracing against something unspoken.

"I hate this part," Lina said. "When the city pretends relocation is neutral."

"It rarely is," Mara replied.

"But you'll come back," Lina said, hopeful and uncertain all at once.

Mara did not answer right away.

"I'll be where I'm needed," she said instead.

Lina accepted the answer for what it was: accurate but incomplete.

Core City announced itself through absence.

Noise thinned as Mara's transit capsule crossed the boundary into its inner zones, the hum of movement quieted by active dampening fields that prized serenity as status. Buildings rose in cleaner lines here, their facades reflective rather than absorptive, light folding back upon itself instead of dispersing freely.

The unit assigned to her was efficient, elegant, impersonal.

Glass, neutral surfaces, adaptive lighting calibrated to suit productivity metrics. The view offered scale rather than intimacy—layers of towers receding into guided haze, a city that preferred to be admired from distance rather than inhabited.

Mara stood in the center of the room and did not unpack immediately.

Her interface chimed softly, presenting a curated list of receptions, forums, and informational gatherings she was expected—encouraged—to attend. None were mandatory. All were strategic.

She scanned them without selection and dismissed the list.

Later.

Her first evening passed without event. She ordered a simple meal from a local service hub and ate standing near the window, watching the city below arrange itself into purposeful symmetry. There were no sudden bursts of sound, no overlapping narratives competing for space. Everything appeared intentional.

Exhaustion crept in quietly.

The kind that followed not action, but sustained vigilance.

The separation made itself felt the following morning.

Mara woke early, instinct unchanged, but the sounds that greeted her were wrong—too uniform, too distant. She dressed and prepared for the day with habitual precision, yet found the motion lacked its usual grounding effect.

On her way to the liaison center, she passed through an atrium lined with adaptive art displays that responded to movement and biometric input. They shifted as she walked, colors rebalancing in response to her presence.

It felt intrusive.

At the center, her arrival was met with polite efficiency.

"Mara Keene," an attendant said smoothly. "We're grateful you could join us on such short notice."

"I'm assigned," Mara replied.

"Yes," the attendant smiled. "Of course."

The distinction mattered here.

Meetings stacked quickly, discussions looping around familiar themes—harmonization, risk mitigation, public reassurance. People spoke at length without saying much, their contributions weighted by reputation rather than substance.

Mara listened.

She spoke sparingly, redirecting conversation when it drifted into abstraction, grounding proposals in feasibility rather than praise. Her input was acknowledged, even respected—but differently than at Midway.

Here, approval came with distance.

Her authority was professional, not relational.

That absence carried more fatigue than resistance ever had.

Elias remained in Midway.

The necessity of it was obvious; so was the unspoken relief it afforded her. Their communication became structured, efficient—updates shared through channels that prioritized clarity over intimacy.

She noted the restraint in his messages, the care not to overstep or inquire unnecessarily. She appreciated it, even as she felt the cost of it accumulate.

Separation clarified many things.

Without proximity, she could see how much the rhythm of Midway had anchored her—how its imperfect noise had offered contrast and context to her own stillness. Core City mirrored her composure back to her without warmth, turning restraint into reflection rather than dialogue.

One evening, Elias sent a brief update.

The spur reopened under limited load. No incident.

Your projections held.

She replied after a pause.

Good. Thank you for the confirmation.

The exchange was precise, complete.

And insufficient.

She set the interface aside and moved to the window, watching the city pulse beneath her with deliberate calm. The light patterns mimicked adherence rather than flow, her own reflection superimposed faintly atop the view.

Muted anticipation crept in—not hope, not dread, but the sense of something deferred rather than denied.

She did not know what shape the separation would take over time. Whether it would sharpen what existed, or soften it into something unrecognizable. She only knew that distance required energy—energy she was not certain she had in abundance right now.

As she prepared for sleep, the Core City's quiet pressed closer, persistent and immaculate.

Mara closed her eyes and let the fatigue settle without resistance.

This, she knew, was not an ending.

It was a holding pattern.

And like all transitional spaces, it demanded patience more than resolve.

Core City did not hurry.

That was its first cruelty.

Mara learned this within days of arrival, as the tempo of her work settled into a rhythm that resisted urgency not through chaos, but through refinement. Problems here did not demand resolution; they invited discussion. Meetings began on time and stretched far past usefulness, their participants curating tone with more care than outcome. The city preferred consensus that felt elegant over decisions that felt necessary.

It wore her down in increments.

At the liaison center, requests multiplied—but none required immediate action. Instead, they arrived as invitations to advise, to contextualize, to frame. Mara's contributions were met with appreciative nods and complementary phrasing, her recommendations placed gently aside until they could be "considered within a broader narrative."

At Midway, that phrase would have sounded absurd.

Here, it was currency.

She learned which words carried weight and which evaporated on contact. She noted how often reassurance was valued more than accuracy, how frequently caution was interpreted as a lack of confidence rather than its expression. Her restraint—once a stabilizing force—became a mirror the city used to admire its own composure.

The fatigue that followed was different from exhaustion.

It felt... diluted.

Social obligations reasserted themselves quickly.

A reception arrived by end of week, its invitation phrased as optional, its attendance quietly assumed. The venue occupied a suspended terrace ringed with polished glass, the city unfurling beneath it with impeccable symmetry. Conversations formed instantly into clusters shaped by status recognition rather than interest.

Mara stood at the edge of one such circle, listening to a discussion about post-incident optics, the speakers' familiarity with the crisis entirely theoretical.

"Handled impeccably," someone said, sipping with satisfaction. "The structure's resilience speaks for itself."

"It always does," another agreed. "There's a certain elegance to systems that don't buckle under scrutiny."

Mara waited.

"And for the human cost?" she asked calmly.

The circle stilled for a fraction of a second.

"Well, of course that's unfortunate," the first speaker replied smoothly. "But incidents contextualize growth."

"They contextualize failure," Mara corrected. "Growth is optional."

A pause followed—not hostile, but distancing.

"Oh," someone laughed lightly. "You're very direct."

"Yes," Mara said. "It's efficient."

She excused herself without apology, moving toward the periphery where the glass cut the city into fragments rather than spectacle. She felt no triumph in the exchange—only the familiar drain of having spoken accurately in a space that preferred comfort.

At night, the separation made itself felt most sharply.

Midway had always resisted silence; even in rest, it hummed with human inconsistency. Core City, by contrast, quieted itself to the point of sterility, sound dampened until thought echoed back at her without distraction.

She caught herself standing too often at the window, watching patterns unfold without intimacy or stake. The city below her was exquisite, unyielding, distant.

She missed the greenway.

She missed Lina's unfiltered pragmatism. Dax's kinetic presence. The way urgency at Midway felt communal rather than curated.

She missed Elias.

The admission arrived without warning, its clarity almost surgical.

She did not miss him as he had been—loud, dominant, insulated by reputation. She missed the quiet recalibration that had followed the fall, the cautious clarity that had replaced certainty. She missed the way their conversations had sharpened rather than soothed, the shared silence that had begun to feel constructive.

Distance, she realized, did not erase motion.

It clarified direction.

Their communication remained deliberate.

Elias did not intrude. He sent updates only when necessary, phrased without flourish. She received them with equal restraint, answering precisely, never asking what he had not offered.

But between the lines, something pressed forward.

One evening, after a particularly draining session debating public confidence metrics, Mara found a single message waiting.

Midway's stabilizers held through the last load spike.

No adjustments needed.

She stared at the words longer than the information required.

Good, she typed back. **That means everyone did their job.**

The response came a minute later.

That's becoming clearer.

She exhaled slowly, the breath carrying more than just relief.

The separation did not dissolve their alignment. It tested it.

Core City repackaged old hierarchies with precision.

Mara recognized them quickly—status rituals softened by technological efficiency, favoritism cloaked in deliberation, deference exchanged invisibly between those who knew how to read it. She moved among these structures with competence but without assimilation, declining invitations that required unnecessary performance, redirecting discussions that drifted toward abstraction without harm.

It marked her.

Not as an outsider.

As an anomaly.

"You're unusually... grounded," a senior coordinator remarked one afternoon. "For someone stationed here."

Mara regarded him neutrally. "Grounding reduces systemic error."

He smiled, faintly uncomfortable. "That's one way to see it."

"Yes," she agreed. "It is."

Her reputation began to take shape—not glowing, not charismatic, but quietly definitive. People learned not to posture around her, knowing the effort would not be rewarded. They brought her real questions, or none at all.

She preferred it that way.

Still, the sense of being held at arm's length persisted. Core City acknowledged competence without fostering belonging; it prized contribution without intimacy. That distance dulled her more than resistance ever had.

She found herself counting days without meaning to.

The disruption arrived unexpectedly.

An allocation shift, minor in scale but revealing in structure, threatened to reroute an entire resource stream through polished corridors rather than functional ones—a decision designed to soothe optics rather than serve need. Mara flagged it within minutes, her objection framed cleanly and supported by data.

The response came hours later.

Appreciated. Under consideration. Will revisit once public response stabilizes.

Stabilizes from what? she wondered.

Nothing was unstable.

Except the narrative.

She drafted a second message—shorter, clearer—then stopped.

Instead, she forwarded the matter to Elias.

No commentary.

Just context.

His response came not immediately, but decisively.

This is misaligned. I'll intervene.

She did not ask how.

Two days later, the reroute was quietly corrected, the change attributed to "updated modeling parameters." No spectacle. No apology. No explanation.

Core City adjusted around the correction as though it had always been inevitable.

Mara closed the notice and sat back, something like relief threading through her fatigue.

It was not control she had missed.

It was *continuity*.

The invitation to return—partial, provisional—came at the end of the third week.

Not from Allocation, but from Torres.

Midway needs your oversight for the next assessment cycle.

Not permanently.

But urgently.

Mara read the message twice.

Then she stood.

The decision did not feel like departure.

It felt like release.

She prepared to leave Core City without ceremony.

The unit returned to neutrality within minutes of her packing, its surfaces erasing the trace of her presence with seamless efficiency. She stood once more at the window, regarding the city that had received her competently and kept her at distance.

There was no resentment.

Only clarity.

Transitional exile, she understood now, served a purpose. It revealed what endured without proximity—and what did not.

As her transit capsule moved outward, the city's polish receded, noise slowly reintroducing itself into the air. She felt something ease inside her as Midway's irregular rhythms came back into range.

Waiting at the platform, Elias did not perform surprise.

He simply nodded.

"You're back," he said.

"Yes," she replied.

"How was it?" he asked.

She considered. "Educational."

He smiled faintly. "That's usually code."

"It is," she agreed.

They walked together across the greenway, the sound of movement grounding rather than distracting.

"I didn't ask you to return," Elias said.

"No," Mara replied. "You didn't need to."

They stopped near the place where the skyway now stood reinforced and quiet.

"This distance," Elias said after a moment, "it clarified things."

"For me as well," she said.

He turned toward her, expression open, unguarded.

"I don't want to lose alignment again," he said. "Not to haste. Not to comfort."

"Then don't," Mara replied. "Distance didn't harm us."

He nodded.

"What would have harmed us," she added, "was pretending proximity mattered more than integrity."

The greenway hummed around them—imperfect, alive, resilient.

Emotional fatigue lingered, but beneath it lay something steadier: anticipation without urgency, hope without illusion.

Transitional exile had done its work.

It had stripped away excess, clarified attachment, and returned her to herself without spectacle.

Mara resumed her place not as someone returned, but as someone reaffirmed.

And this time, she knew—whatever came next would not require her to disappear into polish or noise to be legible.

She would be here.

And that, she understood, was enough.

Synthetic Society

The invitation arrived perfectly calibrated.

Not urgent. Not flattering. Simply *assumed.*

Mara recognized the construction immediately—a summons disguised as an opportunity, routed through Core City's social apparatus but annotated with Midway relevance. Attendance was optional in the way gravity was optional: decline carried no penalty that could be named, only a quiet recalibration of access and assumptions.

Corporate Salon — North Atrium Ring

Theme: Civic Futures & Influencer Alignment

Attendance Encouraged

Encouraged, she noted, was doing tremendous work.

She accepted without enthusiasm.

The North Atrium Ring existed less as a location than as a declaration.

Suspended above a traffic confluence, it appeared to float independent of necessity, its architecture immaculate in the way only structures unconcerned with weather or wear could manage. The glass was self-cleaning, the air filtered to remove all but the most intentional scents. Lighting adjusted in response to reputation metrics rather than bodies, flattering those most frequently observed.

Mara paused just inside the threshold.

The soundscape alone was enough to disorient—voices carefully pitched into audibility ranges that carried without carrying, laughter optimized to signal approachability rather than joy. Every surface reflected a version of someone that had been lightly edited before being returned.

She entered fully.

Immediately, she felt it: the strategic density of proximity. People clustered not by interest, but by visible promise—those whose feeds suggested momentum orbited by those who wished to be seen near momentum. No one stood alone unless they were certain solitude would be read as confidence.

Mara let herself remain unclaimed.

A server passed with a tray of drinks whose colors shifted subtly based on the drinker's biometric profile. She declined without comment and moved toward the edge of the room, where the glass curved downward and the city unfolded beneath it in perfect abstraction.

Below, traffic flowed like data—smooth, continuous, untroubled by the realities it represented.

Above, reputation recalibrated in real time.

Conversation found her anyway.

It always did.

"Mara Keene," a woman said, materializing at her side with effortless precision. "You're the one they sent back from Midway."

The phrasing was not accusatory. It was *classificatory.*

"I returned," Mara replied. "No one sent me."

The woman smiled, unfazed. "Still. You've been... visible lately."

Visibility. That word again.

"It's situational," Mara said.

"Of course," the woman agreed breezily. "Everything is."

She introduced herself as a brand strategist for emerging civic platforms—translation assistance for institutions struggling to narrate their own relevance. Her questions skimmed Mara's work only long enough to establish utility before pivoting toward narrative.

"You don't maintain a personal channel," the strategist remarked. "That's unusual."

"I don't require one," Mara replied.

The strategist laughed lightly. "No one *requires* one. But absence still communicates."

"Yes," Mara said. "It communicates that I'm elsewhere."

That drew a pause—not offense, but recalculation.

"Well," the strategist said finally, "that can be leveraged."

Mara offered a small, neutral smile. "I'm not leveraging myself."

The strategist blinked. "Everyone is."

Mara turned slightly toward the glass. "Not everyone profits from doing so."

The strategist drifted away soon after, her smile never quite dimming.

The salon filled steadily, bodies layering themselves into patterns that felt less social than algorithmic. Influencers—civic, aesthetic, philanthropic—drifted between conversations, trailing a wake of attentiveness that thickened or thinned depending on recent metrics. People angled themselves into visibility cones, careful to be noticed without appearing to seek notice.

Mara watched with detached fascination.

A man near the center spoke at length about post-incident recovery narratives, his analysis polished and hollow.

"Perception leads reality," he said confidently. "Stability comes from belief."

"Or from infrastructure," Mara said mildly.

He laughed. "Naturally. But infrastructure doesn't trend."

"No," she agreed. "It endures."

A few listeners smiled uncertainly, unsure whether they had just witnessed critique or trivia. The man waved it off and continued undeterred.

Mara felt the familiar alienation settle—not sharp, not bitter, just present. This was not hostility. It was tonal mismatch.

She belonged here administratively.

Culturally, she was misaligned.

Elias arrived late.

Not dramatically so. Just enough to reset local gravity.

Mara noticed the shift before she saw him—the way conversations bent imperceptibly, attention tilting with professional interest rather than admiration. His presence no longer drew the ravenous orbit it once had, but it still carried weight: authority stripped of spectacle was rarer, and therefore more legible, than confidence alone.

He did not seek her out immediately.

That, she recognized, was deliberate.

He moved through the salon with a restraint that mirrored her own discomfort, his expressions attentive but unperformative. When people engaged him, he responded thoughtfully and moved on, declining the opportunity to occupy space unnecessarily.

She watched appreciation curdle into confusion in real time.

This was not the Elias they had expected.

Eventually, he joined her near the glass.

"Impressive," he murmured, gaze scanning the room. "In the way controlled environments always are."

"Sterile?" Mara suggested.

"Synthetic," he corrected softly.

She nodded.

"Did you know," he said, "that several people here asked me whether Midway is 'recovering from its authenticity problem.'"

Mara closed her eyes briefly. "I hope you answered carefully."

"I told them Midway doesn't produce authenticity," Elias replied. "It tolerates reality."

She looked at him then—surprised, amused.

"That will not endear you," she said.

"It already hasn't," he replied calmly.

Something like relief threaded through her chest.

They stood together, not conspiring, not performing closeness—simply coexisting in a space that prized appearance over accord. Around them, the salon continued its intricate dance: alliances forming in one breath and dissolving in the next, reputations burnished with borrowed significance.

A civic influencer drifted past, smiling pointedly.

"You should collaborate," she said brightly, gesturing between them. "There's something compelling about visible reconciliation."

Mara turned her head slightly. "Reconciliation implies conflict."

The influencer laughed, uncertain. "Narrative conflict."

Elias responded evenly, "Not everything needs to be narrativized."

The influencer retreated without offense, already redirecting her attention.

Mara exhaled slowly.

"These spaces," she said, "frame every interaction as potential capital."

"And every person as packaging," Elias added.

"Yes."

They watched the city for a moment, letting the abstraction soothe rather than distance them.

"You don't belong here," Elias said quietly.

Mara glanced at him. "Neither do you."

He smiled faintly. "That might be the most comfortable thing I've heard all evening."

The irony sharpened as the night wore on.

Announcements were made—updates on initiatives, partnerships hinted at but never clarified, applause rising on cue. People nodded enthusiastically at ideas designed to signal alignment rather than action. More than once, Mara spotted proposals she had flagged weeks earlier returning in altered language, stripped of substance and padded with optimism.

She felt neither anger nor triumph.

Only distance.

When a panel convened spontaneously near the center—three speakers discussing "resilient futures"—Mara listened briefly before turning away. Resilience was being discussed as brand posture, divorced entirely from adaptation or cost.

"Do you think they notice," she asked Elias under her breath, "how often they praise recovery without mentioning those who absorbed damage?"

"They notice," he replied. "They just prefer abstraction."

"And you?"

"I prefer accuracy," he said. "And accountability."

She nodded once.

That, perhaps, was the real recalibration.

As the salon edged toward its curated conclusion, people began exchanging exit commitments—polite phrases signaling future contact without obligation. The room thinned carefully, leaving behind only those certain their presence had been noted.

Mara felt the fatigue deepen—not physical, but ethical.

She had spoken little, corrected less, resisted the temptation to dismantle what would reform itself regardless. She had observed, catalogued, endured.

That, she realized, was the function of exile.

Not punishment.

Perspective.

As they left the Atrium Ring together, descending through a corridor that filtered out not just sound but pretense, Elias glanced at her.

"You handled that well," he said.

She tilted her head. "By not engaging?"

"By not internalizing," he clarified.

She allowed herself a small smile. "That took practice."

The city beyond the corridor shifted again—less polished, more alive.

And even though the night was quiet, Mara felt the irony settle with gentle precision:

For all its refinement, Synthetic Society had revealed itself as fragile—sustained by consensus, terrified of fracture, and utterly dependent on those who did not belong to it to stabilize what it could not face directly.

Alienation, she realized, was not exclusion.

It was *clarity*.

And clarity, once achieved, could not be convincingly unlearned.

The influence arrived the following morning—not announced, not requested, and not immediately welcomed.

Mara was reviewing a mundane coordination memo in Core City's liaison suite when an unfamiliar identifier blinked in her peripheral feed. The message carried no priority marker, which in this context was itself a signal. It meant someone had chosen subtlety over insistence.

Requesting informal consultation.

Topic: Reputational risk mitigation following Midway alignment shifts.

Mara closed the memo without answering.

The request repeated itself twenty minutes later, routed through a different channel, its wording adjusted to sound collaborative rather than dependent. She let it sit again. By midday, three similar inquiries had appeared—each from a different sector, each carefully avoiding the appearance of coordination.

Synthetic systems, she reflected, panicked quietly.

Elias noticed before she mentioned it. He found her near the third-floor overlook, where the city's deeper layers could be seen intersecting beneath Core City's sheen, their motion ungainly but unmistakably alive.

"They're circling," he said, nodding toward her darkened interface.

"Yes," Mara replied. "They do that when certainty erodes."

"Do you intend to engage?" he asked.

"Only if engagement improves accuracy," she said. "Not comfort."

He smiled faintly. "I asked because they've already decided you're influencing outcomes."

Mara glanced at him, skeptical. "I declined a conversation last night."

"That's why," Elias said. "You broke a script."

The irony was sharp enough to draw a breath of amusement from her. Refusal had not marginalized her here—it had altered the equation.

The salons recalibrated poorly.

A second gathering convened within forty-eight hours, this one smaller, more "authentic" in its advertised framing. The venue was different—less glass, more texture—but the choreography remained intact. Language softened further, speakers foregrounding humility and learning while continuing to avoid specifics.

Mara attended briefly, standing near the exit rather than the glass.

This time, people approached with caution rather than entitlement.

"You raised an interesting point last time," a policy director said, voice deliberately quiet. "About abstraction."

"I stated an observation," Mara replied. "Others elaborated it incorrectly."

The director smiled thinly. "Would you be willing to restate it? On record?"

"No," Mara said.

The smile stalled.

"I don't offer clarity as performance," she continued. "If substance is needed, I'll provide it where consequences attach."

The director nodded, slowly, reassessing. "That might limit your reach."

"That's acceptable," Mara said.

They parted without friction, but when she turned away she sensed attention following—not admiration, not hostility, but something more wary.

Restraint, it seemed, unsettled more effectively than critique.

Elias's experience sharpened the contrast.

Where once he had been courted as momentum embodied, he now found himself questioned—not aggressively, but persistently—about alignment, about philosophy, about whether Midway's recalibration signaled retreat rather than adaptation. He answered honestly, without cushioning his conclusions.

It cost him invitations.

It earned him something else.

"Did you notice," he remarked one evening as they crossed a transit bridge back toward Midway, "that the people most insistent on reassurance never attend implementation reviews?"

"Yes," Mara said. "Visibility is their metric. Durability is ours."

"*Ours*," he repeated, almost amused.

She let the word stand.

The city beneath them felt louder now in comparison—unfiltered, imperfect, insisting on presence rather than image. Traffic stalled and surged unpredictably below, a reminder that systems failed less dramatically when they were allowed to be observed honestly.

She realized, with clarity, that she no longer felt alienation here.

She felt contrast.

The consequences emerged incrementally.

A Core City initiative postponed its rollout after encountering resistance linked—not officially, but perceptibly—to questions Mara had raised weeks earlier. An influencer quietly revised her platform language, shifting from certainty to contingency without explaining why. A corporate board requested "ground-truth verification" before rebranding its resilience metrics.

None of these adjustments were attributed to Mara.

All of them bore her fingerprints.

Lina confirmed it indirectly during a late-night call.

"They're borrowing your language," Lina said. "Stripping it of authorship, but not of effect."

"That's fine," Mara replied. "Language doesn't need ownership to function."

Lina laughed softly. "You terrify them."

Mara smiled faintly. "Good."

The most telling shift came at a public forum.

The event was not a salon, but it had inherited the aesthetic—controlled access, curated attendance, a stage framed for authority. Mara watched the proceedings from a side corridor, having declined a panel invitation she suspected was meant to legitimize rather than engage.

Midway's recalibration was discussed for nearly twenty minutes before anyone mentioned the fall.

When it was addressed, the language was careful.

"Lessons learned," the moderator said smoothly. "Adjustments made."

A younger speaker—evidently less practiced—cleared her throat.

"With respect," she said, "those adjustments came from someone who didn't appear on the platform."

The room stilled.

"She refused to participate tonight," the speaker added, nodding toward the corridor where Mara stood unseen. "But without her intervention, we would still be debating optics."

Mara closed her eyes briefly.

The moderator recovered quickly, redirecting applause toward a summary slide, but something had lodged irreversibly.

Refusal had become reference.

Afterward, Elias joined her as she slipped away into the transit flow.

"You didn't look surprised," he observed.

"I was," she said honestly. "I didn't expect attribution."

"I don't think she meant recognition," he replied. "I think she meant calibration."

The distinction mattered.

They walked in silence for a time, the city's edges blurring with movement.

"You've changed the ambient assumptions," Elias said finally. "Without replacing them."

"Yes," Mara replied. "Replacement creates resistance. Absence creates inquiry."

He nodded, absorbing it.

"You always knew this," he said.

She shrugged. "Knowing isn't the same as acting. Timing matters."

"And now?"

"Now," she said, "the system is unstable enough to accept it."

They returned to Midway together.

The greenway greeted them with noise and motion, people resuming their imperfect choreography with renewed attentiveness. Dax waved from across the way, then hesitated before crossing toward them, judgment recalibrated with care.

"Hey," Dax said. "They were talking about you. Again."

"I imagined," Mara replied.

"This time they didn't sound smug," Dax added. "More... confused."

"That," Mara said gently, "is progress."

Dax rolled her eyes but smiled despite herself.

Later, as night settled and the sounds softened around them, Mara stood once more at the edge of the greenway, watching life resume its uneven pattern. She felt neither triumph nor resentment.

Only clarity.

Synthetic Society, she understood now, was not sustained by deceit or malice.

It was sustained by avoidance—by maintaining surfaces smooth enough that fractures did not demand inspection. Her refusal to polish herself for those surfaces had not isolated her. It had exposed the fragility underneath.

Alienation had become leverage.

Irony had become method.

Elias joined her, hands resting loosely on the rail.

"You don't perform," he said. "And yet they perform around you."

She smiled faintly. "That's the risk of honest presence in artificial spaces."

He looked at her steadily. "You've changed how I understand influence."

"And you've changed how I understand responsibility," she replied.

They stood together, no longer aligned by momentum or opposition, but by something quieter and more durable: shared refusal.

Below them, the city moved without seeking permission.

Above them, layers of polish dimmed, their reflections less convincing in the absence of willing surfaces.

Mara felt something settle firmly into place.

Synthetic Society had offered her visibility on its terms.

She had declined.

And in doing so, she had become unavoidable.

The Polished Stranger

The introduction was immaculate.

It arrived neither loudly nor by chance, but through channels that specialized in inevitability—the kind that made outcomes feel preapproved before they were ever chosen. Mara first heard the name in passing, folded into a briefing note that aimed for comprehensiveness and achieved choreography instead.

Elliot Vance, interim fiduciary adviser.

Corporate mediation specialist.

Reputation remediation consultant.

The verbs were bloodless. The titles clean.

Her father mentioned him that evening as if continuing a thought already well established.

"He's been very helpful," he said, reviewing a ledger view projected faintly above the dining table. "Discreet. Thorough. I should have engaged him earlier."

Mara set her fork down carefully.

"Helpful how?" she asked.

"In clarifying exposure," her father replied, pleased. "Repositioning certain assets. He understands how perception compounds."

Mara felt the faint prickle of attention beneath her calm.

"Perception of whom?" she asked.

"Of us," he said, as if it went without saying. "Of the Keene line. Of continuity."

Continuity again. The word had been reconditioned so many times it barely resembled its origins.

"And?" Mara prompted.

Her father hesitated only briefly—just long enough to signal that what followed mattered.

"He's asked to meet you."

—

Elliot Vance did not look impressive in the ways prestige usually performed in Core City.

He was not overly polished, nor ostentatiously restrained. His suit was tailored but unadorned, his movements calibrated to suggest attentiveness rather than command. He smiled often, but not broadly, as though careful not to claim warmth he had not yet earned.

When Mara entered the consultation suite the following afternoon, he rose at once.

"Ms. Keene," he said, inclining his head with precise deference. "Thank you for making the time."

"I didn't," she replied evenly. "It was requested."

His smile sharpened—appreciative rather than defensive.

"Then I'm grateful all the same," he said. "Efficiency benefits everyone involved."

She took her seat across from him, folding her hands loosely.

Her first impression registered without instruction: he occupied space cleanly. No excess. No clutter. His presence seemed designed to disappear once its function was fulfilled.

"And what function would that be?" she asked.

He rested his hands together, mirroring her posture with deliberate restraint.

"To ensure your family's transitional period concludes without unnecessary friction," he said. "My role is not intervention, but alignment."

"Alignment with whom?" Mara asked.

"With outcomes," Elliot replied.

A safe answer. Imprecise. Impossible to dispute without sounding oppositional.

Her father beamed faintly from his seat beside her.

Mara felt the distinct urge to challenge the framing.

She resisted it.

—

Elliot had done his research.

He referenced Keene Tower without sentiment, spoke of the stewardship transition as a matter of managed optics rather than loss, and acknowledged Midway's recalibration as "remarkably effective under unconventional leadership."

Mara noted the phrasing.

Unconventional.

Leadership.

Titles conferred carefully, just ambiguous enough to flatter without committing.

"I don't consult on operations," Mara said when he paused expectantly. "If that's what you're hoping for, we should recalibrate now."

Elliot shook his head smoothly.

"On the contrary," he said. "Your operational reputation is precisely why I won't intrude upon it."

A pause. Calculated.

"My focus," he continued, "is on translating outcomes into assurance."

"That," Mara said, "often distorts both."

"Yes," Elliot agreed immediately. "Which is why translation must be authored by someone who understands consequence."

Her attention sharpened.

"You're implying you do," she said.

"I'm implying," he replied gently, "that I understand how immunity is constructed."

She did not smile.

Her father did.

—

The rapport built quickly.

Not between Mara and Elliot—she offered no such pretense—but between Elliot and her father, whose relief at speaking fluently about "protections" and "buffers" bordered on gratitude. Elliot did not contradict him. He refined his statements, translated anxiety into strategy, replaced uncertainty with language that felt like control.

Mara watched it happen with clinical detachment.

It was not manipulation.

It was *sterilization*.

"I don't trade in reassurance," Elliot said at one point, as if reading her gaze. "Only in mitigation."

"And how," Mara asked, "do you distinguish between them?"

Elliot folded his hands again.

"Reassurance tells you everything will be fine," he said. "Mitigation tells you what will happen if it isn't."

The answer was solid.

Too solid.

It landed without texture, without human residue. Risk reduced to architecture. Loss reframed as adjustment.

She felt it then—a faint, persistent absence behind his words. Not deceit. Not hostility.

Hollowing.

—

The temptation arrived later.

Not from Elliot directly, but through implication.

He followed the meeting with a message addressed primarily to Mara, copied to her father as practice rather than leverage.

Preliminary modeling indicates your discretion could significantly compress Keene Holdings' exposure timeline.

Your involvement would legitimize transitions others cannot frame credibly.

Legitimize.

She closed the message and leaned back in her chair.

This was the offer, she realized—not partnership, not intimacy, but utilization. Her credibility, borrowed. Her judgment, repackaged. Her authority, made portable.

She imagined it for a moment: how easily the city would accept it, how smoothly reputation would recalibrate around her name shorn of friction. How quickly difficult conversations would become diagrams.

She felt the pull, light but undeniable.

Temptation rarely announced itself as desire.

Often it arrived as relief.

—

Elias noticed her distraction before she realized she had allowed it.

They stood together later that evening along the greenway, the night carrying that soft murmur Midway reserved for transitions that had not yet settled. Dax passed them with a nod and a look that lingered just long enough to register curiosity.

"You're quiet," Elias said.

"Meeting," Mara replied.

He waited.

"Corporate," she added.

That drew his attention fully.

"Who?" he asked.

"Elliot Vance."

A flicker crossed Elias's expression—not dislike, not alarm, but recognition.

"Ah," he said.

"You know him."

"I know *of* him," Elias said carefully. "He's good."

Mara studied Elias's face.

"Define good," she said.

"He stabilizes narratives," Elias replied. "Very effectively."

"And people?" she asked.

Elias hesitated.

"He's efficient," he said at last.

"That wasn't the question," Mara said.

Elias exhaled slowly.

"No," he admitted. "He doesn't seem especially interested in people."

Suspicion sharpened, precise and unwelcome.

—

Elliot moved seamlessly through their lives in the days that followed.

He attended one Core City function in her father's stead "to spare him unnecessary scrutiny." He smoothed over a minor compliance entanglement with language so refined it left no visible residue. He sent Mara updates written with such immaculate neutrality they bordered on apology without carrying one.

At no point did he overstep.

At no point did he ask directly for her allegiance.

And yet—

He waited.

Elliot Vance understood timing.

That was what made him dangerous.

—

The decisive moment came quietly.

Mara returned to Keene Tower one afternoon to review lingering access protocols when she overheard Elliot's voice through a half-open consultation door.

"Ms. Keene's influence is... unique," Elliot was saying, his tone measured. "If she's associated—publicly, even nominally—resistance dissolves. She doesn't provoke opposition."

Provocation. Resistance.

Language of pacification, not respect.

Her father murmured something in response; Mara did not hear the words.

Elliot continued.

"She reduces complexity. People trust her restraint."

Mara stepped back before she could be seen.

That night, she stood again at the greenway rail, watching the city's uneven motion below.

She understood the appeal now.

Elliot offered a future where care could be converted into clearance, where conscience could be deployed strategically rather than exercised continuously. He represented the version of stability that eliminated discomfort rather than engaging it.

And part of her—tired, refined by recent costs—wanted to believe that efficiency could replace vigilance.

Suspicion did not scream.

It whispered.

And temptation did not rush.

It waited.

Elliot Vance never pressed.

That was the first fracture.

Mara noticed it in the days that followed not as absence but as *precision.* He adjusted his proximity with remarkable discipline, appearing only where utility could justify presence and never where sentiment might invite resistance. He sent messages that resolved problems before they announced themselves, offered analyses that closed loops rather than opened debate, arranged outcomes that felt inevitable without ever declaring authority.

It was flawless.

And that, she had learned, was rarely benign.

The turning point came during a family briefing that should have been procedural and became diagnostic instead. Her father requested her presence with unusual insistence, the phrasing betraying concern he did not yet know how to name.

Elliot arrived early, as always, already seated when Mara entered the room. He rose politely, offering her the seat opposite as if this had been agreed upon rather than staged.

"Ms. Keene," he said. "I'm glad you could join us."

Mara did not sit immediately.

"I heard you speak on my behalf yesterday," she said.

Elliot did not appear startled.

"I contextualized your contributions," he replied. "Accurately."

"You advocated for my association," she said.

"I recognized its utility," Elliot said smoothly.

The distinction was crisp. Calculated. Bloodless.

Her father looked between them, tension sharpening the lines at his temples.

"We are discussing the protection of what remains," he said. "Surely that's not objectionable."

Mara sat at last, folding her hands.

"Protection," she said, looking directly at Elliot, "from whom?"

Elliot's eyes did not flicker.

"From misinterpretation," he said.

"And consequence?" Mara asked.

A pause.

"Consequence," Elliot replied carefully, "can usually be managed."

There it was.

Not arrogance.

Not deceit.

A premise.

Elliot believed consequence was an administrative problem.

Mara leaned back.

"You're very good at erasing friction," she said.

Elliot inclined his head. "Friction is inefficient."

"Friction," Mara said, "is where truth accumulates."

Elliot smiled faintly, as though acknowledging a philosophical difference rather than a warning.

"Truth," he said, "doesn't always need exposure."

"No," Mara agreed. "But responsibility does."

Her father cleared his throat, uncomfortable now.

"Elliot has been ensuring our exposure is limited," he said. "That we aren't... punished."

Mara turned toward him.

"Punished for what?" she asked gently.

He hesitated.

"For surviving," he said at last. "For failing differently than others."

Mara nodded. "That isn't punishment. It's context."

Elliot interjected smoothly before the word could land heavily.

"Context," he said, "becomes narrative when unmanaged."

"And narrative," Mara replied, "becomes deception when sterilized."

Silence fell—thick, uncomfortable, irreducible.

For the first time, Elliot did not speak immediately.

The meeting ended without resolution.

Elliot departed with impeccable civility, thanking them both for "productive exchange" and promising revised models "that respected internal values." Her father exhaled only after the door closed behind him, as if a pressure he had not named had finally lifted.

"You were hard on him," he said quietly.

"I was accurate," Mara replied.

"He doesn't mean harm," her father said.

"No," Mara agreed. "He means *immunity*."

Her father frowned.

"Isn't that the goal?"

"Immunity," Mara said, "separates action from consequence. Protection preserves both."

The distinction settled uncomfortably between them.

Later that evening, Elias arrived unexpectedly at Keene Tower, his presence unannounced but not unwelcome. He found Mara alone in the eastern gallery, citylight reflecting across the glass in fractured patterns.

"You felt it too," he said, not a question.

"Yes," Mara replied.

They stood in silence for a moment, the tension between refinement and reality pressing close.

"He's been asking about you," Elias said. "Framing you as the stabilizing constant."

"I'm not a constant," Mara replied. "I'm a participant."

"He doesn't treat people that way," Elias said.

"How does he treat them?" she asked.

"As variables," Elias said. "To reduce."

Mara closed her eyes briefly.

"The danger," she said, "is not that he's wrong about how systems behave. It's that he believes people should behave the same way."

Elias nodded. "He wants your credibility without your friction."

"Yes," she said. "And my silence as consent."

The air tightened with recognition.

The fracture widened days later, the way these things often did—indirectly.

A public statement circulated, attributed to "advisory alignment," praising the city's refined response to recent instability and emphasizing how swiftly uncertainty had been neutralized. Beneath the language, Mara recognized familiar contours—*her* wording, softened and evacuated of weight.

She traced it once.

Then again.

Her name was not attached.

But her voice had been used.

She requested a meeting that night.

Elliot did not delay.

He arrived with composure unbroken, greeting her with the same polished concern that had once suggested safety. This time, she did not invite him to sit.

"You repurposed my language," she said.

"I reframed it," Elliot replied. "For broader acceptance."

"You removed its accountability," she said.

"I made it actionable," he countered.

"No," Mara said calmly. "You made it *inoffensive*."

Elliot paused, then smiled with restraint.

"The city responds to comfort," he said. "You respond to correctness. Those are not always compatible."

"That doesn't give you the right to erase intent," Mara said.

"I didn't erase it," Elliot said. "I preserved it by making it survivable."

She looked at him steadily.

"You don't preserve intent," she said. "You embalm it."

The word landed more sharply than she intended.

Elliot's eyes cooled—not angry, but withdrawn.

"You're idealizing consequence," he said. "Pain is not inherently instructive."

"No," Mara replied. "But removal from consequence is inherently corrupting."

The space between them held.

"This collaboration," Elliot said carefully, "could secure your family's position, redirect scrutiny, and ensure your work scales without friction."

"And in return?" Mara asked.

"In return," he said, "you remain above complication. Untouched by destabilizing extremes."

Mara smiled faintly.

"Untouched," she said. "Isn't that another word for *uninvolved*?"

Elliot did not respond.

"You don't ask whether a decision is right," she continued. "Only whether it survives."

"That's the same thing," Elliot said softly.

"For you," Mara replied. "Not for me."

Elliot left that night under the same immaculate pretense with which he had arrived.

The difference lay in what followed.

The messages slowed. Models adjusted without her input. Her father's relief gave way to uncertainty. Access remained—but no longer invited.

Elliot Vance did not retaliate.

He simply withdrew consensus.

And in Synthetic Society, withdrawal was the sharpest sanction.

Mara felt the shift immediately—not as obstruction, but as *absence*. Requests routed around her. Conversations where her presence would once have resolved debate now continued into abstraction without her intervention.

Yet something unexpected occurred.

Problems began escalating again.

Subtly. Inefficiently. Confusion returned, not dramatically, but persistently.

Elias noticed first.

"They're losing coherence," he said one afternoon as they reviewed two conflicting advisories that should never have diverged. "Without you, their narratives don't close."

"That was always the risk," Mara replied.

"And Elliot?" Elias asked.

"He optimized for silence," she said. "Not continuity."

The irony did not escape them.

The temptation lingered even as its cost revealed itself.

There was comfort in Elliot's calculus. Safety in his erasures. A version of stability that spared her constant vigilance and allowed her correctness to be consumed without the burden of advocacy.

She acknowledged that temptation without shame.

Fatigue, she knew, made order seductive.

But she also knew this:

Elliot's world would function *without her presence*.

It only required her authority.

That was not partnership.

That was extraction.

One final message arrived from him a week later—brief, neutral, offering renewed alignment "under clarified parameters."

Mara read it once.

She did not reply.

Instead, she forwarded the message—unchanged—to Elias and her father, with a single line attached:

I decline to be rendered harmless.

The silence that followed was deeper, and somehow cleaner.

Late that night, she stood again at the greenway rail, Midway alive beneath her with its uneven breath.

Elias joined her, hands resting loosely, unguarded.

"He underestimated you," he said.

She smiled faintly. "He underestimated consequence."

"And temptation?" Elias asked.

She considered.

"Temptation isn't the opposite of integrity," she said. "It's evidence of cost."

He nodded.

"I'm glad you paid it," he said quietly.

"So am I," she replied.

The city moved on without ceremony.

Somewhere beyond them, Synthetic Society recalibrated again—slower now, less certain, deprived of its smooth translator.

Elliot Vance would succeed elsewhere. He always did.

But not here.

Not with her.

The polished stranger had offered Mara safety without substance, clarity without courage, influence without presence.

She had seen through it.

And in choosing friction over sterility, she felt something settle—not triumph, not loss, but commitment.

Suspicion had done its work.

Temptation had been named.

And the space left behind—unshielded, accountable, alive—was one she recognized as home.

The Forgotten Ally

Mara found the message buried beneath system noise.

It arrived not through any channel that mattered to most people—no priority flag, no reputation routing—but through an archive query she had not consciously remembered initiating. The notification itself was unremarkable, its tone neutral to the point of invisibility.

ARCHIVAL ACCESS REQUEST — LEGACY NODE 7C

Origin: Etta Rains

Status: Conditional

Mara stilled.

Etta Rains was a name she had not seen surfaced in years. Not because it lacked relevance, but because relevance had been withdrawn from it with bureaucratic efficiency. In Core City's systems, absence was rarely error. It was outcome.

She accepted the request.

The reply came almost immediately, as though the sender had been waiting—patiently, but without suspension—for confirmation that someone still knew how to listen.

Thank you. I wasn't certain the address still reached a human.

Mara exhaled slowly.

It did.

—

Etta Rains resided in the Lower Reach, in a tier the city's main transit maps had stopped labeling explicitly. The descent took longer than the system estimated, not because of mechanical delay but because infrastructure here was negotiated rather than enforced—lifts pausing for unscheduled stops, passenger traffic sharing space with maintenance routes seldom traversed by executive clearance.

Mara welcomed the delay.

When the lift doors opened, the air was cooler and faintly mineral, tinged with that unmistakable smell of old circuitry and water held back only by vigilance. The corridor beyond bore the marks of continual adaptation—patchwork reinforcements, exposed conduits, hand-labeled nodes overriding decommissioned guidance systems.

A sign near the end of the hall blinked unsteadily.

ARCHIVAL RESIDENCE — DATA CUSTODIAN

Mara knocked once.

The door opened without hesitation.

Etta Rains was smaller than Mara remembered, or perhaps the room made her seem so—wrapped in layered supports that stabilized her posture without disguising its cost. A mobility frame hovered at her side, its movement constrained by careful calibration rather than automation. Her hair, once a uniform dark curl, was now threaded with white, worn back from a face marked more by observation than age.

"Ms. Keene," Etta said, voice dry and steady. "You look like someone who still notices when protocols lie."

Mara smiled faintly. "You always had a way with greetings."

Etta stepped aside. "Come in. The city doesn't archive honesty well."

—

Etta's living space defied categorization.

Old data drives lined the walls—not decorative replicas, but functioning legacy systems stacked with the kind of information long deemed obsolete but never irretrievable. Displays glowed with low-light integrity checks, their interfaces stripped of modern polish in favor of fidelity. Everything here existed for use rather than appearance.

"You're still maintaining personal nodes," Mara observed.

"I never stopped," Etta replied. "Systems forget when they're told forgetting is efficient."

She gestured toward a seat. Mara sat.

"Why now?" Mara asked, without preamble.

Etta regarded her carefully.

"Because Elliot Vance asked me for something," she said.

The name settled like sediment.

"What did he want?" Mara asked.

"My silence," Etta replied simply.

Mara felt something twist—not shock, but recognition given shape.

Etta leaned back slightly, the mobility frame responding with delicate correction.

"He didn't approach me directly at first," Etta continued. "He never does. He sent an intermediary with a request framed as housecleaning—legacy conflicts being resolved, outdated records eligible for archival compression."

She smiled thinly.

"That phrase always means erasure."

"Yes," Mara said.

"I declined," Etta said. "So he came himself."

—

Elliot Vance had once worked in the same strata as Etta Rains, though few now remembered that. Back then, he had not been a mediator or consultant, but a *compiler*—one of those tasked with turning raw institutional truth into narratives fit for governance.

Etta had been an archivist then—one of the last still insisting on preserving *input* rather than outcomes.

"He was charming," Etta said. "He always is. Explained that my data represented phased liabilities no longer applicable to present conditions. Said he wanted to 'unburden' the city."

"And you?" Mara asked.

"I asked him what he was afraid of surviving," Etta said.

Mara's fingers curled slightly.

Etta continued, unfazed.

"He wanted records removed from live reference—not deleted, just... buried," Etta said. "Specifically, those related to transitional fiduciary advisement under Keene Holdings' past restructuring."

Mara's attention sharpened.

"That was before my oversight," she said.

"Exactly," Etta replied. "That's why it matters."

She tapped a control, and one of the darker displays brightened into focus.

Lines of data resolved—old governance matrices, advisory audits, risk transfers flagged and rerouted with language so refined it barely resembled the events it documented.

At the center of several was Elliot Vance's signature marker, subtly embedded but unmistakable.

"He's been doing this a long time," Etta said. "Cleaning the past so the present doesn't have to reckon with it."

"What did he want removed?" Mara asked.

Etta's smile was small but resolute.

"Evidence that he doesn't just mitigate consequence," she said. "He relocates it."

—

The data was meticulous.

Transaction reroutes that transferred liability away from decision-makers and onto peripheral entities. Advisory recommendations that framed cuts as alignment. Post-failure narratives edited to remove references to dissent.

Names were preserved—but contexts were not.

"You were listed once," Etta said gently.

Mara's breath caught. "In what capacity?"

"Anonymized stabilizer," Etta replied. "Your language repurposed without attribution. Your judgments cited without acknowledgment. Your objections reclassified as concurrence where automation filled gaps."

The pattern was devastatingly familiar.

"He uses people who won't perform," Mara said quietly. "Because refusal reads as endorsement when reframed."

"Yes," Etta agreed. "You are trustworthy precisely because you won't promote yourself."

Mara closed her eyes for a moment, letting the weight settle.

"This is why you were erased," she said.

Etta nodded. "I refused to optimize truth."

"What did he offer you?" Mara asked.

Etta laughed softly. "Rest."

The word rang with quiet cruelty.

"He said I'd served the city long enough," Etta continued. "That it was time to let systems carry what they could without my interference. He framed absence as mercy."

"And when you refused?"

"He said nothing more," Etta replied. "He never threatens. He waits for oxygen to thin."

Mara looked around the room at the legacy systems humming softly, stubbornly alive.

"And yet," she said, "you're still here."

Etta met her gaze, something like warmth flickering.

"Because loyalty," she said, "isn't always reciprocation. Sometimes it's preservation."

—

They sat in silence for a few moments, the city's muted pulse threading through the walls.

"Why come to me?" Mara asked at last.

"Because you didn't let him optimize you," Etta replied. "And because you understand what it costs not to."

Mara absorbed that.

"You don't want exposure," she said.

"No," Etta replied. "I want *accuracy.*"

"And consequence?" Mara asked.

Etta smiled sadly. "That's for others to decide."

Mara stood slowly, resolve coalescing.

"He took something from you," she said. "From all of us."

"Yes," Etta agreed. "But he underestimated something."

"What?"

"A system that remembers," Etta said. "And a person willing to carry that memory."

Mara nodded.

Loyalty, she realized, had waited for her in the margins—not loud, not visible, but intact.

And truth, suppressed long enough, had not weakened.

It had only grown sharper.

—

As Mara left the Lower Reach, the city above felt different—less imposing, less abstract. The ascent carried with it a sense of alignment returning, pieces sliding into place without drama.

Elliot Vance had offered safety through erasure.

Etta Rains had offered danger through truth.

Mara knew which she would choose.

Not because it was easier.

But because loyalty, once rewarded, demanded no less.

Mara did not act immediately.

That restraint was not hesitation—it was triage.

Etta's data followed her back into the upper layers of the city like a second pulse, synchronized and inexorable. She uploaded nothing, forwarded nothing, named nothing yet. The archive remained exactly where it was, protected by obscurity rather than force.

Exposure, she knew, was not a single action.

It was a sequence.

She checked for pressure first.

It arrived quietly, as everything dangerous did.

Requests reappeared in her queue within forty-eight hours—questions about her "availability," invitations rephrased as opportunities, interim advisories routed for her "contextual insight." None mentioned Elliot. None needed to.

The systems were seeking re-closure.

She declined them all.

Not brusquely. Not defiantly. Simply without elaboration.

A vacuum forms meaning fast.

Elias recognized the moment before she spoke.

They stood together on the Midway connector platform, watching a maintenance drone align its clamps with exaggerated care. Below them, people passed—unremarkable, uncurated, alive with inconsequence.

"You found something," he said.

"Yes," Mara replied.

"Something that matters."

"Yes."

He didn't press.

"I'm deciding scale," she added.

He nodded, understanding immediately. "Targeted or systemic."

"Accuracy versus spectacle," she said.

"And consequence," he finished.

They fell into silence, not as delay, but as acknowledgment. Whatever came next would not be reversible.

The first disclosure was narrow.

Mara routed a corrected advisory to Allocation—one that cited Etta's preserved data not as accusation, but as *precedent*. It did not name Elliot Vance. It did not allege motive. It simply restored origin links that had been "compressed" out of related documentation years ago.

The correction was boring.

That was its genius.

No headlines followed. No outrage spiked. But several models failed to reconcile under the restored inputs. Confidence metrics drifted. Internal queries proliferated.

Someone asked, quietly, why certain liabilities now reappeared in contexts that had long ago been declared settled.

Another asked who had authorized the earlier deletions.

A third asked whether legacy compression protocols had ever been formally reviewed.

Silence fell where certainty once lived.

Mara forwarded none of those questions.

She left them open.

Elliot noticed within the week.

He requested a meeting—more restrained than before, phrased as clarification rather than alignment. Mara accepted on one condition: that it take place in the same consultation suite where he had first introduced himself.

Neutral ground mattered.

He arrived as always—with composure intact, posture impeccable, a man whose confidence had been refined rather than accreted.

"Ms. Keene," he said, standing. "I was hoping we could address some confusion."

"Yes," Mara replied. "Let's."

They sat.

"I've seen the advisory update," Elliot said carefully. "It destabilizes several continuity models."

"It corrects them," Mara replied.

"Correction is rarely neutral," he said. "It introduces risk."

"It reassigns it," she answered.

His smile tightened, just perceptibly.

"You accessed legacy nodes outside current governance channels," Elliot said. "That's... unconventional."

"She maintained them within her mandate," Mara replied. "You know that."

Elliot did not deny it.

"You've chosen an archivist's reading of truth," he said. "That approach can be... disruptive."

"Yes," Mara said. "It disrupts erasure."

The word landed harder this time.

Elliot's expression cooled—not anger, but recalculation.

"You're jeopardizing equilibrium," he said. "Legacy wounds don't heal when reopened."

"They heal incorrectly when sealed over," Mara replied. "Or not at all."

A pause.

"I tried to spare you this," Elliot said. "Visibility carries consequences."

"So does concealment," Mara said. "You've chosen yours."

He studied her now—not as resource, not as ally, but as obstacle.

"You believe exposure will reform the system," he said.

"No," Mara replied. "I believe *accuracy* will."

"That's idealism," Elliot said softly.

"No," she said. "That's maintenance."

The second disclosure was relational.

Mara returned to the Lower Reach.

Etta received her with the same unvarnished calm, the legacy nodes humming steadily behind her.

"They're asking questions," Etta said. Not hopeful. Simply observant.

"They will keep doing so," Mara replied. "Because the inputs don't reconcile anymore."

Etta nodded. "That's all it ever takes. Friction."

"I won't make this public," Mara said. "Not broadly. Not yet."

"I didn't ask you to," Etta replied.

"I will ensure attribution is reinstated where it belongs," Mara continued. "Your archives will be acknowledged as authoritative."

Etta smiled faintly. "Recognition is loud."

"Accuracy doesn't require applause," Mara said. "Only persistence."

Etta regarded her with something like relief.

"I did wonder," she said, "whether loyalty would cost you leverage."

"It already has," Mara replied. "That's how I know it matters."

The backlash arrived as absence before it arrived as force.

Elliot withdrew fully this time—not just from Mara, but from the circles that had once relied on his quiet absolutions. His presence in meetings thinned. His language disappeared from documents. His models no longer preempted inquiry.

He was not condemned.

He was *bypassed.*

Someone else would emerge, of course. Someone always did. Synthetic Society recycled its smoothers endlessly.

But something had shifted.

Etta's data now anchored enough conversations that erasure required explanation rather than automation. The system had to account for what it had once buried.

Accounting slowed everything.

Mara watched it unfold without satisfaction.

Loyalty, she knew, did not require triumph.

It required endurance.

The reckoning came publicly by accident.

A junior analyst—new enough not to know which absences were intentional—flagged a discrepancy during a live forum. Her question cut through the prepared narrative like a seam tearing under strain.

"This transition appears stabilized," the analyst said, voice uncertain but steady, "but only if we exclude legacy adviser interventions that redirected consequence externally. Shouldn't that context remain visible?"

The moderator froze.

The feeds spiked.

Someone tried to redirect, but the archive reference was already enumerated onscreen, its metadata linking cleanly back to Etta's preserved node.

From names.

To dates.

To decisions.

Elliot Vance's signature marker flared briefly, unmistakable.

No accusation followed.

None was needed.

The room filled with the low, uncomfortable sound of recognition.

—

Afterward, messages flooded Mara's queue—not congratulations, not condemnation, but recalibration requests. Questions. Invitations not to perform, but to *explain*.

She declined most of them.

She accepted only one: a closed review committee tasked with redefining archival compression protocols.

Not because it gave her power.

Because it limited future erasure.

Elias found her that night on the greenway, the city alive beneath them, imperfect and irrepressible. Dax passed with a nod, no longer curious, simply aware.

"It's out," Elias said.

"It was always out," Mara replied. "It just needed context."

"He's finished here."

"Yes," she said. "He'll be welcomed elsewhere."

"And you?"

"I'll stay," Mara said. "Where consequence is allowed to remain attached."

He smiled—quiet, unshowy.

"That's loyalty," he said.

"No," she replied. "That's responsibility."

They stood together, not triumphant, not weary—aligned in the knowledge that truth rarely arrived as revelation.

It arrived as persistence rewarded.

Later, a final message arrived from Etta.

The city feels less quiet tonight.

That's good.

Mara closed the channel and looked out over Midway.

The Forgotten Ally had never wanted spotlight.

Only memory.

And in honoring that, Mara felt the last temptation of sterility loosen its hold.

This was not safety.

It was involvement.

It would cost her.

It already had.

But loyalty—once answered with action rather than sentiment—did not drain.

It steadied.

False Safety

The proposal arrived disguised as relief.

Mara recognized that first, before she recognized anything else—the way the language steadied her pulse instead of quickening it, the way the future it outlined required no vigilance beyond consent. She read the message twice, not because it was unclear, but because it was *comfortable.*

Advisory Pathway — Extended Liaison Term

Scope: Strategic continuity across Core City and Midway

Benefits: Reduced exposure, protected latitude, discretionary influence

Recommendation: Acceptance advised

Acceptance advised.

Not demanded. Not urged. The system never did those things anymore. It had learned that willing compliance outperformed force.

She closed the message and leaned back, the chair adjusting automatically to her posture. Outside the window, Midway continued its uneven breathing—voices overlapping, transit whining just slightly off-tune, a city that refused to smooth itself for aesthetic preference.

False safety, she thought, always sounded reasonable.

The offer carried a name, though it was never presented as such.

Rowan Hale had sent the initial contact hours earlier, phrasing the request as a conversation rather than an appeal. He still respected process even when the outcome concerned him personally.

They met in a quiet atrium between districts—a neutral space with real plants genetically selected for resilience rather than beauty. Rowan arrived early, as he always did, coffee already cooling in his hand.

"You don't have to answer today," he said after they had exchanged greetings and sat. "I wanted you to hear it from me, not through Allocation filters."

"I appreciate that," Mara replied.

He nodded. "They're consolidating roles. Tightening risk exposure after the Elliot fallout. Someone suggested you as anchor."

"Someone," Mara said.

Rowan smiled faintly. "Several someones."

She watched him carefully as he spoke—not for tells of ambition, but for caution. Rowan did not hide behind neutrality; he held it openly.

"It would be stable," he continued. "Shielded. You'd have authority without constant pushback. Fewer emergencies."

"Fewer truths," Mara said.

"Fewer *crises*," Rowan corrected gently. "There's a difference."

She considered that.

"Is there?" she asked.

He hesitated, then answered honestly. "Sometimes."

The air shifted slightly between them, not in conflict, but in disclosure.

"They'd protect you," Rowan continued. "Your work. Your time. They'd stop treating you as an intervention and start treating you as infrastructure."

Mara felt the anxiety thread in—not fear, but urgency sharpened by awareness.

Infrastructure. Not actor. Not challenger.

Enduring. Invisible.

Safe.

The appeal was not romantic.

That was the danger.

Rowan did not promise happiness or fulfillment. He promised *rest*. A future unmarred by constant ethical triage, by the necessity of being present at every fracture point to prevent collapse. A life where decisions would be correct often enough, protected enough, that consequence rarely required proximity.

"You wouldn't disappear," Rowan said. "You'd just stop bleeding into the gaps."

She almost laughed at the accuracy.

"And you?" she asked.

Rowan met her gaze without flinching. "I'd be near you. Working alongside you. Not competing for attention the way others do."

A choice without spectacle.

A future without fever.

Mara felt the gravitational pull of it—not dramatic, not intoxicating, but persuasive in its quiet promise of sustainability.

False safety never arrived shouting.

It arrived offering assistance.

She did not answer him then.

She told him she'd think about it. He accepted that without disappointment, only relief that she had not dismissed the possibility entirely.

After they parted, Mara walked the longer route back to Midway, letting the city's noise erode the polish of the conversation. She passed familiar thresholds: the café where Lina argued cheerfully with vendors, the junction where Kira had once fallen and now bore reinforced lattice lines still faintly visible.

Memory layered itself over the present, heavy but instructive.

Rowan's offer would erase none of it.

It would simply make such things less likely to intrude again.

"That's the point," she murmured to herself.

Elias did not know yet.

That knowledge pressed against her as she moved through her evening routines. He was away on assessment for the north platforms—work that required both presence and recalibrated caution. They had spoken briefly earlier that day, the conversation unremarkable, grounded, easy.

That ease unsettled her now.

She could imagine how this alternative future would unfold: transparency managed just enough not to demand intervention; alignment framed to avoid fracture; her voice consulted only when necessary, never when disruptive.

She would still be effective.

She would no longer be *chosen* for the moments that mattered.

It scared her how tempting that felt.

The city noticed her hesitation, of course.

Systems always did.

By morning, follow-up messages arrived—not pressing, not overt, but encouraging. Clarifying questions. Expanded benefits. Language softening the edges of commitment until refusal would feel unnecessary.

She forwarded none of it.

Instead, she went to Etta.

The Lower Reach was quieter than usual, the corridors humming with subdued maintenance rather than constant correction.

"You're tired," Etta said the moment she saw her.

"Yes," Mara replied.

"That makes false solutions look humane," Etta said bluntly.

Mara smiled faintly. "I was hoping you'd say that."

She explained the offer without embellishment. Etta listened without interruption, her focus absolute.

When Mara finished, Etta leaned back, the mobility frame compensating automatically.

"They want to preserve you," she said.

"Yes."

"Preservation," Etta continued, "is what we do to artifacts we don't intend to consult again."

Mara felt the truth of it settle sharply.

"They won't silence you," Etta added. "They'll just stop listening closely."

"And Rowan?" Mara asked quietly.

Etta considered.

"He's kind," she said. "And careful. He believes safety is a moral good."

"Is it not?" Mara asked.

"It is," Etta replied. "But it's not the *highest* one."

The room filled with the hum of archived truth.

Anxiety crept in that night—not panic, but speed. A sense that something was converging, that choosing delay was itself a decision. She paced her unit longer than usual, unable to still herself.

When Elias returned, it was without ceremony.

He arrived at Midway late, greeted by the city with its usual uneven affection. Mara felt his presence before she saw him, the familiar cadence of alignment reasserting itself effortlessly.

"You look unsettled," he said after only a few minutes together.

"Yes," she replied.

He waited.

"I've been offered something," she said.

He nodded once, neutral, allowing the space between them to hold without assumption.

"A path," she continued. "Stable. Safe. Sanitized."

His brow furrowed slightly. "By whom?"

"Allocation," she said. "With Rowan's support."

Understanding passed between them without explanation.

"That would take you away," Elias said carefully.

"Yes."

"And closer to certainty."

"Yes."

He was quiet for a long moment.

"You're considering it," he said.

"Yes."

The admission landed harder than she expected—but also lighter, freed from concealment.

He did not react the way she feared.

"That makes sense," Elias said instead. "After everything."

She looked at him, startled.

"I won't pretend it doesn't," he continued. "You've carried more than most of us because you refused to trade accuracy for comfort."

"And now?" Mara asked.

"And now," he said, choosing his words with care, "someone is offering you comfort without asking you to stop being accurate. That's compelling."

He paused.

"It's also dangerous."

The tension in her chest tightened.

"Because of me?" she asked quietly.

He shook his head. "Because of *absence*."

She felt the urgency crest—time slipping, consequences approaching.

"This choice," she said, "would simplify things."

"Would it?" Elias asked. "Or just postpone complexity until no one's speaking honestly anymore?"

She turned away to look at the skyway—reinforced, quiet, waiting.

False safety shimmered there, luminous and persuasive.

"I don't want to be tired forever," she said.

"No," Elias agreed, softly. "But I don't want you to be absent either."

They stood there, the city holding its breath—not dramatically, but attentively.

This was the near-miss she felt looming: a future that would *work*, one that would make sense to everyone watching, one that asked only that she stop standing where the fractures were likely to form.

Anxiety sharpened into urgency.

If she chose it, there would be no catastrophe.

No fall.

No scandal.

No obvious loss.

Just a life that traded vigilance for safety—and slowly forgot why vigilance had ever mattered.

Mara closed her eyes.

She knew the decision had not yet been made.

But she also knew she was standing on its edge.

The closing in was gentle.

That was what made it dangerous.

Mara felt it over the next few days as appointments appeared already accepted, as draft schedules populated her calendar with polite finality, as language shifted from *possibility* to *preparation*. No one asked her again whether she intended to take the advisory pathway. They proceeded as though her consent had simply not yet been formalized.

Rowan never followed up directly.

That restraint hurt more than pressure would have.

Instead, he adjusted around the assumption: reassigned his own workload, cleared conflicting rotations, made small structural changes that suggested a future already underway. When they crossed paths, he treated her with the same calm respect he always had—no urgency, no persuasion, only availability.

"You don't look cornered," Lina observed one afternoon, watching Mara scan an interface without actually reading it.

"I am," Mara replied.

"By what?"

"By relief," Mara said quietly.

Lina frowned. "That doesn't sound dangerous."

"It is when it arrives before resolution," Mara answered.

The moment crystallized unexpectedly.

Mara was attending a closed Core City review—one of the last on her provisional assignment—when a scenario simulation failed mid-projection. Not catastrophically. Just enough to interrupt the narrative.

The analyst faltered.

"That shouldn't happen," she said. "The mitigation layer accounts for volatility."

"Does it," Mara asked, "or does it conceal it?"

Silence rippled across the table.

The model resumed, patched visibly by automated smoothing routines. The disruption vanished as if it had never occurred.

The room exhaled.

"See?" a coordinator said, relieved. "The system adapts."

Mara did not look convinced.

"What would have happened," she asked, "if there hadn't been time to smooth?"

The coordinator smiled politely. "That's what redundancy is for."

"And if redundancy masks fragility," Mara pressed gently, "what have we protected?"

No one answered.

The meeting adjourned early.

As Mara gathered her things, she realized what chilled her most was not the failure—it was how quickly comfort returned once the façade was restored.

False safety did not require belief.

Only silence.

She found Rowan waiting when she returned to Midway that evening.

Not at her door.

Not intrusively.

Near the greenway, where the city breathed unevenly and forgot how to perform.

"You look tired," he said.

She didn't deny it.

"They've started preparing the rollout," Rowan added. "Quietly. If you accept, it will happen smoothly."

"And if I don't?" Mara asked.

He hesitated.

"They'll adjust," he said. "Perhaps less smoothly."

"You'd be sidelined," she said.

He met her gaze. "I know."

"That doesn't bother you," Mara observed.

"It does," Rowan replied honestly. "Just not enough to make me pressure you."

The kindness in that answer cut deeply.

"This path," he said, carefully, "wouldn't ask you to compromise. Only to stop standing in the line of impact."

She nodded.

"And eventually," she said, "to stop noticing where the line forms."

Silence stretched between them—not tense, but heavy with meaning.

"You could do so much good from there," Rowan said. "Preventing harm before it reaches people like Kira. Like Etta."

"Yes," Mara agreed.

"And you wouldn't have to exhaust yourself just to keep truth visible."

The appeal was devastatingly reasonable.

Mara felt urgency bloom—not panic, but clarity accelerating toward decision.

"That future," she said, "depends on trust."

"Yes," Rowan replied.

"And trust," she continued, "is maintained there by preemptive erasure."

Rowan closed his eyes briefly.

"They would listen to you," he said. "Perhaps even reshape themselves."

"Until listening became endemic rather than chosen," Mara replied. "Then I'd be preserved instead."

Rowan said nothing.

This was the near-miss—not the wrong man, but the wrong *alignment*.

Elias arrived later, drawn not by schedule but by intuition sharpened through recent loss.

He found them mid-conversation and understood instantly what was at stake.

"I won't argue against it," he said, after Rowan nodded and withdrew with quiet grace. "Not because I agree. But because persuasion would poison the choice."

Mara appreciated that more than she could say.

"I'm afraid," she admitted.

Elias didn't look surprised.

"Of making the wrong decision?"

“Of making the *easy* one,” she said.

He leaned against the rail, gaze trained on the city.

“You know,” he said slowly, “I once believed safety was proof I’d done something right.”

“And now?”

“And now I understand it often meant someone else absorbed what I avoided.”

She turned toward him.

“This future,” she said, “would work.”

“Yes,” Elias replied. “That’s why it’s dangerous.”

Urgency pulsed between them, time converging toward inevitability.

“I don’t want to be heroic,” she said. “Or constantly necessary.”

“No,” he said. “You just don’t want to be absent.”

She exhaled sharply.

“I’m tired of carrying consequence,” she said.

“And I’m terrified,” Elias replied, “that you’ll stop.”

She looked at him then, really looked—no projection, no misalignment left between them.

“That sounds selfish,” she said.

“Only if you think your presence belongs to everyone equally,” he countered. “It doesn’t. It belongs where it matters.”

“And where is that?”

He gestured around them—not theatrically, just honestly.

“Here,” he said. “Where fracture still risks exposure. Where forgetting isn’t automated.”

The city hummed uneasily, alive with imperfection.

Mara felt the decision press closer, urgency resolving into inevitability.

The final signal arrived not from a system, but a person.

Etta.

Her message was brief.

They’ve begun retiring nodes again.

Quietly.

With justification.

Mara closed her eyes.

False safety had started closing behind her even before consent.

This was the clarity she needed—not emotional, not romantic, but structural.

Choosing the safe future would not end vigilance.

It would *redirect* it away from where it could act.

She opened a channel—one she had never used this way before.

To Allocation:

Subject: Advisory Pathway Declination

The words came cleanly.

I decline the extended liaison role.

My work requires proximity to consequence.

Thank you for the offer.

She sent it before doubt could refine it into hesitation.

The system responded automatically with acknowledgment.

No protest.

No inquiry.

Silence.

Rowan accepted the decision as he had promised he would.

He did not withdraw abruptly, nor did he linger. He thanked her for honesty, wished her steadiness, and adjusted his trajectory without narrative.

The sadness of it was acute—but clean.

Mara grieved not a future she wanted, but one she understood too well to choose.

"That was the right choice," Lina said later, eyes searching Mara's face.

"It was the necessary one," Mara replied.

"And Elias?"

Mara glanced toward the reinforced skyway, quiet and patient.

"He understands," she said.

The urgency dissipated slowly, like a fever breaking without spectacle.

The city absorbed her refusal with disinterest at scale and irritation in pockets. Some doors closed quietly. Others opened awkwardly, unprepared for her continued presence outside containment.

Etta's nodes were reinstated.

The archival compression request failed authorization this time—not flagged, just unresolved.

Something had shifted.

Mara stood once more at the greenway, the place of all her recalibrations, watching life proceed in its uneven way.

False safety had nearly claimed her—not through corruption, but through compassion misdirected toward comfort.

She had felt its pull, honored its appeal, and stepped aside anyway.

Anxiety loosened its grip, replaced by something steadier.

Resolve.

There was no applause.

No immediate reward.

Just the certainty that she remained available to truth—not preserved above it.

And as Elias joined her without speaking, fitting his presence to hers rather than reshaping it, Mara knew the near-miss had passed.

The future ahead was uncertain, demanding, unshielded.

And it was hers.

Re-Encounter

The invitation arrived without personalization.

That, Mara thought, was as it should be.

It took the form of a civic bulletin—one of those announcements that passed so frequently through public channels they rarely invited conscious decision. Attendance was framed as communal, nonexclusive, encouraged but not curated.

Public Forum & Sound Assembly — Lower Atrium Amphitheater

Featuring: Modular Resonance Collective

Open Access | Functional Capacity Permitting

Mara read it once and let it sit.

She knew the space. A converted transit atrium whose architecture refused spectacle, where sound behaved unpredictably and gathered communities not otherwise inclined to share attention. It was the sort of place factions overlapped by accident rather than design.

She also knew Elias would be there.

Not because of assurance.

Because avoidance had ceased to be useful.

The Lower Atrium carried sound before it carried bodies.

Mara felt it as she descended: low-frequency vibration traveling upward through reinforced stone, the pulse of something being built collectively rather than performed. The air was warmer here, less refined, textured by breath, metal, and electrical discharge.

The amphitheater was already half-full.

People sat wherever structure permitted—on steps, along rails, leaning against pylons never meant to hold stillness. No elevated platform dominated the space. The performers arranged themselves in a wide circle at ground level, instrument interfaces calibrated to proximity rather than reach.

Mara slipped into a seat near the perimeter and let her posture settle.

She did not look for Elias immediately.

She had learned better.

The music began without announcement.

It was not melody, not rhythm in any traditional sense. It was *assembly*—layers of tone introduced incrementally, pressure applied and withdrawn until resonance formed patterns you could feel more easily than name.

It reminded her of infrastructure.

Of systems learning their own limits.

She closed her eyes briefly as the sound deepened, her breath synchronizing unconsciously with the shifting pulse.

When she opened them again, Elias was there.

Across the atrium, five rows down and one column over, his posture recognizable not by dominance but by stillness. He sat slightly forward, forearms resting on his thighs, listening in a way that suggested effort rather than consumption.

He did not look at her.

Neither did she.

The restraint was not strategy—it was mutual instinct.

The sound swelled.

At the center of the circle, one of the modulators introduced an unstable frequency, deliberately imprecise. The sound wavered, brushing against discomfort before resolving into something unexpectedly cohesive.

A murmur passed through the audience—not applause, but recognition.

Mara smiled faintly.

She felt Elias shift almost imperceptibly at the same moment.

They were not aware of one another's movement.

Or perhaps they were aware and pretending otherwise.

Both possibilities felt electric.

The convergence began in fragments.

She noticed his presence not visually, but peripherally—how proximity changed the acoustic response, how certain frequencies sharpened when he leaned forward, how silence became heavier in shared moments of pause.

Once, he glanced in her direction—just briefly, just enough that she knew it had been intentional rather than accidental.

She did not meet his gaze.

The restraint was excruciating.

And necessary.

The performers adjusted again, tightening the margins, allowing instability to persist longer than comfort suggested. The sound grew brittle, almost too sharp to bear, then softened into warmth as collaboration overtook dominance.

Mara felt the familiar recognition rise—not as memory, but understanding.

This was what recalibration sounded like.

She sensed Elias watching her now—not observing, but *tracking*. Waiting for the moment her attention would break free of the sound long enough to register him fully.

She did not grant it.

Not yet.

During an extended pause between sequences, a child somewhere in the audience laughed softly.

The sound cut through the space like a dropped instrument—unexpected, human, destabilizing. The performers did not react immediately.

Then one of them smiled.

The next tone incorporated the interruption, recalibrating without erasure.

Mara felt her throat tighten.

She saw Elias's head tilt, his lips ghosting into a smile he did not fully allow himself.

It was the most intimate moment they had shared in weeks.

And they did not touch.

The sequence ended without climax.

No final note. No gesture of completion.

Just dispersal.

The audience exhaled as one, the collective holding pattern dissolving into movement. People stood slowly, reluctant to break whatever coherence had briefly formed.

Mara waited.

So did Elias.

When they finally rose, it was not in synchrony—no dramatic alignment, no obvious convergence. They moved among the crowd with practiced ease, paths curving naturally toward one another without declaration.

They met near a structural column etched with old transit coordinates.

"Hello," Elias said.

"Hello," Mara replied.

The word carried far more than greeting.

They stood for a moment, neither stepping closer nor creating distance.

"That was..." Elias began, then stopped.

"Yes," Mara said, saving him.

He smiled, relief threading the edges.

"You feel this sort of thing," he said.

"I notice it," she replied. "Feeling comes later."

"Still," he said. "The noticing is remarkable."

She inclined her head slightly.

"And you?" she asked.

"I'm learning where to stop intervening," he said. "Letting patterns complete."

She regarded him thoughtfully.

"That's new," she said.

"Yes," he agreed. "And uncomfortable."

"Good," she said gently. "Discomfort suggests growth."

He laughed quietly, the sound barely audible over the ebb of departing voices.

They remained there, framed by movement, their stillness anomalous but unchallenged.

"I'm glad you came," Elias said.

"So am I," Mara replied.

The admission felt deliberately placed.

They walked together out of the atrium—not side by side at first, but within the same pace, the same awareness. The city greeted them with layered sound and uneven motion, its complexity familiar and grounding.

People passed them without recognition.

That anonymity felt earned.

"I've been thinking about what you said before," Elias said as they reached the open air. "About proximity to consequence."

"Yes?"

"I don't think I understood until recently how much presence matters—not dominance, not authority. Just... remaining."

"Presence," Mara said, "is a form of accountability."

He nodded.

"And you?" he asked. "Have you regretted staying?"

She considered the question carefully.

"No," she said. "I've felt fatigued. Lonely, at times. Tempted by ease. But not regretful."

He absorbed that.

"There was a moment," she added, "when safe absence almost claimed me."

"And now?" he asked.

"And now," she said, "I hear clearly again."

They stopped at the edge of the thoroughfare, the lights reflecting softly off the reinforced glass above them. For a brief moment, the city's motion receded—not because it had paused, but because their focus had narrowed.

"I won't ask anything of you tonight," Elias said.

"I know," Mara replied.

"That's not restraint," he continued. "It's respect."

"Yes," she said. "It is."

They stood there, the space between them charged but stable—no confession, no collapse, only the undeniable gravity of alignment returning under controlled conditions.

The electric restraint lingered, humming beneath every unsaid word.

As they parted—not reluctantly, not eagerly, simply *deliberately*—Mara felt the convergence settle into something durable.

There would be time.

And when the moment came, it would not require persuasion.

Only recognition.

The convergence did not announce itself.

It accumulated.

Mara realized this later—afterward, when the memory had time to organize itself—but in the moment it felt like standing in a current whose direction only became obvious once she stopped resisting it. The amphitheater emptied slowly, the sound assembly dissolving into residual hum and scattered conversation. People lingered without knowing why. That was the mark of something true having passed among them.

She let the tide move her.

It carried her—not toward Elias directly, not with any intention she could name—but closer, increment by increment. The city opened into a wide concourse beyond the atrium, its ceiling ribbed with old transit arches and dotted with maintenance lights that pulsed irregularly. Here, voices overlapped again. Friction returned. Reality reasserted itself.

They were in the same space now, not adjacent by chance but by gravity.

Elias fell into step beside her without speaking, his pace adjusting unconsciously. He did that now—noticed rhythm before asserting it. She was aware of him without looking, the warmth of another presence contained but undeniable.

They walked in silence long enough for the restraint to become deliberate rather than reflexive.

Eventually, they reached a cluster where people had paused around a temporary installation—one of Core City's attempts at "community engagement," if such things could still be said with earnestness. A small group gathered around a civic moderator fielding questions, the discussion drifting toward recovery, resilience, the familiar vocabulary of adaptation.

Mara stood at the edge.

Elias lingered a step behind her.

The moderator asked something about how societies learned from disruption without becoming brittle in the process. Someone offered a platitude about innovation and flexibility. Another spoke about confidence as a form of energy that could be restored if managed correctly.

Mara listened.

She did not intend to speak.

That was the irony—how often the moments that mattered most arrived precisely when she had stopped performing readiness for them.

A woman near the front asked, "But what do you do when vigilance itself becomes exhaustion? When the people who keep things from failing are the ones who can no longer keep standing there?"

The question hung longer than expected.

Mara felt Elias's attention sharpen instantly—not toward her face, but toward the space where possibility had opened.

She spoke before she realized she had chosen to do so.

"You don't ask them to stand forever," she said calmly. "You change what standing means."

Several heads turned.

Her voice carried—not amplified, not insistent, simply placed.

"You build systems where attentiveness isn't a heroic act," she continued, "but a shared condition. Where consequences remain visible enough that no one person has to hold them alone."

The moderator paused, uncertain whether this constituted an answer or an intervention.

"In other words," Mara added, "you stop rewarding the illusion of safety purchased through silence. Because silence eventually transfers the cost to the least protected."

The concourse absorbed the words the way water absorbs heat—slowly, unevenly.

Elias did not look at her.

He did not need to.

She felt the moment land behind her, felt the recalibration occur where earlier misalignments had lived. This was it—the articulation he had never quite heard, not fully, not all at once.

Not endurance framed as sacrifice.

But constancy framed as design.

The woman who had asked the question nodded, eyes bright with recognition.

"That sounds... expensive," she said.

"It is," Mara replied. "But so is collapse. One just invoices later."

A few people laughed softly—not dismissively, but with the release of seeing something clearly named.

The moderator thanked Mara and redirected, but the conversation never quite returned to abstraction. Threads shifted. Questions became more precise. The tenor changed.

Mara stepped back, no longer needed.

Only then did she realize Elias was looking at her.

Not observing. Not evaluating.

Recognizing.

The look held no urgency. No triumph. Just a quiet recalibration finishing its work.

They moved away together, neither of them commenting on what had just happened.

They did not need to.

Outside, the night had cooled, the city breathing with a steadier rhythm now that performance had been left behind. They stood beneath a skyweb threaded with faint maintenance signals, the glow soft enough to feel earned.

"I didn't know you were going to say that," Elias said finally.

"I didn't either," Mara replied.

He smiled—a small, unguarded curve of understanding.

"I've heard you speak about systems before," he said. "About resilience. But that... was different."

"How?" she asked gently.

"It included people," he said. "Not as inputs. Not as variables. But as the reason the system exists at all."

She considered that.

"I suppose I've stopped separating them," she said. "Once you do, it becomes easier to excuse erasure."

He nodded slowly.

"I used to listen for outcomes," Elias admitted. "For what would work. Tonight I heard something else."

"What did you hear?" Mara asked.

"Commitment," he said. "Without declarations. Loyalty without possession. Care without control."

The words threaded something fragile and precise between them.

They had stopped walking without noticing.

The city continued around them, indifferent to convergence, as cities always were.

"I didn't mean any of that as—" Mara began, then stopped herself.

"As what?" Elias prompted.

"As anything personal," she said.

"I know," he replied. "That's why it mattered."

She looked at him then, really looked, and found no expectation in his expression. No pressure for resolution. Just awareness held carefully, as though he finally understood the cost of mishandling it.

They stood like that for a while longer, the restraint no longer tightening but *holding*—the difference subtle and profound.

"I won't ask you for more than tonight offers," Elias said quietly.

"And what does tonight offer?" she asked.

He gestured around them—not grandly, just honestly.

"Presence. Accuracy. The chance to stand near what's real without naming it too soon."

She felt something ease in her chest.

"Yes," she said. "That's enough."

They parted at the crossing where the greenway curved back into Midway's familiar irregularity. Dax passed with two others, absorbed in discussion, glancing at them only long enough to confirm alignment without probing it. No spectacle followed. No commentary.

Good, Mara thought.

Elias paused before stepping away.

"There will be moments," he said, carefully, "when hesitation looks like failure again. When restraint costs you simplicity."

"Yes," Mara said.

"And when someone will offer safety if you agree to stop standing where things break."

She held his gaze steadily.

"They already have," she said.

He nodded, no surprise in him now.

"I won't be the one to make you smaller," he said. "Not now. Not ever."

The words were not a promise.

They were a boundary—and therefore trustworthy.

"Thank you," she said.

He smiled, warmth returning at last without urgency.

"Good night, Mara."

"Good night, Elias."

She returned to her unit with the electric restraint still humming—no longer sharp, but resonant. The night did not ask her to resolve it. That, too, felt earned.

As she stood at the window, watching Midway's lights blink unevenly into darkness, Mara felt the convergence settle into something unshakeable.

Not romance declared.

Not certainty achieved.

But alignment restored, sharpened by restraint rather than blunted by delay.

Somewhere in the city, systems recalibrated imperfectly. People made choices they would justify later. Safety presented itself again in alluring forms.

But here—now—she had heard herself speak the truth he needed to hear.

And he had listened.

When the moment came that demanded declaration, she knew it would not rely on persuasion.

Only on recognition already achieved.

The city breathed on.

So did she.

Written in Silence

The message was written in silence.

Not the dramatic kind—no storm, no isolation engineered for confession—but the ordinary, late quiet that arrives only after a city has decided it cannot justify staying awake any longer. Elias sat alone in the operations annex overlooking the resecured transit corridor, light dimmed to maintenance levels, his interface dormant beside him.

He had disabled the network cache intentionally.

This was not something he wanted routed, interpreted, or preserved by accident.

What he needed was accuracy without audience.

He started once, erased the opening line, then sat with his hands still for several minutes, letting the familiar urge toward efficiency burn itself out. This was not a briefing. Not an analysis.

He had spent weeks learning the difference.

When he began again, the words came more slowly—and that, too, was deliberate.

I have been wrong for a long time.

He stopped there. Read it. Felt the inadequacy of generalities.

Specificity had been his shield. Now it would have to be his offering.

Not about outcomes. About what they cost, and who paid.

The cursor blinked.

He remembered the skyway's subtle give beneath his boots.

The hollow sound of metal realigning.

The look on Kira's face before gravity intervened.

He continued.

I thought strength announced itself. That it moved first and worried later. I believed restraint was something you adopted when you lacked reach.

That one stayed.

I see now that restraint was the thing I never learned to value because it asked me to remain present when movement would have been easier.

He paused, the weight of it settling properly.

The annex hummed softly around him—systems synchronized, load balanced, everything behaving as designed. Somewhere else in the city, Mara stood where fractures still had access to consequence.

This message was long overdue.

Mara received it while compiling a routing audit she had postponed too many times.

The arrival did not announce itself with urgency. No tone, no vibration designed to pull her attention. Just a single indicator that something had bypassed her filters by consent rather than force.

Direct handoff received.

Encryption: analog-adjacent.

No forwarding path detected.

She stilled.

The method alone told her everything.

She closed the audit and accepted the handoff.

The interface did not render the message immediately. Instead, it required confirmation of receipt conditions—local storage only, no replication, no system redundancy. She authorized it without hesitation.

The text appeared as plain glyphs on a neutral field.

No formatting.

No signature metadata.

No timestamp beyond *now*.

She began to read.

I have been wrong for a long time.

She inhaled once and kept going.

Elias did not speak of love.

Not once.

He spoke instead of philosophy.

I treated safety as something you achieved by removing friction. By acting fast enough that dissent couldn't accrue weight. I see now that what I called decisiveness was often avoidance.

Her pulse slowed, sharpened.

You were never disengaged. You were never absent. You were choosing not to dominate the space where others needed to arrive themselves.

She closed her eyes briefly.

He had heard her.

That night, when you spoke about vigilance not being a heroic act but a shared condition—I realized I had mistaken constancy for endurance and endurance for silence.

Her hands rested flat against the desk.

I see now that your refusal to perform was not indifference. It was fidelity—to truth, to consequence, to the people who weren't in the room when decisions were made.

The words did not hurry.

They did not plead.

They did not ask anything of her yet.

This was not persuasion.

It was recognition.

Elias continued writing as though speaking to the quiet between them rather than to her directly.

I am not asking you to return something we lost. I don't believe it was ever gone. I am asking you to trust that I am capable of standing next to what is difficult without trying to control it.

That line cost him time.

He re-read it, did not revise it, did not soften it.

Then:

If you choose never to come closer than this, I will accept that. Not as punishment. As consequence.

The cursor hovered.

This was the edge.

The place where clarity risked becoming demand.

He let another minute pass.

But if you still believe that presence matters—that speaking accurately is worth the cost of being heard improperly—then I want you to know this: I am here. Not ahead of you. Not waiting for you to adapt.

With you.

He stopped.

There were more words available to him—there always were—but they would not improve accuracy. This was not an argument to be won or a future to be negotiated.

It was an admission of alignment.

He ended it simply.

—E

Not a name.

She would know.

Mara did not move for a long while after she reached the end.

The city continued beyond her window, Midway's irregular pulse stitching together moments of quiet with honest, imperfect sound. She became aware of her breathing only when it shifted—deeper, steadier, unguarded.

He had not asked.

He had not promised.

He had not explained himself into safety.

He had *stood* in it.

Catharsis did not arrive as release.

It arrived as confirmation.

She had been understood—not partially, not sentimentally, but correctly.

Recognition flooded through her with an intensity she had not prepared for, not because it surprised her, but because it *ended something.* A long vigilance, a careful positioning, an internal bracing against misinterpretation that had taken years to develop.

She read the message again.

Slower this time.

Not for reassurance.

For completeness.

Outside, footsteps sounded along the greenway.

Ordinary ones.

Uncurated.

Life continuing.

Her interface shimmered faintly, awaiting response.

She did not type immediately.

She did not need to.

The confession had not demanded symmetry. It had created space for it.

When she finally began, it was not from obligation, but from readiness.

I have never wanted certainty, she wrote.

I wanted accuracy.

That was where she paused.

She felt no rush to justify herself. No need to explain the exhaustion, the near-miss with false safety, the years of standing at fracture points without applause or shelter.

He knew those things now—not as narrative, but as structure.

She continued.

You didn't misread me because you were careless. You misread me because you were rewarded for speed in a world that confused movement with courage.

She allowed herself the smallest smile.

What changed was not your ability to act. It was your willingness to remain.

Her hands rested briefly in her lap before returning to the keys.

I will not accept a version of us that requires silence to survive. Or safety that asks me to leave the margins unobserved.

Another pause.

This part mattered.

If you are offering presence without containment, and fidelity without possession—then yes. I recognize myself there.

She stopped before it could become something else.

No poetry.

No flourish.

Just alignment stated plainly.

She closed with what felt sufficient.

—M

She sent it before doubt could enter and ask for polish.

The confirmation returned silently. No receipt. No echo.

Just completion.

Across the city, Elias read her reply once.

Then again.

He did not sit back. He did not exhale dramatically. He leaned forward, forearms resting against the desk, the weight of recognition settling into his shoulders not as relief, but as responsibility accepted.

They had not resolved anything.

They had not promised ease.

What they had done—without performance, without audience—was acknowledge the same horizon from different positions and decide to walk toward it without rearranging the terrain.

That was enough.

For now.

Outside, the city continued its imperfect choreography.

Inside two separate rooms, something precise and deliberate had aligned—not through persuasion, but through truth delivered at the moment it could finally land.

The letter had done its work.

What came next would not need to be written.

They did not meet immediately.

That was the first mercy.

The city did not compress time to accommodate revelation, and neither of them tried to force it. The letter existed now—complete, deliberate, irrevocable—altering the internal geometry of everything that followed. It did not demand response in real space, did not request proof through presence or gesture.

It waited.

Mara moved through the next day with a steadiness that surprised her. Tasks aligned. Decisions sharpened rather than scattered. The city's background noise—maintenance cycles, informal conversations, the rough cadence of Midway—felt less intrusive than it had in weeks. Not because anything was quieter, but because nothing was pressing against unspoken uncertainty anymore.

Recognition had settled the most exhausting question.

When she walked the greenway that evening, people nodded as they always did. Dax waved from across the way. A maintenance drone hummed overhead, recalibrating its approach after a minor correction. Life continued.

So did she.

Elias waited until night fell properly before he reached out—not by message this time, but by proximity. He took the longer route back from the upper platforms, letting chance sharpen into intention without announcement. He did not come to her door. He stood instead near the edge of the reinforced span where the skyway met ground, a place that remembered fracture without demanding it be reenacted.

She felt him before she saw him.

He turned as she approached, expression composed but unguarded, the careful alertness of someone who knew the moment mattered and would not try to shape it.

"Hello," he said.

"Hello," she replied.

The word landed differently now—no longer a gesture, but an acknowledgment held in common.

They stood for a moment without stepping closer. The city flowed around them, imperfect and unconcerned, the air cool with the promise of rain later. Neither of them remarked on the letter. They did not need to name what was already present between them.

"I read your reply," Elias said finally.

"Yes," Mara answered.

"Thank you," he added—not perfunctory, not anxious. "For its accuracy."

She inclined her head slightly. "It was due."

They shared a small smile, the kind that arrived without rehearsal.

They began to walk.

No destination. No route chosen in advance. Their footsteps fell into alignment naturally—not because either adjusted, but because both noticed.

"I don't want this to feel like a conclusion," Elias said after a few minutes. "Or an absolution."

"It won't," Mara replied. "It shouldn't."

"Good," he said. "Because what I'm learning now doesn't feel like relief. It feels like obligation."

She regarded him thoughtfully. "That's the version that lasts."

He nodded.

They passed beneath a string of low lamps, their light unassuming, utilitarian. The skyway rose above them—not dominant anymore, just present—its repairs visible if you knew where to look.

"I used to think confession was about urgency," Elias said. "About seizing the moment before it slipped away."

"And now?" she asked.

"And now I think it's about patience," he said. "About ensuring the moment exists at all."

She stopped walking.

He did too, instantly.

"That," she said, "is not something many people learn."

"I didn't," he replied. "Not until it cost me something I couldn't optimize away."

She looked at him steadily. "And now?"

"And now," he said, "I want to choose the version of responsibility that doesn't make me smaller."

She smiled faintly. "Nor anyone else."

"Yes," he agreed.

They resumed, the night deepening around them.

A public board flickered to life nearby, updating transit advisories. The language was plain now—no flourish, no reassurance engineered into the phrasing. Mara noticed and did not comment. Elias noticed too.

"I changed that," he said quietly.

She met his gaze. "I know."

The acknowledgment felt intimate without trespassing.

They reached the place where the greenway bent toward the Lower Reach, the air cooler there, city sounds layering into something almost musical. Elias slowed.

"There will be pressure again," he said. "For ease. For safety framed as absence. I don't want you to feel like you'd have to leave to protect yourself from that."

She answered without hesitation. "I won't."

"And if proximity becomes heavy?" he asked. "If standing near me makes your work harder?"

She considered the question honestly.

"Then we'll adjust positioning," she said. "Not alignment."

He absorbed that, relief threading through his posture.

"I can do that," he said. "I can learn."

She laughed softly. "You already are."

They stopped where the path divided—one route back toward Core City's distant glow, the other deeper into Midway's lived texture. Neither took the branching step immediately.

The pause was deliberate.

Elias turned toward her fully now, no longer guarded against the possibility of misreading. The city's light caught his face at an angle that softened rather than clarified, the way shared moments often did.

"I won't ask you to promise anything," he said. "Not time. Not closeness. Not certainty."

"Good," she replied. "I don't believe in promises that ask us to stop paying attention."

“What I can ask,” he continued, careful, “is whether you’re willing to let this be... present.”

She did not look away.

“Yes,” she said. “I am.”

The air between them shifted—not with resolve fulfilled, but with consent granted.

He stepped closer then, the distance closing by inches rather than intent. He did not touch her. He did not need to. The choice itself carried weight enough.

Across the greenway, laughter rose and fell. Somewhere, a door opened and closed. The city remained indifferent to their convergence, as cities always were.

“I don’t feel triumphant,” Elias said quietly. “I feel... oriented.”

Mara nodded. “That’s what truth does when it’s finally placed.”

They stood together for another minute, perhaps two, letting the alignment settle into something that did not require naming to be real.

When they parted, it was without reluctance or hurry.

“Tomorrow,” he said.

“Yes,” she replied.

Not as schedule.

As fact.

He stepped onto the path toward the platforms. She turned back toward Midway. Neither watched the other leave. Trust did not require surveillance.

Inside her unit, later, Mara paused by the window and allowed herself a long breath. The letter remained open on her interface—not glowing, not demanding, simply *there*. She did not reread it. It had already done what it needed to do.

She understood now: the emotional climax had not been the words exchanged, but the space they had created—wide enough to stand within without erasure, precise enough to hold without pressure.

Whatever came next would not be built on persuasion.

It would be built on the patient work of staying present where truth insisted on being seen.

And for the first time, she did not feel she was doing that work alone.

Chosen Constancy

They chose the edge of the city because neither of them trusted centers anymore.

Not institutions. Not crowds. Not places designed to amplify meaning rather than contain it.

The path Elias suggested followed the old maintenance belt that curved along the perimeter of the Lower Reach—where transit infrastructure thinned, where the city's vertical insistence gave way to long, horizontal spans. Here, the city did not try to impress. It simply endured.

Mara arrived first.

She stood near the barrier rail, watching water slip between reinforced pylons, its movement steady and untheatrical. The smell of metal and damp stone grounded her, a reminder of systems that answered to physics rather than narrative.

When Elias approached, she did not turn immediately.

Neither did he speak.

That, she realized, was already different than it would have been once. Silence no longer braced itself for interpretation. It simply existed.

They began walking without ceremony.

Footsteps echoed softly against composite decking, spaced naturally—a half-meter between them that neither rushed to close nor guarded. Overhead, maintenance lights cast wide cones of amber illumination, leaving large pockets of shadow untouched.

"This used to be a service route," Elias said after several minutes.

"I know," Mara replied. "It still is."

He smiled faintly. "Exactly."

They walked on.

The city's edge revealed layers the Core never acknowledged: conduits rerouted and rerouted again, weld marks visible beneath newer plating, signs of failure not concealed but reinforced around. Nothing here pretended to have been immutable.

Mara found herself breathing more steadily than she had in days.

"I want to talk about what I didn't say," Elias said at last.

She inclined her head slightly. "So do I."

He considered where to begin, then chose not to optimize the opening.

"When I left," he said, voice level, "I told myself it was temporary. Necessary. That I would return once I had something solid enough to offer."

She did not interrupt.

"I believed stability was something you achieved first," he continued, "and then shared. Like an asset."

Mara watched the water below them break itself against old concrete and reform without complaint.

"And you believed I didn't want to share risk," she said.

"Yes," Elias admitted. "I thought you wanted certainty more than possibility."

She nodded. "And you mistook my caution for fear."

"Yes."

The honesty settled cleanly between them, neither heavy nor absolving.

"I didn't end things because I doubted you," Mara said quietly. "I ended them because I was afraid of what would be demanded of you if I didn't."

Elias slowed.

"What do you mean?" he asked.

She stopped walking.

He did too, immediately.

"When you left," she said, turning to face him now, "you were already carrying more than you acknowledged. Risk, responsibility, expectation. You had access to danger I couldn't remove—but I could add to."

He frowned slightly, listening.

"My family," she continued, "my context, my need for stability at that moment—it would have made your choices heavier. And you hadn't learned yet how to put weight down."

Elias absorbed that, his gaze fixed not on her face but somewhere just past it.

"I wanted to be strong," he said.

"You wanted to be unencumbered," she replied gently. "There's a difference."

He exhaled through his nose, not defensive, just recognizing something late.

"And you?" he asked. "Why didn't you say any of this then?"

Mara's answer came without hesitation.

"Because you weren't listening for nuance," she said. "You were listening for permission."

The words were precise. Kind. Unforgiving.

Elias closed his eyes briefly.

"You're right," he said. "I'd learned to hear only approval or obstruction. Anything else sounded like doubt."

"That wasn't your fault alone," Mara said. "The city rewards people who mistake certainty for leadership."

He nodded once.

They resumed walking, their pace slower now, more deliberate.

Ahead, the path narrowed where one section had never been properly rebuilt. The original guardrail remained—pitted, scarred, reinforced pragmatically rather than replaced. Elias rested his forearm against it as they passed.

"I thought that going away was choosing growth," he said. "I didn't see how much of it was avoidance."

"Growth without accountability often is," Mara replied.

There was no accusation in it.

Only clarity.

"And you," Elias said, turning slightly toward her as they walked, "you stayed. You endured the consequences everyone else outsourced."

"Yes," she said simply.

"Do you resent me for that?"

Mara considered the question carefully.

"I resented being misread," she said. "I still do. But I don't resent constancy. It's not a sacrifice when you choose it consciously."

That distinction eased something in him he hadn't realized was still taut.

They reached a point where the city fell away into a wide basin of water crossed by staggered light reflections. It was quiet here—not empty, but settled. Elias stopped again.

"I need to say this," he said. "Not as apology—but as reckoning."

She waited.

"I didn't return hoping to recover what we lost," he said. "I returned thinking I had outgrown it. That I was better now. Larger."

His mouth moved in a humorless smile.

"I see now that what I gained was scale, not depth."

Mara studied him, the low light drawing careful lines across his expression.

"And what do you see when you look at me?" she asked.

The question did not tremble.

Elias met her gaze fully.

"I see someone who never stopped standing where others stepped aside," he said. "Not because she had to, but because she believed the system wouldn't survive otherwise."

She felt something inside her release—not a knot, but a long-held posture.

"And you never asked me to be smaller to accommodate you," he continued. "You only asked me to be accurate."

Mara breathed out slowly.

"I asked myself that first," she said. "Everything else followed."

They leaned together against the rail, not touching, but close enough that awareness replaced distance.

"What scares you now?" Elias asked.

She answered without artifice.

"That ease will be mistaken for safety again," she said. "That people will keep trying to protect me by removing me from consequence."

"And you won't accept that."

"No," she said. "But resisting it alone is... expensive."

Elias nodded.

"I can't promise it will stop," he said. "But I can stop participating in it. I can refuse to let my presence be a buffer that erases you."

That mattered.

She turned slightly toward him.

"And I won't make myself smaller to make proximity easier," she said. "Not for you. Not for anyone."

He smiled—quiet, unguarded, deeply present.

"I wouldn't want you to."

They stood there as the city edge held them steady, neither demanding resolution nor threatening collapse. The relief that settled between them didn't come from absolution but from alignment—a recognition that they were finally speaking from the same layer of understanding.

"We're not the same people," Elias said.

"No," Mara agreed. "But we're finally accountable versions of them."

That felt true.

They began their walk back along the maintenance belt, their pace aligned now without effort. The city did not shift to accommodate them. It didn't need to.

Chosen constancy, Mara realized, did not announce itself through endurance alone.

It was shaped in moments like this—when explanation replaced performance, when presence was offered without condition, and when the past was neither erased nor allowed to dominate the future.

They had not solved everything.

They did not need to.

They had done the harder thing.

They had chosen one another with eyes open.

And that, she felt with a quiet certainty, was enough to keep walking.

They did not turn back when the maintenance belt narrowed to a single ribbon of light.

The city's edge grew quieter the farther they went, not empty but unbothered—no advertising layers, no curated sound, only the patient cadence of water meeting barrier and withdrawing again. Here, the Reach forgot itself long enough to become honest.

Elias broke the silence first, not because it pressed him, but because he had learned when to place weight.

"When I think about the years between," he said, "I see how much I mistook motion for progress. I believed I could outpace what wasn't resolved."

Mara listened with the attentive stillness that had always made space rather than filled it. She did not nod. She did not soften his words by preempting them.

"And what did you leave unresolved?" she asked.

He considered the question, turning it over until it stopped glittering and began to hold.

"The cost of being admired," he said. "And the comfort of being unchallenged."

They stopped again where the belt widened into a viewing platform—one of the old kind, its surface patched and repatched, its rail bearing the abrades of hands that had gripped it long before anyone thought to photograph the view. The water below ran darker here, less reflective, moving with no concern for spectacle.

"I learned to accept praise in place of correction," Elias continued. "It felt earned. It felt efficient."

"And now?" Mara asked.

"And now I see how often efficiency canceled judgment," he said. "I thought I was removing friction. I was removing witnesses."

Mara leaned her forearms on the rail, the cool metal steady beneath her skin.

"You were isolating yourself from consequence," she said. "And isolating others from study."

He nodded, the admission unguarded.

"I wasn't alone in that," he added. "It's how the city teaches some of us to survive."

"Yes," she said. "But survival isn't the same as continuity."

The word settled in him—*continuity*—different from preservation, different from stasis. It implied endurance with memory intact.

They stood there a moment longer, letting the concepts arrange themselves into something usable.

"I want to talk about what happened when you stayed," Elias said. "And I left."

Mara straightened, meeting him in the low light.

"Then talk about it," she said.

He did not rush.

"When I was gone," he said, "I told myself you had chosen safety over risk. That you wanted your world bounded."

"And what did that allow you to believe?" she asked, not harshly.

"That I was the only one willing to jeopardize certainty," he replied. "That I was braver."

She did not let the silence rescue him.

"That belief," she said, "let you absolve yourself of what my staying actually did."

He looked at her carefully. "Which was?"

"Visibility," Mara said. "I remained where failures could be seen and named before they hardened. I didn't make myself safe. I made myself *accountable*."

The relief that crossed his face was brief, followed by something more sober.

"I didn't understand the labour of that," he said. "I thought it was passive."

"No," she replied. "It was sustained."

They began moving again, slower now, their steps coordinated by an ease that required no attention.

"I don't ask you to regret leaving," Mara continued. "You became who you needed to become."

"I do regret the way I defined return," he said. "As arrival rather than repair."

She considered, then nodded. "Repair is quieter."

"And slower," he added.

"Good," she said. "Speed confuses completion."

They passed a node where the belt crossed a spillway, the sound of water deepening into a low thunder before flattening again into movement. Elias lifted his gaze to the horizon, where maintenance lights marked the boundary of the Reach like a modest constellation.

"There's something else," he said.

Mara waited; she had learned when waiting mattered.

"I've been afraid," he said, "that closeness would require me to be certain again. To make promises I couldn't keep without repeating old patterns."

The admission surprised him as much as it surprised her.

Mara slowed, then turned fully toward him.

"Certainty isn't what I want from you," she said. "Responsiveness is."

He frowned slightly. "Explain."

"Certainty fixes outcomes in advance," she said. "Responsiveness keeps adjusting when outcomes change. One excludes people. The other includes them."

He absorbed that with care.

"So if I said I would remain," he said, "but also remain willing to change—"

"That would be presence," she finished. "Not containment."

The distinction settled cleanly between them.

They walked until the platform looped back toward Midway, the city's texture sharpening as lights multiplied and small sounds returned. The world did not feel intrusive anymore; it felt appropriately scaled.

"I need to say this clearly," Elias said. "Because it's not something I've practiced."

She watched him, the corners of her mouth lifting just slightly.

"I don't want you here because you stabilize *me*," he said. "I want you here because you destabilize complacency where it forms."

She offered him an unguarded look.

"That's not a romantic reason," she said.

"Good," he replied. "It's a durable one."

They shared a quiet laugh, relief without release.

They stopped where the path divided again—this time closer to Midway, where voices carried and the smell of street cooking drifted up from a lower tier. Life, insisting.

"I'm not asking for your forgiveness," Elias said. "Or to be trusted without proof."

Mara nodded. "Then this will work."

He blinked. "Because I'm not asking?"

"Because you're not," she said. "Trust grows where it isn't extracted."

They stood there, neither leaning away nor moving closer, the space between them no longer charged with tension but with consent.

"And you?" he asked. "What do you want, now that this is clear?"

Mara did not need time to search for the answer, but she gave it care anyway.

"I want to keep standing where the work is," she said. "I want companionship that doesn't ask me to leave when standing gets hard. I want disagreement that sharpens, not eclipses. And I want to be chosen without being packaged."

Elias smiled—slow, sincere.

"I can do that," he said. "And when I can't, I can say so."

She held his gaze. "That's all I need."

They started back toward the heart of Midway together, their pace aligned without calibration, the easy kind of togetherness that followed shared reckoning.

Near the greenway, Dax waved from a bench, her grin unmistakable. Lina emerged from a doorway, mid-argument, broke off when she saw them, and offered a nod that contained no questions.

"No audience tonight," Mara said quietly.

"Good," Elias replied.

They parted near her building, not because anything needed to end, but because endings believed in their own importance too much lately.

"Tomorrow?" he asked.

"Yes," she said. "After the review."

"I'll walk you here," he offered.

"You already have," she replied.

The smile he gave her then was not triumphant. It was patient.

Inside her unit, later, Mara paused again by the window. The city's sounds felt properly distant, the way stars did when you recognized a constellation but did not need it to guide you anymore.

Chosen constancy, she realized, was not a vow spoken aloud.

It was a sequence of decisions made visible to one another—decisions to remain present, to correct without conquering, to accept consequence without dramatizing it.

She did not feel swept.

She felt anchored.

And when she turned away from the glass to rest, the quiet that met her was no longer lonely. It was complete.

Social Reactions

The reaction was retroactive.

Mara understood that before she understood anything else—the way certainty moved backward through memory, reassigning meaning to decisions that had once been questioned. Society rarely admitted to learning. It preferred to claim it had *always known*.

She first noticed the shift in tone rather than statement.

A message from Allocation arrived late morning, its language subtly altered from prior correspondence.

Acknowledged: recalibrated advisory alignment.

Observation: sustained stability metrics.

Status note: association risk downgraded.

Association risk.

The phrase had once felt like indictment. Now it read like absolution nobody meant to name.

She closed the message without reply.

The acceptance spread quietly, as these things always did.

No one apologized. No one acknowledged previous concern. Instead, former hesitation was quietly reclassified as prudent caution, and Mara's choices—once framed as obstinate, premature, or inconvenient—were rehearsed as evidence of prescience.

It was being rewritten.

At Keene Tower, the change arrived through her father first.

He did not announce it. He never would. But at dinner that evening, he referenced Elias casually, as though continuity had never been in question.

"Calder was mentioned in the review council," he said, selecting a data display filter with more care than necessary. "Apparently his handling of the post-incident protocols has earned... renewed confidence."

Renewed.

Mara kept her expression neutral.

"I imagine the city appreciates clarity," she said.

"Yes." Her father hesitated, then added, "And consistency."

The word landed with unfamiliar warmth.

A year ago, that consistency had been something to worry over.

Now, it was suddenly an asset.

The shift accelerated.

Invitations arrived that no longer required justification, their phrasing careful not to suggest concession but unmistakably revised all the same.

Joint attendance would be welcome.

Shared presence anticipated.

Mara observed the language with professional detachment.

The love had not changed.

The *context* had.

That was the irony that stayed with her longest: nothing about her alignment with Elias had shifted except the city's assessment of its safety. Their closeness was now acceptable not because it was understood, but because it had been *validated by outcome*.

Success had conferred respectability retroactively.

She felt the quiet triumph of it—not vindictive, not celebratory, but edged with something sharper.

This was how power trained perception.

Elias noticed, too.

They spoke of it one evening in passing, the observation framed with the same care they now brought to most things.

"They're warmer," he said neutrally, watching a group redirect course slightly as they crossed the greenway, making room without acknowledging the adjustment.

"Yes," Mara replied.

"They were not," he said.

"No," she agreed.

He exhaled softly. "It's remarkable how consistent affection becomes once uncertainty resolves itself into approval."

Mara smiled faintly. "It was never uncertainty they objected to."

"No," he said. "It was exposure."

They shared a look—quiet, calibrated.

"Now that exposure has yielded something they can quote," Elias continued, "they're comfortable again."

"And if it hadn't?" Mara asked.

His answer was immediate. "They would still call their resistance principled."

She nodded.

This, too, was something she had learned a long time ago.

The clearest recalculation came from her family.

Not in words, but posture.

Her sister—who had once worried openly about optics, about practicality, about the wisdom of attaching romance to uneven ground—now spoke of Elias as though he had always been part of the structure.

"He makes sense," she said one afternoon, following a brief mention of shared logistics oversight they'd recently implemented. "In hindsight."

In hindsight.

Mara noted how often that phrase appeared in conversations now, how generously it absolved past doubt.

"Yes," she said lightly. "It does."

Her sister paused, then smiled—a smile that carried relief rather than apology.

"I suppose you saw it earlier than the rest of us," she said.

Mara did not correct her.

Seeing earlier was not the same as being supported earlier.

But the concession mattered.

Elias's acceptance followed a similar pattern.

His decisions—which once disrupted comfort—were now praised as strategic restraint. Where hesitation had been questioned, prudence was now highlighted. Where adaptability had been mistaken for retreat, maturity now filled the gap.

A senior civic coordinator remarked publicly, "Calder's strength lies in measured consistency."

Measured.

Consistency.

Words that would have sounded like compromise before the fall, before the letter, before the reckoning had shifted what those terms were allowed to mean.

Mara felt the irony deepen.

He had changed.

But what had finally won approval was not transformation—it was *proof*.

Proof soothed.

Principles unsettled.

The social recalibration culminated in a reception that would, once, have felt dangerous.

Now it felt inevitable.

It was hosted in a mid-tier Core City forum—polished, not gaudy—framed carefully as a review of adaptive civic response models. Mara attended with Elias not because it was expected, but because absence would now have been noticed differently.

They entered together.

Not hand in hand.

Not postured for attention.

Simply aligned.

The room responded in increments.

Glances lingered longer than necessary. Conversations shifted course subtly, making space without acknowledgement. People who had once watched from a distance now approached directly, their faces relaxed by the safety of approval.

One woman—connected distantly to Allocation, Mara noticed—smiled warmly and said, "It's good to see you both today."

Good.

Not interesting. Not surprising.

Acceptable.

Elias nodded in polite recognition. Mara inclined her head.

The encounter passed without ceremony.

But Mara felt it all the same.

Later, amid discussions that now included them both without qualification, Mara caught fragments of old concerns reframed as virtues.

"You know," someone said, gesturing lightly toward Elias, "his independence once caused quite a stir."

"Yes," another replied. "But that perspective was necessary."

Necessary.

Mara wondered briefly where necessity had been when cost outweighed comfort.

She wondered, and then let it go.

The room didn't require confrontation.

It required observation.

They left early.

Outside, the air felt cleaner not because the city had changed, but because she no longer needed to assess it for threat.

"Well," Elias said lightly as they descended toward the greenway again, "I believe we've crossed some invisible threshold."

"Yes," Mara said. "We've become reasonable."

He laughed quietly. "The highest honor."

"According to them," she added.

He glanced at her, understanding threading beneath the humor.

"It doesn't change what we chose," he said.

"No," she replied. "It changes how others narrate it."

"And how does that feel?"

Mara considered.

"Validating," she said truthfully. "And revealing."

He nodded. "Of the system?"

"Yes," she said. "And of its limits."

They walked in silence for a moment, the city repairing itself around them as it always did.

"Would you trade it?" Elias asked softly. "The difficulty before."

Mara shook her head.

"No," she said. "I wouldn't want acceptance that costs accuracy."

The quiet triumph settled—not exuberant, not boastful, but steady.

What they had built did not depend on social sanction.

It simply survived it.

As they neared Midway, familiar sounds rose to meet them—unfiltered laughter, a street vendor arguing cheerfully with a patron, footsteps overlapping in disordered rhythm.

This was where constancy had been chosen, not rewarded.

"You realize," Elias said, "we're now being used as an example."

"Yes," Mara replied. "That will last until the next disruption."

"And after?"

"After," she said, "they'll forget again."

He smiled. "That's all right."

She looked at him questioningly.

"We'll remember," he said.

And that was enough.

The city recalculated around them as cities did—absorbing, reframing, declaring inevitability where there had been resistance.

Mara let herself feel the quiet triumph of having endured it.

Not because she had been proven right.

But because she had not been persuaded to leave.

What others now accepted had always been there.

And the irony—that respect arrived only once danger passed—did not sour the victory.

It clarified it.

She had not waited for approval.

Approval had arrived late.

And she felt no obligation to reorder her life to meet it.

The recalculation completed itself without ceremony.

By the time Mara realized it had settled, the city had already moved on to applying it—as cities did. What had once required explanation now required only reference. What had drawn concern no longer triggered interest. She and Elias were no longer an uncertainty to be managed, but a precedent to be cited.

That shift, Mara knew, was the final stage.

Not acceptance.

Normalization.

She noticed it on the morning review feeds when her name appeared beside his in a joint context, unmarked by qualifiers. No parenthetical caution. No procedural framing. Just adjacency, presented as though it had always belonged there.

She did not correct it.

The family acknowledgment arrived later, quieter, and more personal.

Her father called her into the eastern gallery under the transparent pretext of reviewing access reassignments. They stood side by side as the city glinted below, their silhouettes reflected faintly in the glass.

"You've done well," he said finally.

The phrase carried history.

"Yes," Mara replied.

"I was... concerned," he continued, adjusting the display's brightness without needing to. "Once. About the instability."

She let him speak.

"It seems," he added, "that concern was misplaced."

Misplaced.

Not wrong.

"That instability," Mara said carefully, "was rarely where we thought it was."

He nodded slowly, as if testing the idea against newly comfortable evidence.

"I find," he said, "that my colleagues speak of you with considerable confidence now."

"Because it's safe," Mara replied—not unkindly.

He looked at her then, really looking, and smiled faintly.

"Yes," he agreed. "Because it is."

The admission did not feel like surrender.

It felt like alignment delayed by caution.

The broader social absorption followed its familiar pattern.

People who had once regarded Mara with careful distance now spoke of her as a linchpin. Those who had worried aloud about Elias's independence praised his restraint as maturity. Quiet decisions became strategic choices in hindsight; resistance rebranded itself as discernment.

At one gathering, a senior liaison remarked breezily, "Of course they make sense together—they represent continuity."

Mara noted the confidence with which the statement was delivered.

Continuity.

The word had traveled far.

She did not object. She did not correct.

She understood how fragile such declarations were—how quickly they would reverse if circumstances changed again. Stability, once assumed, was always conditional.

She felt neither bitterness nor gratitude.

Only clarity.

It was Elias, unexpectedly, who named the absurdity of it.

They stood together at the edge of a civic terrace during a midweek forum—one of those events that now welcomed them without explanation. The city's low hum carried upward, the sound of approved systems in motion.

"You realize," he said quietly, watching a group angle toward them with studied casualness, "we've become exemplary."

"Yes," Mara replied.

"For having done nothing differently," he added.

She smiled faintly. "For having survived long enough to be declared inevitable."

He laughed under his breath.

"I used to think inevitability was something you engineered," he said. "Now I see it's something declared only when no one feels threatened anymore."

"That's the danger of it," Mara said. "It erases the cost."

They lingered long enough to be polite, then withdrew before the evening required more of them than observation.

They had learned, together, when presence mattered and when it merely sustained a narrative.

The true resolution came not in applause but in omission.

One afternoon, Mara noticed that an ongoing advisory discussion—one that would previously have dragged her into justification—concluded without needing her clarification at all. The proposal had been revised preemptively, its language adjusted to reflect constraints she had once fought to make visible.

Someone had learned.

Not necessarily *who* she was.

But *how* she worked.

That distinction mattered more than recognition.

Later, when she and Elias crossed paths in the corridor outside the oversight wing, he noticed it too.

"They anticipated you," he said.

"Yes," Mara replied. "That means they've stopped reacting."

"And started integrating."

"Perhaps."

He regarded her thoughtfully.

"That must feel like victory."

She shook her head. "It feels like relief."

He nodded.

"And irony," he added.

"Yes," she said. "That too."

What she found most telling was how easily dissent had been forgotten.

The voices that had once questioned her presence now cited her as standard. The memory of resistance dissipated with remarkable speed, archived in the collective consciousness under the category of *resolved concern*.

It was antiseptic.

Efficient.

And entirely predictable.

She spoke of it one evening to Etta during a quiet check-in, their conversation routed through the preserved legacy channel that had become their default.

"They're comfortable now," Mara said.

Etta's reply came after a pause.

"Comfort," she sent, "has a short memory."

"Yes," Mara typed back.

"But remember," Etta continued, "discomfort always knows where you stood."

Mara closed the channel with a small, grateful smile.

Loyalty did not require validation.

Only accuracy.

The final seal of social sanction arrived, inevitably, as invitation.

A formal dinner—moderate scale, unremarkable guest list, curated neutrality. It was not an honor. It was a signal.

They attended.

Not because it mattered.

But because absence would now carry consequence of its own.

They arrived together and were received with the smooth grace of familiarity, no one requiring reassurance or explanation. Conversation flowed easily, calibrated to comfort now that uncertainty had been smoothed away.

At the table, a guest remarked lightly, "It's refreshing to see alignment that feels... settled."

Mara met Elias's gaze for a fractional second, then returned her attention to the speaker.

"Yes," she said. "Settlement has its advantages."

"And its risks," Elias added.

The guest laughed politely, unsure whether to treat the comment as humor or commentary.

They did not elaborate.

When they left, the night air greeted them like an honest collaborator.

"I don't feel triumphant," Elias said as they descended toward the greenway again.

"That's because this wasn't a contest," Mara replied.

"No," he agreed. "It was a filter."

They walked in companionable silence for a while, letting the city reassert its texture—less curated here, more alive, less concerned with how events were framed for observation.

"This acceptance," Elias said eventually, "does it change anything for you?"

She considered.

"It changes how I'm treated," she said. "Not how I choose."

He nodded, approval unspoken but clear.

"That's what frightened me at first," he admitted. "That social validation would erase the precision of what we've built."

"And now?" she asked.

"And now I see that validation doesn't erase anything," he said. "It just arrives late."

Mara smiled at that.

"Yes," she said. "Far too late to be instructive."

They reached the place where Midway's lights grew irregular again, where people moved without choreography and sound carried without amplification.

This, she thought, was where constancy had been chosen.

Everything else was commentary.

As she prepared to rest that night, Mara felt the quiet triumph fully—not as satisfaction, not as vindication, but as release from vigilance that no longer needed to be total. She did not confuse acceptance with truth, but she allowed it to exist without bracing against it.

The city had recalculated.

It always did.

What mattered was that she had not.

And that when recognition finally came, it did not demand concession in return.

The irony of it remained sharp enough to keep her honest.

The triumph remained quiet enough to endure.

Neon Horizon

The horizon looked different at night.

That was what Mara noticed first as she and Elias stood on the upper platform where the city thinned into transit and water, where Neon lines bent toward departure rather than containment. By day, the Reach declared itself with clarity—routes visible, thresholds labeled, risk measured and countermeasured until it resembled intention. By night, it softened. Light refracted. Motion became suggestion rather than statement.

The future, she thought, looked like this when you stopped asking it to be safe.

They had not planned to come here together. The platform existed because it had always existed—a convergence of outgoing routes, refueling arrays, and evaluation lanes that made mobility appear orderly by cutting it into schedules. Elias's work required him here. Mara's presence was not required.

That was the difference.

He did not ask her to come.

She did.

The night air carried the scent of coolant and salt, a mingled proof of boundary and passage. Far below, the water caught and broke the city's light into scattered signatures that drifted outward, uncoordinated and persistent.

"You don't have to stay," Elias said quietly.

Mara smiled faintly. "I know."

That was the point.

For years, she had calibrated her life around necessity—where she was needed, where absence would be interpreted as failure, where presence could prevent collapse. The places she chose now were fewer and more deliberate. This one was not strategic.

It was honest.

"I wanted to see it," she said. "Not as an abstraction."

He nodded, understanding without needing clarification.

Beyond them, a departure vessel slid free of its docking clamps, movement so smooth it barely disturbed the air. Motion indicators pulsed once, then faded as the craft aligned its vector and joined the slow curve outward.

It would not return on a predictable timeline.

That, too, was familiar.

"I don't need to tell you what this means," Elias said. "My schedule. My range."

"No," Mara replied. "You don't."

They stood together, not touching, the gap between them occupied by shared sight rather than distance. She could feel the hum of the platform beneath her feet—the subtle vibration of a system designed to endure passage rather than prevent it.

Elias shifted slightly, resting his forearms on the rail.

"When I was younger," he said, "I thought movement was freedom. That the farther I could go, the less anything could pin me down."

"And now?" she asked.

"And now I think freedom is consent," he said. "To movement that doesn't pretend permanence."

Mara considered that.

"I once believed safety meant staying," she said. "Staying put. Holding ground."

He glanced at her, attentive.

"I learned it wasn't the same as fidelity," she continued. "It was only fidelity when I chose it—and when it didn't require others to do the leaving for me."

A quiet passed between them, not heavy, not expectant—simply full.

The city exhaled again as another craft aligned and departed, leaving behind a widening pocket of light that slowly rebalanced itself.

"It would be easier," Elias said, carefully, "to ask you to want something settled."

"Yes," Mara agreed. "It would."

"And you don't?"

She shook her head.

"I want something chosen," she said. "And choice doesn't promise stillness."

He absorbed that, relief and gravity threading through his posture together.

"I can't offer you safety," he said. "Not in the way others mean it."

Mara smiled then—not ironically, not bravely. Just clearly.

"I don't need to be protected from instability," she said. "I need to know it's named."

"And agreed to?" he asked.

"Yes," she replied. "And revisited."

He let out a breath he hadn't known he was holding.

There was melancholy in this, she knew. Accepting a life that would stretch and compress unpredictably, that would demand recalibration again and again, that might carry absence like weather—sometimes clearing, sometimes persistent. The city understood that kind of pact. It had been built on it.

She understood it too.

They walked along the platform's curve, passing a series of illuminated markers that tracked outbound routes as living lines rather than schedules. Each one represented a future in motion. None pretended to be safe. All pretended to be necessary.

Elias stopped near a marker tagged for a corridor that ran beyond the Reach's regulatory envelope.

"I'll be needed out there," he said. "Not always. But repeatedly."

"Yes," Mara said.

"And I won't structure my return around comfort anymore," he added. "Or timelines that make other people feel secure."

She considered his words—and the work behind them.

"Then tell me this," she said. "What would you do if staying became the harder choice?"

He did not answer immediately.

"If staying meant presence rather than accommodation," he said slowly, "I would stay."

She nodded. "That's all I need to hear."

They resumed walking, their shadows stretching and folding beneath the platform's lights. The city seemed to recede as they moved outward, not because it vanished, but because it no longer demanded interpretation.

At the far end of the platform, the noise thinned to a low, encompassing hum—power flowing, routes opening, systems agreeing to be permeable.

This was where travelers paused before final notices appeared, where decision outran announcement.

Mara turned back toward the city once more.

"I don't romanticize this," she said quietly. "The leaving. The uncertainty."

"I know," Elias replied.

"And I won't pretend it won't cost me," she continued. "There will be nights that feel longer because you're not there to shorten them."

He faced her fully now, the neon light from the horizon tracing deliberate lines across his expression.

"I don't want you to bear that alone," he said.

"I won't," she replied. "But I won't ask you to dismantle your life to avoid it."

Something decided itself between them then—not as contract, not as vow, but as alignment recognized and accepted.

This was not the acceptance of safety.

It was the acceptance of movement as a shared condition.

They stood together as the horizon shifted again, the light reorganizing itself into a new pattern that would last only until something moved through it.

Melancholy settled—not sorrow, not regret, but the acknowledgment that what had ended was not risk, but the illusion of closure. Peace followed it, not triumphant, not serene, but durable.

Mara turned to him, her voice steady.

"I don't need you to promise me return," she said. "I need you to promise me presence when we stand in the same place."

"And honesty when we don't," he added.

"Yes," she said. "Especially then."

He smiled—soft, sincere, unobstructed.

"That," he said, "I can do."

The platform lights dimmed slightly as the system cycled down for the night's quieter hours. The horizon remained—neon and unresolved, waiting for motion to define it again.

Mara did not feel afraid.

She felt prepared.

Love, she understood now, did not always choose certainty. Sometimes it chose instability—knowingly, deliberately—because stability without truth was simply another form of disappearance.

She rested her hands on the cool rail and watched the next vessel depart, its trajectory clean and unclaimed, its future unreadable and real.

This was the horizon they were choosing together.

Not because it was safe.

But because it was lit enough to see, and wide enough to walk without pretending the ground beneath them would not shift.

And for the first time, that felt like peace.

The horizon did not wait for agreement.

It never had.

Mara learned this in the weeks that followed—not through rupture or absence, but through accumulation. Elias left as scheduled, his departure unmarked by ceremony and remarkably free of the weight that once clung to such moments. The platform accepted him, the city absorbed the motion, and the neon curvatures of retreat realigned themselves without pause.

She watched until the light lines thinned into suggestion, then turned back without theatrics.

This, she understood, was the first test of chosen instability: not lingering where departure asked for completion, not rehearsing absence until it became significance. She allowed the moment its place in time and let the city claim the rest.

Life continued.

Midway did not falter in his absence. That mattered.

The greenway remained noisy and ungovernable in its particular way, conversations overlapping and resolving themselves without coordination. Lina argued cheerfully with a vendor over delivery windows. Dax laughed too loud, too freely, a sound that still startled Mara with relief. Etta's archived nodes hummed reliably in the lower layers, their truth unoptimized and intact.

Presence, she reminded herself, was not proximity alone.

It was attention.

The days acquired a different rhythm—not lesser, not diluted, simply reweighted. Mara moved through her work with the same precision, but without the underlying tension that once required her constant triangulation between contact and loss. The work did not intensify to fill the space Elias's schedule had vacated. It remained what it was: difficult, necessary, insufficient alone.

Sometimes, late in the evening, a message arrived—not long, not intimate in form, but attentive in tone. Elias never described danger. He did not dramatize movement. He named locations, asked measured questions, shared observations rather than reassurance.

When they spoke, it was never to bridge distance.

It was to maintain alignment.

"This corridor isn't stable yet," he wrote once. "The city's confidence is outpacing reality."

She replied without delay. "Then let it wait. Confidence is cheaper to restore than trust."

There was no flourish in his response.

"Understood."

That, she realized, was the texture of their connection now. Not intensity. Not constant affirmation.

Understanding that did not require repetition.

One night, the city surprised her.

A power redistribution error rippled outward from an under-maintained junction near the Lower Reach, dimming whole sections of Midway for several minutes. Not long enough to disrupt systems entirely. Long enough to unsettle assumptions.

Mara was already moving when the first alerts failed to escalate.

She reached the junction on foot—faster that way—her senses adjusting to reduced light as instinctively as breath. A small crowd had gathered, uncertain, their phones glowing uselessly with delayed diagnostics.

Mara stepped forward.

"Stay where you are," she said calmly. "This isn't dangerous. It's just unfinished."

The words landed not as reassurance, but recognition.

She rerouted manually, hands steady, voice even as she coordinated response from memory and observation rather than feed. The lights returned gradually, not all at once, and the crowd dispersed with mild embarrassment rather than panic.

She stood alone at the junction when it was done, the quiet settling naturally around her again.

Her interface chimed.

A single message.

"Proud of you," Elias wrote. "Not for fixing it. For naming it honestly."

She smiled, leaning briefly against the warm casing of the restored node.

He had understood what mattered.

Time unspooled further.

Not every day was clean. Some carried weight she did not share. Some nights pressed harder than others. There were mornings she woke with the edge of fatigue already sharpened, days when vigilance felt less like choice and more like muscle memory refusing to relax.

And yet—

She had not mistaken stillness for safety, or movement for escape. The horizon they had chosen remained as it was meant to be: open, lit unevenly, honest in its refusal to promise what it could not deliver.

When Elias returned—briefly, unpredictably—the reunion carried no adjustment phase. They fell back into proximity without rehearsal, their awareness of one another quiet and durable.

They walked the greenway once, passing beneath the same lights where they had first acknowledged the cost of staying visible. No audience formed. No narrative demanded punctuation.

"I nearly asked you to come with me," Elias said as they walked.

Mara did not look startled.

"I know," she said.

"And then?"

"And then I realized that asking you to follow would have been asking you to leave where you matter," she replied.

"Yes," he agreed.

They walked on.

The city recalibrated again, because that was what cities did.

New risks emerged. Old models failed in minor and instructive ways. Leadership shifted without fanfare as comfort gave way to competence. And in the background—quiet, persistent—the answer to a question the city rarely admitted to asking continued its work.

What happens when you stop pretending stability is earned by absence?

Mara did not articulate it publicly.

She lived it.

At a mid-tier forum months later, asked to comment on long-range civic resilience planning, she offered a single sentence that redirected the entire discussion.

"We'll adapt better when we stop asking who can act fastest and start asking who stays longest with the outcome."

There was conversation after that. Debate. Some resistance.

But no dismissal.

Her words now landed where once they had slid.

One evening, when the city leaned heavily into its quieter hours, she found Elias again at the platform's far end—the same place they had stood months earlier, watching departure nets shimmer and settle.

This time, she arrived second.

"You came back sooner than expected," she said.

He smiled. "Not everything needs to be linear."

They stood together, hands resting on the rail, shoulders nearly touching in the way of people who did not need to claim space from one another.

"I still won't promise you return," he said, without looking at her.

She nodded. "Good."

"And I still won't ask you to leave," she added.

"That's better," he replied.

They watched as another vessel slipped free, its outline dissolving into the city's outward glow.

The melancholy returned—not sharp, not demanding—but this time it brought peace with it. Acceptance without resignation. Love without bargaining.

"This," Elias said quietly, "feels like standing on the weather rather than hiding from it."

Mara smiled.

"Yes," she said. "And like knowing when to come inside."

They remained there a while longer, letting the horizon be what it was.

Lit.

Unfinished.

Shared.

When they finally turned away, Mara did not feel that anything essential had been concluded or deferred. The story did not require closure in that sense.

What mattered had already been decided.

She had chosen not safety, but fidelity.

Not permanence, but presence.

Not assurance, but alignment.

And in doing so, she had found something that did not need to hold still to endure.

The neon lights bent again toward departure.

The city adjusted.

And in the quiet between motion and return, Mara walked forward without illusion—steady, awake, and never alone.

About the Author

G. J. Stein writes speculative fiction about attention, consequence, and the tension between human judgment and the systems built to replace it. His work blends emotional precision with near-future settings shaped by power, memory, and adaptation.

Learn more at www.gjsteinbooks.com.

You can connect with me on:

- https://www.gjsteinbooks.com

Subscribe to my newsletter:

- https://sendfox.com/gjsteinbooks

www.ingramcontent.com/pod-product-compliance
Lightning Source LLC
LaVergne TN
LVHW100524110826
845146LV00002B/767

* 9 7 9 8 9 9 5 3 2 9 4 2 8 *